'This is masterfully done.'

The Times

'Arnold writes with such muscular flair the characters stride off the pages.'
Peterborough Telegraph

'Intelligent plotting, historical accuracy, heart-pounding battle scenes and a memorable cast of characters are the hallmarks of Arnold's remarkable series.'

Pendle Today

'Mike Arnold hooks the reader with the clash of steel and the roar of gunpowder. Rollicking action and proper history combine in this cracking series.'
Anthony Riches, author of the bestselling "Empire" series

'Mike Arnold has caught all of the passion, urgency, fear and exhilaration of men in battle. Not only that, he's writing in a period that he obviously knows intimately and in to which he has breathed new life.'
Patrick Mercer, author of 'To Do and Die' and 'Dust and Steel'

'Captures the grittiness, as well as the doomed glamour, of the Royalist cause.'
Charles Spencer, author of 'Prince Rupert: The Last Cavalier'

'You can smell the gunpowder and hear the cannon fire as you're thrust into the mud and blood of the battlefields. Arnold's passion… suffuses every page.'
Robyn Young, author of the Brethren Trilogy.

By the same author:

The Civil War Chronicles

Stryker and the Angels of Death (Novella)

Traitor's Blood

Devil's Charge

Hunter's Rage

Assassin's Reign

Warlord's Gold

The Prince's Gambit (Novella)

Marston Moor

The Highwayman Series

Highwayman: Ironside

Highwayman: Winter Swarm

Michael Arnold's interest in British history is lifelong, and childhood holidays were spent visiting castles and battlefields. He became a Sharpe junkie at the age of 13, and his particular fascination with the seventeenth century was piqued partly by the fact that his hometown, Petersfield, is steeped in the history of the period. Michael is the critically acclaimed author of The Civil War Chronicles, featuring the indomitable Captain Stryker, and is also the creator of the bestselling Highwayman sequence of novellas. In Corpse Thief, the first in a major new series, he turns his attention to the dark underworld of London's resurrectionists.

You can find out more about Michael Arnold, Joshua Hawke, Captain Stryker and the rest, by visiting the following places online:

www.michael-arnold.net

Facebook: MichaelArnoldBooks

Twitter: @MikeArnold01

CORPSE THIEF

PART ONE

MICHAEL ARNOLD

First published in 2019 by Bad Baby Press

www.michael-arnold.net

For Maisie, with love

PROLOGUE

LONDON

SEPTEMBER 1821

"The good Lord blesses me," Varney Tapp muttered, sketching a cross in the foul air with his long hoe, "for I wade in rivers of gold."

"Get on wi' yer!" a retort, friendly if brusque, carried to him from another part of the crumbling brick tunnel. "We're first down, Varn! Do not squander!"

"I shall not, old cock!" Varney called back. His wry laugh was corrupted almost immediately by a bout of racking coughs, but still the water, stretching away to a lazy bend, glimmered yellow under the attentions of his lantern. He spat away the acrid mass that had erupted into his mouth and waded on, placing his feet carefully as sewage sloshed about his tall boots, splattering the canvas trousers and the hem of his voluminous coat. Every yard gained earned a pause as he prodded the ground delicately with the hoe, exploring the filth for valuables. He coughed again, managed to hawk up more mucus, and said a quick prayer that he would live long enough to find something of value. Of true worth. A legacy for his children.

For time was running out. He was not yet fifty, but he sensed the decline in his bones. He could feel the burn in his chest. Could taste it too, the taint of decay that lingered upon his breath. His body was failing, infected and enfeebled. But what could he expect? Toshers saw out their lives under the feet of other folk - quite literally. They dwelt amongst the swarming rats and voracious wild hogs in London's labyrinthine sewers, searching, ever searching, inhaling the stink, feeling it seep inexorably into every pore. This work that was his livelihood would eventually compel him to his death. Just one more find, he told himself as he pushed on through the viscous piss and shit of the greatest city in the world. One more treasure.

It was only just dawn. The cold had come early this autumn, and the putrefied liquid that seethed between his boots seemed to bite at his very marrow. His few remaining teeth, clinging stubbornly to the soft and shifting foundations of long collapsed gums, chattered excitedly, and he alternated the hand that carried the little lamp so that the tiny flame's meagre warmth might be shared as far as possible in advance of the day's scavenge. He pictured his desires, as if seeing them in his mind's eye might make them real beneath the ink-black water. Diamond necklaces, bejewelled rings, glittering pendants.

The dreams still swirled in his mind like the flotsam at his ankles when he saw it. A hint of something precious, glimmering like a cat's eye in the murk. It winked at him, some thirty paces distant, reflecting his soft light from a point just before the vile river vanished round the sweeping bend. It was a break in the brickwork, perhaps a small alcove, a relic of construction that served no modern purpose but in the snagging of debris. Such curiosities might not help the natural flow of sewage to the Thames, but they were a Godsend for a tosher. A trap for trinkets.

Varney Tapp gathered the straps of his large bag and tugged them further up his shoulder. He set off, gripping the lantern harder and building speed by the leverage of the hoe, a rushing wake marking his path. From on high, the westernmost extent of Upper Thames Street, came the muffled clatter of coach and horses upon cobbles. The day above ground was beginning. He drew nearer to the alcove, squinting as he raised his arm to cast light upon its deep drift of waste. Movement shifted on the surface, like a black shawl sliding away. Rats, dozens, skittering for the shadows in fright.

He saw the hand before anything else, for it was from its clawed grip that the metal shone. Tapp froze five paces short, his breaths rasping painfully, cacophonous in the lonely tunnel. He stared at the waxen form for a minute or so, though it felt as though hours raced by. Glancing back, he saw no sign of his friend, and knowledge that he was alone sent an icy spear up his spine. The metal winked at him again. It was enough. He swallowed hard and decided to edge closer.

The corpse was that of a girl. Probably little more than a child, though it was difficult to tell amongst the vines. At least they looked like vines, or stalks of some kind, wrapped about her from ankles to head as if the roots of trees had risen from the earth to devour her whole. Only that extended arm had managed to work its way free in some final, tragic gesture.

Varney stooped a little, avarice trumping trepidation. The glint had come from some kind of button, he now saw, for the white fingers held it up as though it were a trophy, clear above water and vine, dry despite the stinking scum lapping gently over the rest of the entwined flesh. He propped the hoe against the sewer wall and squatted, parting some of the bindings to get a better look at the girl. It was already obvious that she was naked within her strange harness, for enough of her was exposed to the fetid air to see that she had not the parts of a man, but he pushed the vines away to expose more flesh. She had been laid flat on her back, skinny as a rake and pale as candle wax. Her legs were long but shapeless, like a pair of tapers, while her pearly breasts were no more than small mounds amongst skeletal ribs, spring buds on winter branches. He realised that she was too young to have reached womanhood. A street urchin, he supposed, consigned to a hopeless life and a lonely death.

He hooked fingertips beneath the vines covering the cadaver's head, tearing them easily away to release a mass of thickly curled hair that cascaded about the filth in a wide fan the colour of honey, still vibrant in this cold hell. And then Varney Tapp vomited. His guts erupted like a volcano, juddering up through his body in a torrent, steaming bile spewing down his velveteen coat, spattering the body. He recoiled, staggering backwards, caring nothing for the effluent slopping up his thighs, thinking only of clean air, wishing only for daylight. Yet he could not turn, nor even look away. The girl's face was gone. No eyes stared back at him, only black holes like the sockets of some ancient skull. The nose had come away too, sliced cleanly to leave a red mass, as if a fat ruby had been plunged into her face in its stead. There were not even any lips to hide the girl's ghoulish grin, simply ragged scraps of matter draped like a fiendish curtain over the exposed teeth.

"Oh, good Christ," Varney managed to blurt. "Christ."

Varney was gasping like a landed trout, his ribs more agonised than ever, and he feared his heart was finally poised to expire. He tore his gaze away, lest the very image of the girl's ruined face be the last thing he ever saw, and turned his back on the corpse. The wan light quivered around him, painting shapes that were suddenly strange and frightening on the slime-stained walls. He realised the hand clutching the lantern trembled and he clamped his free palm around the wrist in an effort to keep it still. He waited for several moments, allowing his pulse to calm and his breathing to steady.

"Leave, Varn," he urged himself aloud, his words echoing up and down the oozing brick. "Get the devil out of this place."

And yet.

Varney turned back, resolving to brave the corpse one more time. After all, it was the lot of a tosher to spend his days searching the putrid depths beneath the metropolis for things that glittered, and the girl – what was left of her – promised just such a bauble within her decaying palm. Besides, he thought, what did she need with it now?

He did not look directly at her face this time, for those sepulchral eyes were too much to behold. Instead he rushed to her side, shooing away a trio of returning rats. He stooped for the raised hand. Her skin was cold, it made him shudder, but he pulled all the same, prising the fingers apart and wrenching free his reward.

It was only when he straightened that he felt the pain. His chest again, worse this time. More intense, in fact, than he had ever experienced. He stood stock still, unwilling to risk enraging his plaintive heart. The excitement, he thought. Too much excitement for one morning. At least he had the trinket.

But the pain increased, and then the bitter taste of rot that seemed an ever-present drizzle at the back of his tongue was replaced by a torrid downpour of tangy metal, as though he had licked a lead pipe. It was a curious taste, one he was unused to, and only when he felt the blood well over his bottom lip and down the sides of his chin did he understand that something was amiss. He tried to breathe, but nothing would come. His arms felt suddenly numb, then his legs and his neck and cheeks. And Varney Tapp knew he was dying.

He turned, trying to leave, but his path was blocked. A great silhouette loomed, black and massive, filling the tunnel as though it rose out of the toxic morass at Varney's feet. At the creature's centre there was a symbol, shining bright in the lamplight. The tosher tried to cry out but his lungs refused to respond, and in that moment he knew that he was not having the heart attack he so feared.

He looked down at the fine tip of smooth steel that protruded through the coat at his sternum. At that same moment he felt the weight at his back, and knew that it must be the hilt of the weapon, dangling out beyond his spine like some perverse tail. He stared again at his killer's metal heart.

Then he was falling.

CHAPTER ONE

DECEMBER 1821

WEDNESDAY

"Hawke. *Hawke*!"

Joshua Hawke arched his aching back. It always hurt more in the cold, and this night was more biting than most. He stared down at the three-man working party. "Aye?"

"Jesus wept, Hawke!" one of the men hissed. "Keep your crapulous god-damned head steady."

"I've not touched a drop all day, Blackbird," Hawke protested.

A face tilted up, illuminated suddenly by tremulous light. It was pulpy, the dark skin damaged and healed too many times to count, the nose canted violently to one side. The black eyes, gleaming like nuggets of jet, regarded him nastily, brimming with repressed violence. "You're a fucking liar."

"That I am," Hawke said as jauntily as he could.

"Well?"

"All quiet," Hawke replied, glancing briefly over his shoulder to check for the chink of light at the far corner of St George's Bloomsbury burying ground. "No alarm as yet."

"Lucas had better not be dozing," Blackbird warned, his gravelly voice a curious amalgam of Wapping and the West Indies.

Hawke shook his head. "Not him, Blackbird. He's caught on quick."

Blackbird snorted to show his disdain and went back to the task. They grunted and swore in the marrow-numbing blackness, voices soft, discreet in their terrible business. The ground was hard. It might have been impossible to dig, but for the patch of freshly turned earth that marked their target. Even here the pale shroud had descended in the hours after nightfall, gossamer frost creeping over the newest of the graveyard's mounds as it had the grassy expanse between the crooked tombstones and the slanting rooftops all around. But in this dark place, where the earth was so recently disturbed, it could be scraped quickly away to reveal the loose soil beneath. They wielded wooden shovels, a deliberate choice to muffle the scraping of stones, shoulders working like tandem timber-saws as they hauled back debris.

Joshua Hawke waited silently for the hole to deepen. He blew out his cheeks, watching the trail of hot breath rise in a plume against the sky, pleased for the cold, for it meant the rank vapours kicked up by the myriad shallow graves were frozen to a musty whiff. The place stank enough to bring tears to a man's eyes in the summer months, for overcrowded plots disgorged what they failed to contain, spewing their decayed residents to the surface, the resulting noxious miasma free to corrupt the lungs of the living.

Hawke lifted the iron bars he grasped in each gloved hand. They were dark as the heavens, heavy and hooked, lethal in a scrap. But not tonight. Tonight they would be employed in a task of skill. When the time was right.

“Through?” another member of the party asked. He was standing to the side of the excavation, craning his neck to see into the crumbling shaft. His voice was a strained whisper behind the lantern in his raised fist, though Blackbird heard him well enough, for he returned a sour glance.

“Not yet, Gilroy. Keep your bloody britches on.”

All but one of the lantern’s sides were covered so that it would illuminate the prize without betraying those engaged in the search, and the single beam quivered manically as Gilroy replied in a hoarse whisper. “Well get on wi’ yer!”

Blackbird dropped his spade and twisted back, squinting into the light. “Give us a chance!”

The lamp-bearer set his jaw. “God’s bones, but you’re slow as a lame bullock.” He glanced around, eyes searching for the lookout’s lamp near the burying ground’s main gates. “They have paid watchmen here. Christ, but I heard they’re all veterans. Warty-loo, Tally-vera, Bada...”

“Pah!” Blackbird spat contemptuously. He was sitting back on his haunches now, rubbing hands against heavily muscled forearms. “Every bugger twixt here and the river would claim the same if it got them the job.”

The second digger nodded. His was a narrow face, lop-sided, almost hollow on one side, as though the greater part of his left cheek had been removed, while his chin tapered sharply into a pointed beard that he now tugged between thumb and forefinger. “Most guards are tumbledown old gin-hounds, Gilroy.” His voice, nasal and pitched high, carried the hard crackle of London’s eastern suburbs. “Worry not.”

Gilroy blew a gust of air through his hooked nose. “You’d better be bloody right, Goaty. Dawn’s not far off.”

Blackbird nodded at that. “Best get on.”

The third digger, a fellow in his forties, with salt-and-pepper hair and a wiry beard, panted, “We’re almost there. Ain’t deep.”

“Finish it off, then, Harlowe,” Blackbird said.

It was only moments after Harlowe's nodded response that one of the battered tools hit upon something with a low thud, dull but distinct from the surrounding loose earth. Unmistakably wood upon wood. Blackbird glanced up at Gilroy with a grin. "What was you saying?"

Hawke smirked as the lamp-bearer hacked up a wad of phlegm and deposited it at the foot of a nearby tombstone. "To business, then."

The five converged on the grave, peering along the lantern's modest beam. They had dug what amounted to a narrow shaft. It was the width of three spades, and no more than two feet deep, ending abruptly where, they now saw, dark soil gave way to the pale flatness of timber. Blackbird dropped his spade again and delved into the hole, rapping the coffin lid lightly with gloved knuckles. "Wake up, sirrah. You're late for work."

The others sniggered.

Blackbird slunk away from the fresh tunnel and straightened slowly, dropping the tool and stretching his back like a waking tomcat. "If you please, Mister Hawke."

Hawke moved to the edge of the hole and dropped to his knees. The world swam for a second, and he screwed his eyes tight shut, waiting for the gin-haze to drift away. Head clearing, he thrust both crowbars into the abyss, hooking the timber lid firmly. Only a small portion of the coffin was exposed, but quite enough for their purpose this night. He sucked a huge breath into his lungs, the cold air racing up and down his ribs. And then he pulled.

Hawke had been strong once, but all that had gone, ebbed away to leave him a brittle shell of former glory. But the wood used for such a coffin was cheap, more rotten than the body it contained, and it snapped easily, splintering between the force of the bars and the weight of remaining soil. For a heartbeat the group fell silent. The snapping had sounded unnaturally loud in these smallest hours, and, though none said it, Hawke knew that they each would be listening for the dread tone of a rising hue and cry. Nothing came. Stillness only. Suffocating silence.

Hawke looked down. The shape of a head leered back at him, shadowy features of a man's face staring up sightlessly at the scudding clouds. A sharp smell greeted him too, like musty books and mouldy grain, wafting up between his knees. It was not bad, for the bloating rot was not yet upon this flesh, but the knowledge of whence the scent came did not help Hawke's stewed stomach. Not for the first time he vowed never to touch a drop again.

At Blackbird's impatient prompt, Hawke withdrew the bars, careful not to let them clang against one another as he set them on the frozen grass, and quickly removed his gloves. He hated this part. Had dreaded it the first time, and, after so many successful lifts, acknowledged that it would probably bring bile to his throat for the rest of his life. He gritted his teeth, leaned down, and plunged his hands into the coffin. The body was solid. For a dreadful moment he wondered whether rigor mortis would prove their undoing, but he reminded himself that three days and nights in a wintry grave would take a stiffening toll on the warmest of flesh. The skin was slippery as he slid his palms over the shoulders, inserting his fingers between the arms and the upper ribs so that he might cleave apart the armpits. "Ready."

At once the end of a stout rope appeared at his ear, dangling like a poised viper. Hawke took it, instructed Gilroy to adjust the direction of the light, and carefully looped the thick hemp under the cadaver's arms and behind its back. He pulled it tight, looked back at the waiting faces, and nodded to the man whose skin was the shade of strong coffee. "All yours."

Blackbird was tall, and that alone made him imposing, but what really sealed his formidable reputation was the brawn that encased his frame. His muscles strained beneath his shirt, shifting as his arms moved like round-shot in a sack, and now he replaced Hawke at the head of the grave, clasped the rope in both massive hands, and hauled.

The body rose immediately, torso lurching upwards even as the arms hung loose and free, as though Blackbird were some macabre puppeteer. He pushed up with his broad legs, the power too great for the limp corpse to resist, and the callow marionette slid free, drawn from the small hole like a thorn from a pricked thumb.

Hawke watched in silence. He was always reminded of the birth of a calf he had once seen. The pale form slipping out of its mother as the farmer drew back his gore-spattered arm. Here there was no gore, of course. Not even blood, for the dead did not bleed, but the movement of the body as it worked free of the narrow shaft always brought back that same memory. And now the pallid, almost translucent corpse lay before them. Goaty and Harlowe were already backfilling the shaft as the rest stared at their prize. The body was that of a grown man with dark hair and beard. Known in the trade as a *large*, it would fetch them eight guineas; if they could get it out of the cemetery unseen.

"Well?" Blackbird said.

Hawke crouched beside the body. The dead man looked to be in his mid-twenties, roughly the same age as himself. He lifted one of the porcelain-white arms, shook it roughly, let it drop, and turned back to glance up at the expectant faces. "Rigor's passed."

A collective sigh seemed to whisper through the group while Blackbird went to join Hawke. Being by far the strongest among them, it was an unspoken fact of their work that he would be the one to shift the cargo into place. A swift nod exchanged, Hawke took the shoulders, repulsed once more by the slippery coldness of the dead skin, while his companion grasped an ankle in each vast hand. He wriggled forwards on his knees, lifting and pushing the legs so that the shins folded inward against the thighs. As he moved, Hawke twisted the body onto its side, easing the head down into the chest. It was not easy to force a large cadaver into the foetal position, even one now beyond the steel-limbed resistance of rigor mortis, but this was far from their first experience of the task, and it was achieved with little fuss. Blackbird took the rope in hand, and he looped it around the back of the knees, pulling tight so that they were fastened firmly to the chest. Goaty and Harlowe had finished returning the grave to its former neatness, and one of them produced a large cloth sack, unfurling it as though it were a flag. When Hawke had used a thinner cord to bind the wrists, he stepped away, giving Blackbird room to move. In a single motion, the huge man scooped up the trussed corpse like a new-born babe, hoisted it into the air and stuffed it inside the waiting sack. Goaty pulled the cord at its throat smartly shut.

"Good," Blackbird intoned as the light was snuffed and the shovels and hooks collected. "This one goes to Doctor Vine." He licked his full lips slowly, drew the bulging sack up and over his shoulder, and began to walk towards the cemetery gates where their lookout's own lamp still shone in the dark.

And then it flickered.

They all saw it, clear as day in the depths of night. The light that young Lucas had been dangling during their efforts, solid and assured, was winking, one moment bright, the next black as the sky. Which meant trouble.

Blackbird stole a glance over his shoulder, first checking for menaces in the shadows, then making sure his gang were at his back. With silent acknowledgement, the five men and their heavy cargo pressed on. They moved between the stones of the dead, quiet as the bones beneath their feet. The ground was lumpy and treacherous where the soil of centuries had mingled with shallow graves, shifted and risen into so many tufty mounds. But the men were experienced in this most clandestine enterprise, experts in excavation, but also in evasion. Blackbird negotiated a path that kept them in the darkest recesses of the burying ground, unseen by any but the keenest eyes, and soon they were pressed up against the bricks of the wall that enclosed St George's cluttered plot. They snaked along beside it, all the while listening for the sounds of watchmen cocking pistols and searching the grass for the primed jaws of man-traps. If a man made his living by stealing the dead, the threat from vigilant and vengeful kin was a very real hazard.

But no clicks came from the dark. No steel teeth slammed closed about their legs, and up ahead they spotted a flaxen-haired youth, crouching low behind a steeply slanted tombstone. Hawke and the others followed Blackbird to the temporary shelter of a cluster of stones nearby.

Lucas was the newest member of the gang, and had yet to graduate past lookout duty, but he was a sensible lad and had killed his light as soon as he felt his warning would be heeded. He stared back at his companions from the gloom, the whites of his eyes visible as tiny grey orbs. With a jerk of his head he indicated a point away to his right.

Hawke stared out into the cemetery. At first he saw nothing but a darkness only penetrated by the moon-gilded outlines of mossy stones. He wondered for a moment whether the green young man had allowed his imagination rather too long a leash. A lapse that would see him corrected at the end of Blackbird's mallet-like fists. Then the shadows began to shift. It was barely perceptible at first, but, as his eyes drilled into the inky near distance, he knew that the movement was real. Arms gestured, heads bobbed. Two figures, it seemed, locked in animated discourse, some thirty yards away. They were both men, Hawke guessed, for though he could discern no features, both were tall and broad at the shoulders. One pivoted a half-step, and his silhouette, outlined for a split second by the moon, appeared to have a hook in place of one hand. Fortunately neither seemed to have noticed the faces hidden in the shadows.

Hawke made to move, but a thick forearm swung across his chest like a sailboat's boom.

"Wait," Blackbird growled softly.

"Should we not take our leave?"

"If they're res-men," Blackbird replied, "we need to send out a message." He took his free hand from Hawke's chest and placed it upon his own waist. It was where he kept his knife. "This is Szekely's turf. He'll not thank us for letting his rivals find profit at his expense."

That was true enough, Hawke conceded, but still he shook his head. "Only two of them?"

"Might be others," Goaty whispered from a little way behind.

"And where are the tools?" Hawke persisted. "Shovels, hooks. Not even a sack between them."

Blackbird considered his words for a moment, staring hard at the two silhouettes. He adjusted the bulging sack at his shoulder, finally betraying a sign of discomfort. "If they ain't here for a dig, what's their business?"

Hawke shrugged. "What do we care?"

Eventually Blackbird nodded, looking at the others. "Hawke's right. Let us take this bugger to market."

Θ

Theophilus Vine's anatomy school was one of the smaller establishments in the city. A terraced house, mid-way along Stanhope Street, of blackened bricks and dilapidated windows, it seemed a far cry from the ostentatious institutions with which it competed. But compete it did, for the simple reason that Doctor Vine paid well, and, as a result, his students always had fresh corpses to poke and prod and cut.

The six men and their newly excavated prize entered Vine's premises through a little side door away from the prying eyes of the main street. They were sheltered by the night, but that did not tempt them to recklessness. After all, it was not legal to dissect a human being unless that hapless person had been condemned to the fate after the gallows.

They grunted and hissed their way through the passage at the rear of the building, following Vine's assistant, Clementine, who had opened the door wearing a thick woollen robe pulled tight over her nightgown and a sour expression on her face. She was a ruddy-cheeked woman of middle age, with flat features, an unnaturally depressed nose and gnarled hands that should have belonged to a prize-fighter. She had a fussy, discontented air, and bustled along quickly, clearly peeved at the hour as she showed them through a yellow and white door that bore a hand-written sign: Anatomy Theatre.

Light filled the space within as Clementine lit a trio of oil lamps. The room had once been a kitchen, Hawke reckoned, for it still had a giant iron hearth at one end, a deep sink at another and hooks and shelves on all the walls. For its most recent incarnation, however, the cooking utensils, jars and pans had been supplanted by all manner of wicked looking implements, the tools of the dissector's trade. Tongs and blades and callipers, bone saws of varying size and shape, drills, scissors, scalpels and little curved knives, all beautifully crafted, all marked with their owner's initials, and all capable of eliciting a deep shudder within Hawke.

At Clementine's surly order, Blackbird, Hawke, Harlowe and Goaty manhandled the sack through the score of empty chairs that were strewn about and laid it out on the cold tiles at the room's centre. They cut it open without delay, the body slithering free like a giant baby torn from the grisliest womb imaginable. Blackbird spoke briefly to Clementine, coins chinked between them, while Hawke and the others unbound the dead flesh, hefted it onto one of the theatre's two stained and knife-scarred tables and pulled each limb straight. In the light Hawke found himself staring at the face of the dead man. He had been right in his guess. A man of perhaps twenty-two or twenty-three, just a little younger than himself, with fresh, unblemished skin beneath the whiskers. His eyelids had peeled back, revealing hazel eyes that stared serenely at the low ceiling. What had killed him?

"Puncture wound," a high-pitched, nasal voice rasped in startling answer.

Hawke turned on his heels, half expecting to see some black-cloaked warlock standing behind, evil eyes boring into his mind. "Doctor Vine?"

Theophilus Vine was a taciturn fellow of small stature, thinning pate and burgeoning midriff. He was in the process of putting on a filthy apron, brown with dried blood, and peered down at the body through thick spectacles that perched daintily on the end of his sharp little nose. "Here, d'you see? That was what you were considering, was it not? How the poor fellow met his maker?"

"Aye, sir," Hawke muttered, embarrassed at his transparency.

"Stabbed," Vine declared. He placed his forefinger on the lily-white abdomen, indicating a thin red line that was perhaps an inch across. It looked to Hawke like nothing more than a scratch.

The youngest of the gang, Lucas, moved up to stand beside Hawke. He was in his late teens, tall and thin, with a shock of unkempt hair that reminded Hawke of a straw thatch. "Don't look much."

Hawke shook his head. "Never do."

"Quite," Doctor Vine agreed, pushing his wire-rimmed lenses further up his nose. "The entry wound is often surprisingly nondescript. But it is the depth of the thing, d'you see?"

With that, he went to one of the wall hooks and selected a slender probe that was as long as his forearm, with a sharp point and a bone handle. Returning to the subject, he teased apart the livid surface skin with thumb and finger, inserting the probe into the wound. It stopped when about half its length had been swallowed by the flesh. "A proud six inches. It'll have pierced a vital structure." He straightened suddenly, the glint of enthusiasm twinkling across his eyes. "Still. We must make certain!"

Make certain? Hawke knew a deadly stab wound when he saw one. He had seen too many. Had come from a place where swords had cut down families, where the streets had run with the blood of innocents. He felt like weeping at the memories, seared onto his mind for as long as he drew breath, only dimmed when he was in his cups, and then for so fleeting a time it was hardly worthwhile.

"Turn 'im, lads," a voice growled. Hawke looked up to see that it was Blackbird, and he quickly set himself to the task.

Blackbird and Doctor Vine oversaw matters as the other men slid hands beneath the body, Hawke and Lucas at the thighs, Goaty, Harlowe and Gilroy at the shoulders. In a well-practised manoeuvre, and on the count of three, they lifted and turned the deceased - pale, naked flesh shimmering in the warm light - so that he rested face-down on the table.

"Looks like he's had a beating," Lucas noted in a rich East Anglian burr, pale eyes snaking across the mottled blue patches that covered the skin from shoulders to buttocks.

Vine shook his head, running his fingers almost tenderly along the spine. Pale tracks were left in their wake, scored where his nails moved through the sickly sweet liquid that had already begun to ooze through the skin. "The blood pools after death, young man."

Gilroy scratched at his crotch, rolling his eyes at the naive youth. "They all look like this, Lucas. I'm a porter over at The London, and I can't tells you 'ow many I seen like it." He left his genitals alone long enough to sniff his hand. “And now they’ll shave him so he looks like one o’ them wax models, and they’ll start slicin’ him up.”

“But that is not our work,” Blackbird’s voice echoed around the room. All eyes moved to see that he was already at the door. “We’re done here, lads. Let us be away.”

Θ

The day was bright for all that it was cold.

Hawke walked briskly along Bow Street, digging at a rotten gum beneath one of his molars with a sharp length of wire. The pain came in pulses, making him bite down on the metal strand. He welcomed it, for it cleared his mind.

A short distance later, and he was running up the steps leading to the door of the Dog & Bull. Shouldering it open, he was immediately forced to squint against the pungent fug of tobacco and stale beer. The inn was quiet at this time of day, unlike the less salubrious establishments he frequented amongst the rookeries around

Seven Dials. A few pairs of eyes glanced through the smoke at him in half interest, but most gazed implacably into their pots, oblivious to another face in the sprawling city.

Hawke turned to his left, moving quickly to a rough wooden table pressed up against the alehouse's only window. Taking a seat, he stared out through the dirty glass at the street beyond. He kept his greatcoat fastened while his body thawed, but took off his topper and placed it on the adjacent chair. Absently, he still prodded at the ragged and swollen gum while he observed the world go by. A costermonger pushed a barrow full of wizened red pippins over the cobbles, its load wobbling precariously as the front wheel bounced. Hawke watched in silence until the costermonger trundled past one particular group of buildings. They were handsome structures, he supposed, if stern-faced and austere, looming over Bow Street like the sentinels they spawned. Numbers 3 and 4. He stared hard.

A shadow startled him and he looked up. The man was tall, with fists like bear paws and the frame of a wrestler. One might, Hawke had often thought, forgive the assumption that he was a pugilist or navvy, but for the fellow's elegant attire. His blue coat, yellow waistcoat and jet-black cravat were the clothes of a man of means.

"May I sit?" the huge man asked as he took off his hat, his voice rounded by education, if forged unmistakably among the smoky, gas-lit streets of the capital.

Hawke nodded at the chair opposite, as though he had any choice in the matter. "My guest, Mister Ruthven."

George Ruthven was around the age of thirty, though his bearing and demeanour spoke of a man far older. His sandy hair was oiled neatly against his scalp, his mutton-chop side whiskers were pristinely trimmed to form a precise frame for his florid face, and his manner exuded confidence. He had small eyes that never stopped moving, twinkling with an unnerving intelligence, and his shoulders were permanently squared to keep his frame at its most imposing. He slid onto the bench opposite, setting his badge of office, a gilt-topped tipstaff, upon the table. Somewhere about his person, Hawke knew, there would be a William Lacey pistol, though he kept that concealed.

"Well?" Ruthven said.

"Gin," Hawke replied, coiling the wire and putting it in a pocket. He glanced out the window, at the brown leaves tumbling along the road before a bitter wind. "With some hot water," he added with a slight shiver.

"It'll be the death of you," Ruthven said. His thick red brows twitched. "Again."

Hawke ignored the barb. "So be it."

Ruthven's bulky arm shot up and he clicked his fingers.

A girl scurried smartly over. She did not look at Hawke. "What'll it be, Mister Ruthven?"

"Gin with hot water, Maggie. Small beer for me."

Maggie turned away. "Certainly, sir."

"And two slices of pigeon pie," Ruthven called after her.

Hawke's stomach seemed to have ears of its own, for it grumbled at the mention of food. "Thank you, sir."

Ruthven picked at something between front teeth that were like twin tombstones; big and flat and grey. "Can't let my favourite informant starve now, can we?” He sat back, folded his arms, his face settling into a half-smirk that spoke of a man very comfortable with the trajectory his life had taken.

The dagger at Hawke’s belt seemed suddenly heavy. Christ, but he hated the smug bastard. George Ruthven was a Bow Street Patrol Officer, a Runner to most, though he would never deign to use the unofficial moniker, and his name was known across the capital. As Principal Officer, Ruthven was a big cog in the thief-taking machine established in the middle of the last century, but his real fame had come from his part in the arrest of the Cato Street conspirators the previous winter. The group of ultra-radicals, known as the Society of Spencean Philanthropists, had planned to overthrow the government, beginning with the assassination of the cabinet, most of whom, they had discovered, were due to dine together at the house of a privy councillor, Lord Harrowby. Ruthven had learnt of these plans and led a party of Bow Street personnel to the conspirators’ hiding place in a stable in nearby Cato Street. In the fight that followed, one Runner had died, the Cato Street gang had been smashed, and Ruthven had made his name. Now, a year and a half on, the principal Officer was the darling of the great and good of London, and the nemesis of the rest.

"I hear the Caribbee fellow's taken the reins," Ruthven said.

Hawke nodded. "Blackbird."

"Looks a brute."

"Jack Tar, as was. Then into smuggling."

Ruthven fiddled with the rim of his hat, his expression one of wry amusement. "A life as colourful as his complexion. And now he slits throats and steals corpses." He looked up sharply. "What did they do with Sheepy's body?"

Hawke waited while Maggie came over with their drinks. She set them down and returned to the counter to fetch two plates. Bending slowly, so that the fulsomeness of her bosom could not be ignored, she laid the crumbling segments of cold pie in front of each man. Hawke almost laughed at the brazenness of the gesture, for she might have been mistaken for one of the whores that flocked about the taverns of St Giles. Not that she had any interest in him, of course. Her eyes were firmly fixed upon the dashing officer and, he felt certain, the wealth it was rumoured he now possessed. Hawke caught her coquettish smile as she backed away, and his amusement soured. Girls like her had once reserved their winks and pouts for him. Back when he had been tall and handsome. Before it had happened. Before everything changed. Now he was just tall. His muscles had withered away, his skin turned as pasty as the corpses in which he dealt, his teeth decayed to mottled amber, his blue eyes dull. He felt like a faded man. A silhouette of what once he had been.

Ruthven cleared his throat noisily. "Sheepy?"

"Into the river," Hawke said, blinking away his reverie, "like all the rest." Sheepy Johns, dubbed so on account of his curly white hair, had been the leader until a quarrel in a rookery soup shop had ended with a rusty knife slammed deep into his belly. It had taken a long time for him to die, but die he had, writhing and puking, shitting himself and calling for a mother he had probably never laid eyes on.

"Does that make you number two?" Ruthven asked thoughtfully as he lifted the ale pot to his lips.

Hawke nodded, scratching the dark stubble at his skull. He had had to take a razor to his head to keep the lice at bay. “For the time being.”

Ruthven raised his cup in mock salute. “Then I toast your promotion.”

Hawke felt his face flush. He gritted his teeth. “Szekely seems to favour me.” He shrugged. “Thinks I’m useful on account of my letters.”

“Does he know your,” Ruthven pursed his lips as he searched for the word, and the corners of his mouth twitched, “story?”

Hawke said that he did not. “Such news would not be welcome, I suspect.”

Ruthven chuckled. “But he knows you can fight.” His little eyes raked appraisingly over Hawke’s torso. “Despite your obvious frailties.”

Hawke bridled inwardly at that, not so much in response to the mockery, but because it was a thrust that was painfully true. He glared at the table, his bony arms feeling suddenly more brittle. He wondered if they could even wield a sword any more. “Aye.”

“Then you are useful for that alone,” the Principal Officer said. He waited for Hawke to meet his gaze. “And yet?”

“And yet Blackbird has a particular friend who eyes my place.”

Ruthven drew a handkerchief from his sleeve and dabbed the corners of his mouth. “The hospital porter?”

“Gilroy Penley?” Hawke shook his head. “He’s useful for his connections with the anatomists, but he hasn’t the wit.”

“The one they call Goaty, then?”

“The same.”

Ruthven screwed up his mouth in distaste. “Appears to have had half his face ripped off.”

“You have it precisely, sir. Mastiff down at one of the Southwark pits. Jumped the fence.”

Ruthven snorted. “Mistook him for a bear, did it?”

“Evidently.”

Hawke looked down at his drink. Just the sight of it made him salivate. It was life itself. Pure, unadulterated life. He worked for the stuff. Lived for it. Though he despised what it had done to him, how it had gnawed away at his insides and his mind, that did not stop him yearning for the next drink as though it were a secret lover. He felt the fingers of his right hand gently tremble, and he wrapped them about the glass, squeezing harder than necessary, hurrying the liquid to his mouth as though the world depended upon it.

The gin, strong and bitter, burned remorselessly at his tongue and lips. He swilled the liquid about his mouth, raised as it was to a pleasant warmth by the water, bathing his teeth, feeling his pulse thump at their roots where his gums were suddenly lambent. The ache in his molar was muffled, the frayed edges of his nerves tied away, and, in a single, glorious moment, the memories of home were washed distant. Purged to half-formed wraiths. He closed his eyes.

"You'll continue," Ruthven said as he watched the drink he had purchased disappear down Hawke's throat.

Hawke opened his eyes, lowered the glass, his face feeling the warmth of the gin, pulsating and welcome. He stared at the Bow Street Runner, wondering whether the words had been meant as a question or a statement. Ruthven seemed careless of the scrutiny, concentrating instead on the pie that he now greedily devoured.

Hawke had decided to follow suit when Ruthven said, "Grubbing in the mud again?"

He looked up from the pie cradled in his palms, realising Ruthven had noticed the grime beneath his fingernails. He licked crumbs from his lips. "We made a lift last night, aye."

"Flesh only, one hopes?"

Hawke took a bite of the pastry-flecked pigeon meat as he nodded. A corpse was not considered property in the eyes of the law, and the grave robbers – the Resurrection Men as they were often called – who obtained fresh cadavers for the insatiable anatomy schools, were careful to take only what they required. To dig up a naked body would see you rapped across the knuckles by the magistrates, perhaps fined if you were unlucky, but little more. A man caught stealing goods from a burial – clothes, jewellery, anything – might be tried for theft, and that would see him transported to the colonies, or worse.

"Flesh only," Hawke said after another mouthful.

"Good. Wouldn't wish to see so useful an agent strung up."

"I am not your agent."

Ruthven wrinkled his flat nose to show that he cared little for Hawke's belligerence. "My eyes and ears, then. My window on to the underworld." He set down the pie crust and took a swig of beer. "It was successful, this lift?"

"Aye," Hawke said, thinking back to the night's work. He stifled a shudder. Not for the act itself, but for the oppressive knowledge that he found the theft and sale of corpses so simple a thing. He had been in London two years, a resurrection man for half that time, and already the work had become mundane to him.

"What was the trade?" Ruthven asked.

"One large."

"Receiver?"

"Doctor Vine, out at Stanhope Street."

Ruthven tapped his forefinger lightly against his temple. "Good to know. How much did he pay?"

"Eight guineas."

"I'm pleased for you," the big man said dryly. "Or rather, I'm pleased for Szekely. I hope he remunerates you well."

"You would not be speaking with me if that were the case."

Ruthven's broad face split in a grin. "Touché."

"Why am I here, Mister Ruthven?" Hawke said quickly, for he did not wish to dwell upon Szekely. The mere mention of the name made his blood run chill.

"I summoned you." Ruthven tilted back his lantern jaw and quaffed the remainder of his beer.

"I got the note, sir, but I have no news of significance," Hawke persisted. He leaned in a touch. "So it must be you who have something to impart."

Ruthven set down the pot, placing his elbows on the table and making a steeple of his hands. "I would ask you to keep your ear to the ground."

"Don't I always?"

Ruthven's small eyes became suddenly tiny in that vast skull, his face sagging. "Two weeks ago, a pair of bodies were pulled out of a sewer beneath Upper Thames Street. One was a tosher named Varney Tapp, the other a little girl, who we believe to be one Betsy Milne, daughter of a Smithfield slaughter-man."

Hawke stared back at the officer, barely able to contain his incredulity. "That's what you've dragged me over here for? A sewer sucker and a gutter snipe? You expect me to believe the Runners are interested in either of those poor bastards?"

Ruthven's jaw twitched. "We are not Runners, Hawke, we are Bow Street Patrol Officers." He sat back, cracked his knuckles. "The girl was wrapped."

Hawke frowned. "Raped?"

"Wrapped."

"In a shroud?"

"In stalks," Ruthven said. "Two kinds." He fished briefly inside his blue coat, producing a pair of what looked to be plant cuttings, each between six and eight inches long, one green and the other light brown. He placed them on the table. "Taken from the body."

Hawke picked up the greener piece. It had the texture of celery, but its aroma struck him instantly. "Fennel?"

"What say you of the other?"

Hawke inspected it, then shrugged. "Tell me."

"We cannot identify it. The victim was woven within the stuff. Like a cocoon." Ruthven traced an invisible line with a finger beneath his chin. "That's how she died. Throttled with the stuff. But-"

"But?"

Ruthven seemed to hesitate, then blew out those ruddy cheeks as though his head were a huge set of bellows. "She had no face," he said eventually, his tone unusual for its sudden discomfiture. "Or rather, it had been ripped off."

Silence followed. Hawke stayed leaning in, Ruthven remained as he was. “Ripped off?” Hawke echoed the words slowly, hoping he had misheard.

The tension in Ruthven’s face told him his ears functioned as well as ever. “Eyes gouged out, nose cut off, that kind of thing. You can appreciate why such a find has come to our attention.”

“The tosher-man?”

“Not he. His end came by way of a knife in the back.”

Hawke slumped backwards, rubbing his palms hard over his eyes, as though the images could be purged from his mind. “Jesus wept,” he whispered, and now the faceless girl faded, only to be replaced by other children. Cleaved and bloodied. Their mothers too. All hewn by steel and rage and hate. Not again, his mind muttered, and he planted his hands on the table top and pushed himself upright. “Not for me, Mister Ruthven,” he said blearily, as though waking from some nightmare. “Not this time.”

But George Ruthven's tipstaff was immediately up, flashing across to press against Hawke's narrow waist, barring his escape. "Stay, Mister Hawke," Ruthven intoned. "I said stay."

The words were laced with threat, and Hawke did as he was told, but as soon as he had checked for prying eyes he hissed, "Fuck you, Ruthven. You do not own me." He moved round the edge of the table, easing back the tipstaff, and craned over the pots and the remnants of pigeon pie to look down upon the man in the expensive silken waistcoat. "You pay me to pass you information so that you and your bastard Runners can stay ahead of the villains. I do that. Happily so, for I once observed things from your side of the wall. But this? A child mutilated?" He shook his head slowly. "Not this."

Ruthven laughed, though it was a dark sound, devoid of mirth or empathy. "My side of the wall? Your delusions demean us both, you gin-soaked wastrel. You do as you're told because Szekely does not pay you enough to keep you in drink and opium, and because you are not fit for employment elsewhere."

“I will give up the gin,” Hawke spluttered, “if it will keep me from this task.”

Ruthven laughed again, lowering the tipstaff. “Is that right? Tell me, Joshua. How are the good folk of Droylsden?” He put the stave to his lips, blowing warm breath across the shining end and polishing it with his sleeve. When he was satisfied, he glanced up. “Your mother? How about dear Uncle Jack?”

Hawke thought he would be sick there and then. He swallowed hard, felt his eyes prick with heat. “You wouldn’t.”

Ruthven stood suddenly. Hawke was not a short man, nearly six feet, but the lawman looked down upon him, his boxer’s face brutal in the smoky air. “Try me,” he replied slowly. “You are a member of Colan Szekely’s organisation. Ghouls, traders in death. You disgust me. But your position is useful, so I allow you to continue. I pay you for your whispers, Hawke, but you are not my employee. You are my creature. You’ll do as you’re damn well told. Not because of this,” he jabbed the tipstaff into Hawke’s ribs, then nodded at the empty gin glass on the table, “or even that. But because I know who you are." He leaned closer, the smell of beer and meat and pastry on his breath. "Who you really are, Joshua Hawke. And don't bloody well forget it." He backed away suddenly, the aggression ebbing. "I've a great deal riding on this case. If you do not offer your assistance freely, I will be left with little choice but to dig up your roots and place them in the palm of Colan Szekely. If ever he discovered your duplicity, he would weight your ankles and dump you in the river." He indulged in a triumphal smirk. "If he were to learn of your past as well, your death would not be so easy."

Hawke slumped back, deflated and defeated. "Bastard."

"Be sure to set about your work promptly. The penny bloods are full of the tale. Sensationalised, of course. Witches and sorcerers and demons, stalking the night and preying upon beautiful young maidens." He rubbed his face, suddenly looking exhausted. "But the newspapers will duly follow, and I shall have a riot on my hands."

"And my work is what, exactly?"

"Our officers have encountered something of a dead end," Ruthven said bleakly, the corner of his eye flickering. It was evidently not easy for him to admit Bow Street's shortcomings, and that fact alone cheered Hawke immensely. "It is imperative that this matter is resolved swiftly, and to the satisfaction of the mob, but no one will speak with us." He shrugged. "There are no witnesses."

Hawke folded his arms. "Do I get a tipstaff?"

"You get to live a little longer," Ruthven said flatly. "I need a man with a modicum of wit, experience in the detection of villainy and the requisite connections within the city's criminal fraternity. You may have fallen far, Mister Hawke, but you once served under Joseph Nadin."

"The man was as crooked as Szekely."

"The man was an excellent thief-taker and Deputy-Constable of Manchester. If you worked for Nadin, then you can work for me."

Hawke shook his head. "Those days are long behind me. I'll pass you information, as I have always done, but no more."

Ruthven fished in his coat, pulling out a small but bulging leather bag that chinked loudly as he set it on the table. "You will learn who killed Betsy Milne. This bounty will free up whichever axles may need greasing. The remainder is yours, to be invested in as much gin and laudanum as you can consume."

Hawke stared at the money. It was a small fortune. He licked his lips greedily, like a wolf eyeing a lamb, and instantly chided himself, yet there was little point in playing it coy. He slid out a hand that quaked slightly, gathering up the purse as though it contained the very secret to salvation.

Ruthven smiled coldly down at him. "There's a good chap."

Hawke forced his mind back to the matter in question. "Two weeks, you said. Since the bodies were discovered. Can I see them?"

Ruthven shook his head. "Long since buried. But they were not killed a fortnight ago. They were much decomposed. The coroner believed the crime took place back in the autumn."

"Who found them?"

"Another tosher-man, named Mayhew."

"I will need to speak with him."

"Be my guest. You'll find him with the mudlarks and beggars down on the north foreshore. Do not think my men have omitted him from our enquiries. He was questioned."

"And?"

"A fool and a sot. Worthless."

"Even so," Hawke began, but Ruthven cut him off.

"A word to the wise. Rumour has it that Boris Milne sniffs vengeance."

"Milne?" Hawke replied, nonplussed. "The girl's father? The butcher?"

Ruthven nodded. "He believes his poor dead daughter was the victim of resurrection men requiring fresher corpses than usual."

"Is he right?"

Ruthven sucked his teeth. "You tell me."

"Not that I have heard," Hawke said truthfully. "Might be another gang, but not one of ours."

"As I suspected," Ruthven said. "She was shredded and slashed, not anatomised, though a layman would not know the difference." He took a lingering breath through his big nostrils. "Butcher Milne blames you and your kind, and why wouldn't he? And he has repute, Mister Hawke. He is known to slaughter more than livestock. You had better expedite your investigations, or he'll soon be knocking at your door." With a wink, Ruthven turned on his heels. "Maggie! One more here!"

The serving girl brandished a blushing smile. "'Course, Mister Ruthven, sir. What shall you 'ave? Same again?"

Ruthven shook his head. "Not I, Maggie. For my friend, here. Gin. Just gin." He grinned nastily. "Always gin! Place it on my account."

Maggie smiled sweetly, though it was obvious she had no interest serving Hawke if the hero of London was not to remain. "Right away, sir."

Ruthven cast Hawke an uncompromising stare. "A girl with her face ripped off." He set his jaw as if bracing himself against the image. "Something evil lurks, Hawke, and I'll not have it in my town." His gaze flickered to the table, where the stem cuttings lay side by side. "Keep those. Find their significance." He went towards the door, hesitating to glance across his wide shoulder. "You were someone once. A man of justice, like me. I am not asking you to turn thief-taker. Merely pose a few discreet questions. You know people who might have heard something. Sniff about in the taprooms, listen at dark doorways. Wade in the filth you call home. Tell me what you discover."

And with that, he was gone.

Θ

The stink of the Thames, of open gutters, of horse shit and smoke was ripe in Hawke's nostrils as he trudged home. It was dusk now, gaslight casting a wan cloak over the streets and buildings. The shadows at the road's edges seemed all the deeper for it, as though forced to work harder against the tremulous glow, and Hawke made certain to stay in the very centre of the cobbled thoroughfare. He looked left and right with every pace, senses as keen as the knife sheathed at his belt, eyes and ears searching the penumbra for sinister shapes and sounds. A shadow shifted beneath one of the towering lamps. Hawke put a hand to his new purse, let the other hand slide to the dagger's bone handle, his jaw suddenly tight, but he soon saw that a pair of children huddled there, draped in rags, pressed together for warmth. They would not likely survive the winter, and he wondered if he would soon be pulling them from a shallow pauper's grave, destined for the schools and their scalpels.

A discordant symphony of hooves and wheels rose up behind him, smashing the children from his mind's eye, and he leapt to the side as a hackney carriage clattered past. He spat in its wake, curses drowned by the din.

"Waste o' hot air, friend," a man's voice called from a florist's bolted doorway. "They wouldn't hear if you were perched on their shoulders."

Hawke squinted into the gloom to see the toothless visage of an elderly man with slate-grey hair and a beard fringed in white. He was wrapped against the cold in a woollen shawl, a garment doubtless long discarded by some high-class lady, though his feet were bare and berry-red in the feeble light. "You're right, of course."

The old man stooped, hunching against the chill breeze, but he straightened a touch, watery eyes widening. "Well strike me down, sir, if you do not hail from God's own country!"

"Lancashire, friend," Hawke said.

"Yorkshireman, me, and proud in it! But not an educated fellow like thysen, m'lord!" His dry-looking lips peeled back in a rictus grin. "Got a coin or three for a fellow northerner?" He gave a mock salute. "And a veteran o' Waterloo!"

There but for the grace of God go I, Hawke thought. A bitter internal voice sneered, there but for the indulgence of Messrs Szekely and Ruthven. Not wishing to display his newfound funds, he plucked a clipped and worn farthing from the pocket of his greatcoat, tossing it to the beggar. "I applaud the effort, friend, but you're too old to've fought at Waterloo."

The man shrugged. "Worth a throw, was it not? Were you there, m'lord?"

“I was too young.” But you saw fighting, the disembodied voices whispered around Hawke’s skull, cackling, mocking. He shook his head as though it were full of bees. “And don’t call me lord.”

His voice, he had hoped when first he reached London, would be his saving grace. Clipped and disciplined by pricey education, but warmed by the tones of his native county, Hawke had expected it to keep him in the right strata of society. He wanted to find work in a law firm, or as a clerk for one of the big trading companies out at the docks. But he had found matters to the contrary, for he could not prove his credentials, had no letter of recommendation, and was deliberately vague about his background. Furthermore, he had come to the city with only modest funds, and none of the better kind of folk would deal with him in attire made shabby by the long hike south. He had quickly been forced to scrape for work of a humbler nature. Clerking in a less well-heeled establishment, perhaps, or shop work, if only to get his new life started. In the event, even that proved difficult, for the whiff of schooling in his tone worked against him when dealing with London’s poorest. It was only six years since the defeat of Bonaparte’s forces, and former soldiers still flooded the metropolis. The threat of civil strife simmered in the alehouses and gin shops, and the government were alert to any potential trouble makers. The common folk of London mistrusted a man asking for a pauper's wage with the voice of the gentry. They took him for a spy. Which, of course, he was, Hawke reflected ruefully as he turned into Plumbtree Street. But not in the way folk assumed.

He took a left and paced into Phoenix Street. He was in the place he called home now, the slum known as St Giles rookery, and he slipped his hand beneath the hem of his coat and gripped the hilt of his knife again. It was eerily quiet. There was almost no light here, the shadows growing in confidence as the lamps became fewer, their black talons lengthening to steal more of the dying day. Here was Hawke's new world; the one he had received in the ill-fated trade for his former self. The one, he now accepted, awarded him as penance. Punishment for sins he knew he would never erase.

It had not started badly. A job as an assistant in the London Hospital out at Whitechapel had seen him earn enough to fill his belly.

He cleaned floors and moved patients and emptied buckets of excrement. It was hard enough work, but not entirely to be disliked. And yet his mind would not let him be at ease. It maintained a state of worry, replaying the old memories over and over, keeping him from sleep, barring him from happiness. He had turned to drink. Successfully to begin with. A perfect balance of hospital and gin shop, allowing him to work and sleep and function as a genuine member of society for the first time since he had fled Droylsden. But then the scales had begun to tip, so gradually that he had not foreseen the change until the balance was weighted fully on the side of the drink, and soon he had stopped eating, preferring to spend all of his coin on the liquid that had become a life-giving elixir. In a matter of a few short months he was missing work altogether, preferring to spend the days in gin shops and opium dens rather than hospital wards, and before he knew where he was, the job had been given to a more reliable man. A sober man.

Hawke lodged in a cramped, dank, mouldering room nestled in the roof of an ancient tenement on Buckbridge Street in the very heart of the rookery. The whole building leaned severely so that a man could almost touch the eaves of the rooftops on the far side of road, and he glanced up as he negotiated the steps to the entrance, making sure no piss buckets were poised above. He moved quickly inside, shouldering open the door that was never locked, and up the splintered, crumbling staircase that was the structure's decrepit spine. He scaled three floors, each with its own landing and several doorways, some of which seemed to speak to him as groans and shouts and laughter and sobs emanated from the rooms beyond. Tonight, like every night, there would be screams. He reached the attic rooms. There were two doors, one on either side of the staircase, and he went right. He wondered if Lucas would be awake. He had not wished to share with the straw-haired stripling, but the lad was new to the city, having walked barefoot all the way from a fishing village on the Norfolk coast, and Szekely had taken the lad under his wing. And what Szekely wanted, he got. He was not a bad employer, Hawke mused. Indeed, the man had saved Hawke's life just as he had saved Lucas. Hawke's time at the London Hospital had put him in contact with a porter named

Gilroy Penley, and Penley, it transpired, was a resurrection man, who happened to be part of a gang working the cemeteries during the blackest nights of winter. At first Hawke had baulked at the idea of partaking in such a grim business. The sack-'em-up men, as they were often called, were hated as much as they were feared, and it was dangerous work. But it was work. And Hawke, above all, needed funds, because the gin shops called to him. The memories needed smothering.

The door to his room was ajar, which was not unusual. Hawke pushed it open, called to Lucas, expecting the spotty-faced pup to grin up at him from his raggedy bed in the far corner.

Instead, Joshua Hawke froze. Lucas was there, lying flat as he had expected, and at first it looked as though he was grinning as he always did, but as Hawke's eyes adjusted to the gloom, he saw that it was not a natural smile that greeted him, rather one made by man. A man with a blade, who had torn a broad, ragged slash across the lad's windpipe. Blood had coursed down Lucas's narrow chest, so that his shirt was as dark as the grubby sheets in which he was bundled.

Hawke moved closer, hearing himself swear. It was obvious there was nothing he could do, for Lucas was long dead. A fan of crimson droplets stained the rest of the bed, describing the pulse of his rapidly emptied jugular. The whole place stank of coppery blood.

Hawke staggered back, feeling the damp wall against his shoulder blades. He slipped in something wet, toppling onto his rump, and realised with horror that the floorboards, too, were thick with blood. He sprawled where he fell, scrabbling to find purchase, eventually inching to his feet like a fawn on an icy pond. He needed to leave, but he could not move his legs properly. He knew he should summon Szekely, or even Ruthven, but what if they accused him? He decided to hide the body. Make the whole horrific mess disappear. Tell everyone that Lucas must have done a midnight flit. He looked again at the corpse. The world swam before him, his feet and hips and guts all turning to water. He slumped heavily to his knees. There was a loose floorboard nearby and he reached for it, levering up the plank with savagely bitten nails. A lifeline glinted in the shallow, rectangular chasm beneath. He lunged for it, grasping the cold glass as a drowning man might grasp a floating spar. Then he reeled away, thumbing open the stopper and jamming the bottle between his lips. Nothing else mattered. Lucas could wait.

CHAPTER TWO

THURSDAY

The icy water felt like shattering glass against Hawke's skin. He gasped, flailing wildly, for a split second fearing he had been dumped in the Thames like the hapless Sheepy Johns.

His eyes sprung open and he sat up with a start. It appeared to be daytime, for a feeble grey light bathed everything. His head pounded, hammer on anvil, and he thought he might pass out to the tune of his own blood rushing in his ears. The sight of a round, cleanly shaved face staring at him from beneath a high quality beaver hat brought a sudden, chilling clarity. The man was ghostly in his pallor, save the eyes which were glittering and baby-blue. The nose was pinched and arrow-straight, while the lips, pursed in curiosity, were narrow and purple. A thin, white scar bisected the left cheek from eyelid to mouth, the legacy of some long healed but never forgotten violence.

Hawke realised where he was, not that it took a great deal of deduction. He had not moved since the night before. He had lain beside the hole in the floor, empty gin bottle cradled close like a lover, and now he was sitting, rump numb, beside a pool of his own vomit. There were more figures in the room, faces he recognised, and from their mouths came low mutterings as they surveyed the chamber. He realised they were looking at the bed on which a cadaver still rested, stiff and mottled.

"My dear *Sólyom*," the man in the beaver hat was saying, the strange concoction of Irish and Hungarian parentage brewing a famously exotic accent. He was dressed in an expensive looking suit of fine black wool that was expertly tailored to his narrow frame. "You look poorly."

"Mister Szekely?" Hawke managed to croak.

Szekely held up a staying palm that was upholstered in spotless kidskin the colour of cream. "Shh, now, *Sólyom*," he said softly, using the pet name reserved for Hawke. "Rest." The blue eyes flickered to the bloodstained bed and back. "You must be exhausted after so strenuous a night."

"Christ," Hawke rasped, panicking as he caught the intimation like a punch to the guts. He tried to stand, shaking his head as vigorously as his pulsating skull would allow. He trod in the vomit and slipped. "Christ, Mister Szekely, I..."

"You look poorly," Szekely cut him off, indicating for him to remain seated, "but perhaps not as poorly as he." He jerked his chin towards the bed. "Tell me, *Sólyom*, what did young Lucas ever do to you?"

One of the other men sidled into view, still clutching the bucket that had been used to dowse him. It was the hulking form of Blackbird, his scalp almost scraping the tie beam that held up the roof. He set down the empty pail and glowered grimly from above folded arms that looked like entwined gun barrels. "This had better be good."

Hawke shook his head again. "I..." he searched, desperately, for words that would exonerate, but he knew he had none. There was no alibi at all. "I did not..."

Szekely tutted slowly. "Come, come, *Sólyom*, waste not your breath on denial." He adjusted the flamboyant white cravat that bloomed like petals beneath his narrow chin. "Cleanse your conscience."

"I did not do..." Hawke twisted, levelling a trembling finger at the bed, "... that. I did not kill him, I swear. Mister Szekely, please believe me."

"It appears you are determined to waste your breath," Szekely said, resigned to hearing what he evidently considered to be a futile argument. He stepped forwards a touch and crouched low before his prone subordinate. "Very well."

"I returned last night," Hawke said, mind sifting frantically through the silt of disjointed and half-formed memories.

"From?" Szekely asked patiently, as though speaking to a child.

Ruthven! Principal Officer George Ruthven! Bow Street Runner, hero of London's thief-takers! Scourge of men like Colan Szekely! Hawke clamped shut his eyes, screwing the lids hard down as though they would dam the stream. A stream, if articulated, that would surely see his guts teased out through his nostrils. "A tavern," he answered at length.

"Which?"

"I forget," Hawke answered.

"And?" Blackbird chimed in.

"And that is the fact of the matter," Hawke retorted hotly, managing defiance when not addressing Szekely. "I drank until I was in my cups. I came home." He shrugged. "I found Lucas."

"You did not quarrel?" Szekely asked. He removed his hat to reveal an entirely bald pate. Not shaved to stubble, like Hawke's, but as smooth as an egg. The gesture made Hawke flinch. "You did not fly into a rage?" He blew gently on the hat's upturned rim. "Blackbird says you have a temper."

A thought struck Hawke and he reached for his belt. "Here."

Blackbird and the others, men Hawke now recognised to be Goaty and Harlowe, converged as one, instinctively moving to protect their master. But Szekely, not remotely flustered, held up the hat like a barrier. “Hold.” The gang froze in place. The pale face regarded Hawke and nodded. “Continue, my dear *Sólyom*.”

“My dagger,” Hawke said, inching it free as slowly as he could. He turned it so that the blade shone in the weak light. “It is clean, see?”

“So you cleaned it,” Szekely said, unimpressed.

Hawke got up, slowly so as not to trigger the others to violence, and staggered over to Lucas. He stared down at the corpse. His guts twisted cruelly but there was nothing left to bring up. “He lies flat,” he managed to mutter through the gasps. “There are no wounds to his hands.”

“What’s that got to do,” Goaty said angrily, scratching the beard that only partially masked the misshapen tangle of scars that was his lower face, “with ‘is fackin’ neck?”

"The suggestion," Szekely answered calmly, "is that Lucas put up no fight."

"And I am uninjured," Hawke went on, sensing with relief that the Hungarian was gradually questioning his own initial reaction. He made himself look into Szekely's chill gaze, desperate to seize upon what little momentum had gathered. "Do you think neither of us would have suffered defensive wounds had we fought?"

"Hark at him," Blackbird muttered, dockyard iron softened by sugar island drawl. "He sound like a coroner."

Szekely's delicate eyebrow arched at that.

"The craven bastard offed him while he slept," Goaty remarked before his leader could speak.

Hawke shot him an acidic look. "Then we were not quarrelling."

"So you waited for him to fall asleep," Goaty sneered. "Planned it."

"Precisely. You must ask yourself why I would do such a thing. Do you think me so cold blooded?"

"Aye," Goaty said nastily. "I do."

Hawke looked instead at Szekely. "Do you?"

Szekely gnawed briefly at his upper lip, staring hard at the waxen cadaver, before turning back to fix that glittering gaze upon Hawke. "I am undecided."

"And look at the floor," Hawke blurted, letting his mind tumble, studying the room for the finest detail in the knowledge that it might just save his skin. "It is covered in blood. Would it be so, if he had been attacked in his bed?" That got him to thinking. He bent down to inspect Lucas's neck wounds, which were savage and undoubtedly lethal, but it was true that the spatter, congealing and fading to brown, was far too extensive to be the consequence of an assault confined to the bed area. Yet, as he had stated to Szekely, there was a conspicuous lack of defensive wounds. Could Lucas have been sleeping when he - they? - had come for him? Examining the scene after abject terror had sharpened Hawke's wits like a whetstone to a blade, he suddenly did not think so. Then he saw the marks. Below and to the side of the gaping slash, just above the dead man's right collar bone. He stooped closer, narrowing his eyes to resist the gloom. At first he took them for tattoos, for they were circular in nature, about an inch apart, and etched in a zig-zag pattern, almost like a pair of wheels. But they were tiny, each the size of a well-fed tick, and hardly worthy of the effort of ink and needle. He touched his fingers to one of the marks. It was crisp where the blood had dried. He applied a little pressure, cracking the seal, and wetness gleamed underneath. A fresh wound in its own right.

"Why did you not summon me immediately?" Szekely was saying.

Hawke straightened. "I keep a gin bottle stashed beneath the boards," he answered truthfully. "It was the first thing I thought to do."

"You are truly pathetic, *Sólyom*," Szekely said.

"I do not deny it."

Szekely leaned in. "Look me in the eye. Did you kill Lucas?"

"No. I came home, found him. I did not know what to do. In the end, I chose to drink it away."

"He lies," Goaty said.

The Hungarian ignored his mastiff-mangled acolyte, glancing instead at the man who led the gang in Szekely's name. "Blackbird?"

Blackbird shrugged those powerful shoulders. "What does it matter? We've all done worse."

"It matters," Szekely replied, "because good workers are hard to come by." He looked back at Hawke. "Let us say I believe you, *Sólyom*. Would that please?"

Hawke nodded vigorously, relief flooding his body like laudanum. He had seen, and done, enough bad things in his life to know that men were wicked, but this man, this pallid, slightly built and softly spoken figure transcended such simplicity. For all his urbane manners, he was terror incarnate. "It would, Mister Szekely, that it would."

Szekely sighed heavily, standing straight. "You are a sot. A husk of a man."

"I know it."

"But you are clever, I think. I know you can read and write, which is more than most, and you speak well. But there is something else behind that gaze." Szekely cocked his head to the side, examining Hawke as a hawk might examine a sparrow. "A wit within. Once sharp, now dull, but not yet blunt. If you did not kill Lucas, I would be glad to know who did." He replaced his hat, and said, "There; your opportunity."

"Opportunity?" Hawke echoed, baffled.

"Find the culprit," Szekely replied as though it were obvious.

"If it ain't Hawke," Blackbird spoke now, "then it's the Giltspur Boys."

The Hungarian nodded thoughtfully. "Aye, you are probably right. And perhaps that is precisely what *Sólyom* will discover. I should like to know for sure."

Blackbird seemed perturbed. "I will discover the truth of it, Colan."

"No, my friend, you will not," Szekely said. "Subtlety is required here, not brute force. I would avoid a war with the Giltspurs if possible. You are a cudgel. Our associate, here, might just prove himself the scalpel I need." When Blackbird's proud chin essayed a reluctant nod, Szekely eyed Hawke. "You know our world and the folk within it, yet you do not cut so distinct a figure as we. Move among the shadows, vanish therein. Turn over a few rocks. See what crawls out."

"I will, Mister Szekely," Hawke said, for he had no other choice. "Which den do the Giltspur Boys frequent?"

"*The Bell*, at Smithfield."

That final word resonated in Hawke's mind like the toll of a gong. He found himself in the *Dog & Bull*, staring into the laconic gaze of George Ruthven. What had he said about the dead girl? He knew the matter was a risk to pursue, but nor would he again be afforded so ripe an opportunity. He said, as lightly as possible, "Funny. They were talking of it in the tap-house."

"Talking of *The Bell*?" Blackbird said.

Hawke shook his head. "Smithfield."

"Oh?" prompted Szekely.

"Something Milne," Hawke went on. "A butcher."

"Boris, aye," Szekely said. "What of him?"

Hawke met his eye levelly. “His daughter was killed.”

“You heard this in the tavern?”

Hawke nodded. “Gossip only. But it sounded bad. Murdered, they were saying.”

“Boris Milne is a known man,” Szekely said slowly, evidently running the implication through his mind as he spoke.

“Runs protection rackets,” Blackbird elaborated. “A fearsome cove.”

“I had not heard tell of his girl’s demise,” Szekely said. He laughed briefly, grimly. “Jesus, but I would not like to be in the perpetrator’s shoes.”

The others laughed too, though a vein of anxiety seemed to subdue the sound. They were scared of Butcher Milne. With good cause, Hawke thought, though they were ignorant to it. If Ruthven spoke true, the man blamed London’s network of grave robbers for the death. He glanced back at Lucas’s broken body. Perhaps Milne had already exacted revenge. But how could he articulate his concern to Szekely? It was all too tenuous for a half-heard rumour in a nameless drinking den, and he could hardly disclose his real source. "*The Bell*?" he repeated the name of the tavern he would visit.

"*The Bell*," Blackbird repeated the name irritably, "you dullard."

Hawke mouthed the word a couple more times, making a show of committing it to memory. "I do not know the area well."

Colan Szekely was already walking towards the door. He looked back briefly. "That is why you will take Corissa."

Θ

The man and woman moved with one mind, darting through the alleys like shoaling fish, silently, instinctively, inseparable. To anyone who cared notice, they were a couple, lovers, linked by hand and intent on an evening of shared company, the rest of the world an irrelevance to be blotted out. They ignored the calls of the meat vendors as the last of Smithfield's myriad stalls were packed away in the rimy dusk. They leapt an offal-clogged gutter that was already skeined in new frost, skirted a cluttered repository for empty barrows, and moved swiftly between tables upturned in preparation for folding. The butchers bellowed to one another, smeared pink hands on crimson aprons, wiped cleavers and packed away blades of every length and severity. Kites, gulls and crows circled above, biding their time for the feast of fleshy scraps over which they would do battle with a legion of rodents. The district lamplighter tramped over the cobbles nearby, heading for the lamp that stood on sentry duty at the centre of the market, while smaller lights illuminated many of the shadowy tributaries that funnelled London's population in and out of the area.

The man and woman took one such path, scuttling quickly so as not to tarry in the dangerous gloom. The city was as alive at night as it was by day, but the creatures abroad were a different breed all together. It was wise never to linger. At the end of the alleyway, where the buildings on either side gave way to a courtyard that was littered with animal dung, the couple came to a halt by a low door, above which creaked a hinged sign. It was daubed with a rough picture of a golden bell. The man, wrapped from chin to knees in a long greatcoat, shoved it open, propping it with a booted foot for his companion to cross the threshold. He doffed a silk top hat, the dents on the crown betraying hard use. She looked back as she stepped into the murky interior, pulling the blue shawl from her head to reveal a complexion that was exotically tanned, like creamy cinnamon, the mingling of Europe and the Orient. She winked coquettishly, her eyes large and almond-shaped. “Thank you, kind sir.”

Joshua Hawke followed her to a sticky table pushed hard against one of the tavern’s tobacco stained walls. “What’ll it be, Miss Lott?”

Corissa Lott licked lips that were plump and dark. “Gin?”

Hawke found himself transfixed on her glistening mouth as he waved a hand to summon service. “Gin, twice,” he said, sensing the pot-girl’s arrival but not looking round. When the rustle of skirts faded to nothing, he leaned in a touch. “What now?”

“We wait and watch,” Corissa said, her sharp local accent a stark contrast with Hawke’s. She took a moment to arrange the curls at her ears, making sure the rest of her long, coal-black hair remained pinned in its chignon knot at the nape of her neck. “The Giltspurs are hard to miss. Irish stock. All red heads and mad eyes." She made a theatrical shiver, though she was wrapped snuggly enough within a fur-lined pelisse coat that stretched all the way to her ankles. "Cold out there."

Hawke would have leapt over the table there and then if he thought his warming embrace would be remotely welcome. But she was a trifler, he thought. A game-player. She had always been kind to him, a little too friendly, given her relationship with Colan Szekely, and he half suspected her duty was to weed out those with the temerity to chance their arm with their employer's woman. Szekely valued loyalty almost as highly as he valued discretion, and it was probably good policy to test prospective newcomers to his organisation with the sweetest bait imaginable. Consequently, Hawke had to make do with staring at Corissa Lott from afar, and stare he most certainly did. She was a natural wonder, as far as he was concerned, a radiant flower that had somehow bloomed in this most barren, corrupt soil.

"You're a strange one, Joshua Hawke," Corissa said, the intense light from a newly stoked hearth dancing across eyes that were like nuggets of polished obsidian.

"Oh?"

Corissa waited a second as the serving girl appeared, taking the moment to pluck free her gloves. Two cloudy looking glasses full of gin were set down, and she clasped one with delicate fingers, wincing as she sipped. "Goaty don't like you," she said as the girl vanished. "Harlowe neither. They reckon you're stuck up your own arse."

"Kind of them," Hawke said, putting his own glass to his lips.

She chuckled, sipped. "On account of your voice, see?"

Hawke swilled the gin round his mouth, letting it blaze at his decaying gums. "My voice is different," he said when he had swallowed the welcome fire down, "because I am from the north."

She shook her head. "Plenty from the north hereabouts, and from a sight further off than that. Not so many with good schooling." She looked him straight in the eyes, spearing him. "Colan thinks you're hiding something."

He swallowed hard, though there was no drink this time. "He said that?"

"Didn't 'ave to. I can tell in his eyes."

"And what do you think?"

The corners of Corissa's mouth upturned a fraction and she wrinkled her small, slightly squashed nose. "I ain't made up my mind yet." She had thick eyebrows that shifted together as she frowned, examining him. "You're skinny as a runt, pale as a ghost and you shake like a shitting whippet."

"Please, Corissa, compliments make me uncomfortable," Hawke joked, though the brutally truthful assessment cut him to the quick.

She laughed. Little dimples excavated her cheeks, transporting her instantly from mid-twenties to late teens. "I was going to say that, in spite of it all, you make me curious. You walk too straight, your eyes are too busy, and you ain't stupid. It's like there's a man - a real man - trapped inside that scrawny body, just waiting to leap out." Her eyes narrowed suddenly, as if she hoped to penetrate his very soul. "Or maybe it's hiding."

If he had hitherto wished she knew there were hidden depths to Joshua Hawke, he now prayed that she was guessing. "Your head's full of bees, girl," he blurted, almost too quickly.

She pushed a glossy black ringlet away from her left eye, her gaze roaming over his face. "Maybe. Colan's ain't, though."

That was true enough, Hawke thought. The leader of one of the most powerful crime syndicates north of the river had come, so legend told, from almost nothing. He was self-taught and self-made, ambition, wit and a propensity for violence serving as triple engines that drove him out of the gutter in a rise that was as rapid as it was stellar. If Szekely was frightening for his ruthlessness, he was formidable for his intellect.

"How many gangs does he run now?" Hawke asked, desperate to deflect Corissa's attention from his own provenance. "Four?"

"Double it!" she corrected him, pride invigorating her tone. "Not all sack-'em-uppers, mind. Pickpockets, house breakers, fences.

Owns the whole o' Bloomsbury and St Giles. Now he's looking south. Latest was Uriah Todd's operation down at Blackfriars."

Hawke fell silent as he sketched a rudimentary map of the area in his head. "Giltspur Street's not so far removed from there. That's what's riled them?"

She nodded. "Old Uriah owed Colan money. They say he paid up eventually, but only after Colan had deprived him of his bollocks."

"What became of him?"

"Bled out, tied to a tree outside St Andrew by the Wardrobe."

"Christ," Hawke muttered, quaffing the rest of his drink in a single breath. He wondered what horrors would be reserved for him should his own secrets ever come to light.

"Colan had bought off or killed Todd's lads before the corpse was cold," Corissa went on.

"And before the Giltspur Boys could move in."

"That's about the size of it," Corissa said. "Blackfriars should've been theirs for the taking, or so they claim."

So that explained Blackbird's accusation against the Giltspur Boys. Hawke said, "Szekely has a goodly number of men in his employ now."

"And women," she chided.

"And women," Hawke repeated. But you are more than Szekely's employee, he thought jealously. "It is an empire, of sorts."

She shrugged. "He's ambitious. Wants to rule London's dark heart."

"There are many who would stop him," Hawke ventured. "Bow Street and the like."

Her laugh was mocking. "He don't give a stoat's cock for the Runners, Joshua, you knows that. The law does not work for the little man. For the poorest of the poor." Her nose wrinkled in a sneer of pure malevolence. "The authorities despise the common folk. Would be rid of us all if they could. You're from up north. You must have heard what they did to that crowd at..." she clicked her fingers, "where was it?"

“I cannot think,” Hawke said quickly. “Does Szekely not fear rival gangs, then?” he prompted, hauling the conversation firmly back to the south of the country. “Not just the Giltspurs. The city is overrun.”

The ghost of concern shifted across her delicate features. “Don’t ever air your misgivings to his face, Joshua. I once saw him skin a fella for lack of faith. He may be small but he’s deadly.”

“I have seen him with a blade. He is quick.”

“Quick? That ain’t the half of it. He is cruel. He will go further, cause more pain, more suffering, than his enemies. There are plenty o’ bad apples in London town,” she warned quietly, “but Colan Szekely is more rotten than all the rest.”

A fact you rather like, Hawke thought bitterly. He supposed he could hardly blame her. Not because she was Szekely’s woman, but because she had come from the same unlikely place. Szekely’s rise had dragged his associates out of the slums on his coat tails. Corissa Lott was one of those who had clung on tightest.

The door swung suddenly open at Hawke's back. The flames in the nearby hearth reared madly in response. He could not see who entered, but read all he needed in Corissa's face. She immediately seemed to sink in her chair, dipping her head and reaching out across the table to take Hawke's hands in her own. Lovers again; he wished it was no charade.

"Giltspurs," Corissa whispered. "Four of them. Drinking small beer."

"Must be on a job later," Hawke said.

"Or they've murder in mind," she replied, raising her soot-black brow questioningly.

"One way to find out."

The door opened again, another gust of chill night air blasting the nape of Hawke's neck. This time he turned, a matter of instinct, to be greeted by the sight of a huge man. He must have been at least six and a half feet tall, and as wide, all the way from shoulders to waist, as the doorway through which he now stooped. He was alone, but seemed undaunted by the gazes that fell upon him, striding confidently into the room. Hawke knew that he and Corissa were supposed to keep their presence concealed, but he could not help but twist as the big man sidled past, unable to wrest his gaze from so dominating a figure.

A voice whispered close to his ear. "Boris Milne."

Hawke stared at Corissa, startled by her sudden appearance on the bench at his side. "The butcher?"

She nodded, sliding up against him so that their legs touched. He caught her scent, gentle lavender, as she slipped a hand between his thighs. "You know him?"

The girl was doing nothing but her duty, merely maintaining the pretence of courtship to discourage second glances, but that did not stop Hawke from feeling himself stiffen at her touch. He swallowed thickly. "Szekely mentioned him before."

They watched Milne as he reached the bar, turning back to face the room as he did so. He slowly rolled up his sleeves, revealing forearms like shoulders of ham. His hands, Hawke noticed, were stained red, and there was a large cleaver thrust into a belt at his hip. He was bathed fully in the light from the tavern's half-dozen oil lamps now, and for the first time Hawke could discern his features. Milne's face was wide and round, framed by thick side whiskers, his complexion pock-pitted and his eyes narrow. He had a high forehead, with copper-coloured hair that was cropped short in wiry curls, save a bald patch at his left temple where an old wound had slashed the skin barren. That same injury had accounted for the bottom half of his left ear, a ragged patch of scar tissue all that remained of the lobe. Hawke knew the type; the ascendant male in any pack. He had encountered and subdued plenty in his old life. With a pang of shame, he realised the Smithfield butcher could snap the new incarnation of Joshua Hawke like a dessicated twig. He stared at his boots as Milne cleared a grinding throat.

"My girl is dead," Milne announced, his hard accent, like Corissa's, forged in the rookeries of the capital. "My Betsy." The narrow eyes were red and bleary, but they searched the room, lingering on each table in turn, making even the most belligerent-minded patron look away. "I would know who done the wicked deed." With impressive speed for so large a man, he spun to engage the tapster, who, protected though he was by his deep oaken serving slab, jolted rearward as if he had been shot. “This place is the haunt of resurrectionists, is it not?”

The tapster, hardly a waif himself, flinched at the tone. “I...” he stammered, “I would not...”

“By Jesus, cully,” Milne snarled with sudden fury, “you will not dissemble!” The cleaver was in his great paw in a flash. “Else I shall flay you alive and feed you to the hungry masses.”

“All sorts, Mister Milne,” the quivering tapster bleated querulously, shying from the glinting tool as though it was the grim reaper’s scythe. “We gets all sorts in here.”

Butcher Milne turned the cleaver, admiring its edge. “The Giltspur Boys drink here, so I understand. The Parkers and the Williamsons too.”

“They ain't here now,” the tapster said, and Hawke, hitherto transfixed on the encounter, realised with horror that the man spoke truthfully. The gang had vanished.

He felt Corissa lean in. She had not been so inattentive. Her gin-laced breath was warm at his ear. “They’ve high-tailed it, the lucky bastards.”

Milne had put away his cleaver and was stalking towards the door. His eyes were full of tears. “I will have words with them!” he called to all who might listen. “My Betsy was hurt bad. Cut most vile. Anatomists and their knives. Well I’ve a knife for those who supplied my daughter’s flesh for the ghouls’ table!” His voice broke, as the tears rolled. “Tell them.” He stopped with the door half open, staring into the room once more. Sobbing, he shouted, “Tell them, damn your hides! Butcher Milne will find those responsible!”

Θ

“Where did they go?” Corissa asked as she leaned across the bar. Hawke, loitering a pace behind, felt sure she would have taken the tapster by the collar if her arms could reach. “Did they say?”

The tapster, lounging against his hogsheads, a grubby cloth balled in one hand, seemed amused by the question. “Come again, my love?”

“The Giltspurs,” Corissa pressed. “I saw them, you old weasel, so speak plain. How’d they get past the butcher?”

The Bell’s landlord glanced at the doorway, as if to make certain the butcher was truly gone. “I didn’t tell Milne, my love, so why would I tell you?” He raked her with his gaze, licking his lips suggestively. “That said, I am partial to mulatto meat.”

Even in the gloom, Hawke could see strain tighten Corissa’s cheeks. “Listen to me, you...”

Hawke stepped up, placing a hand on her shoulder. She flinched, twisting sharply like a startled cat, but held her tongue all the same. He let his eyes lift above her to regard the tapster. “Because what we learn here,” he said levelly, “will be relayed to Mister Colan Szekely.”

The tapster, who had plunged the rag into a rinsed ale pot, immediately ceased his rhythmic wiping. “Szekely?”

Hawke offered a sympathetic smile. “What we tell Mister Szekely is entirely your choice, though I cannot promise a sanguine reaction if he learns the folk of this establishment are...” he paused, letting the silence scream between them, “less than helpful.”

“I could have wrung it out of him,” Corissa grumbled as they left *The Bell* and made their way into the now empty expanse of Smithfield Market.

“Aye, you could,” Hawke conceded, “but we’ve not the time to dally.”

The sky above was falteringly star-studded, blankets of darkly scudding cloud obscuring and revealing the tiny lights in turn. The pair had used the same exit as the Giltspur Boys - a small service door at the building’s rear - allowing them at once to follow in their quarry's footsteps and avoid crossing paths with the rampaging Milne, and Corissa dragged him by the hand across the increasingly icy cobbles and into a narrow alleyway.

"You're a cool cod," she said as they picked their way through the gloom, damp brickwork close on both flanks.

"He fears Milne," Hawke said, "and he fears the Giltspur Boys more. But he fears Szekely most."

"Still, you knew how to deal with him," she said with evident admiration. "Impressive for a hospital skivvy. What did you say you did up north?"

"That way," Hawke indicated a sharp left-turn. "He said the Hockley pit, did he not?"

"You're learning, Joshua," Corissa said, adding a soft whistle. "Very good. North and then west."

Hawke let himself be guided, feet tumbling in Corissa's panting wake, but his mind was elsewhere entirely. All he could think of was the irate butcher's words. "Did you not hear him?" he said at her back as they snaked their way through London's sooty arteries. "Milne blames the resurrection men."

"So?"

"It's him. He killed Lucas."

She guided him swiftly through a labyrinth of arches and unlit passageways, her eyes always fixed dead ahead, tracking her prey with uncanny instinct. Hawke's knowledge of the city might well have shown improvement, but he knew he would have been utterly lost by now, had he been alone. "Milne said he hunts the killers," she answered over her shoulder. "He did not say he already took revenge. My shilling's still on the Giltspurs."

"But..." Hawke began.

"What?" she said, exasperated, and finally stopped to turn. "What is it, Joshua?"

What indeed, thought Hawke? Should he tell her that the foremost lawman in London had tipped him off about Milne? That Ruthven, the arch thief-taker himself, had foretold the danger the butcher represented? And yet Corissa's words rang true. He had been convinced that Milne had killed Lucas, yet there was something in the butcher's threat that implied the grief-stricken man had yet to take any reprisal. Certainly there was nothing in his words that suggested he had already killed one of their number. Thus, Hawke would still have to investigate his friend's death on behalf of Szekely, all the while conducting secret enquiries as to Betsy Milne's true killer. And what of the tosher found in the sewer with poor Betsy? Coincidence? A murder committed elsewhere, a body washed along the capital's subterranean arteries along with the rest of the detritus? Or a part of the same event? An eyewitness, perhaps. Offed by Betsy's killer to silence a wagging tongue. In the end, Hawke simply shook his head. "Nothing."

She tutted, pulled hard at his wrist, and moved on apace. It took less than fifteen more minutes to reach the location whispered by *The Bell's* frightened landlord; An insalubrious patch of slum-land to the north of Hatton Garden, perpetually flooded by the Fleet River. The area had officially been renamed Ray Street at the turn of the century, but its ancient title stubbornly persisted, the moniker under which it had gained infamy.

Hockley-in-the-Hole was a warren of unlit alleys and tumbledown tenements that served as home for some of London's poorest inhabitants and the headquarters for all types of villainy.

Despite the fresh construction work that seemed ubiquitous in this part of the city, not even the Runners, it was said, ventured into these streets after dusk, and Hawke was fairly certain they did not wile away many daylight hours here either. The place reminded him of his home in St Giles. But what put Hockley-in-the-Hole truly on the map was the large bear garden that staged blood sports on almost the same scale as the establishments across the river at Southwark.

"There," Corissa said, her face immediately obscured by vapour.

Hawke followed her outstretched finger. A four-storied tavern dominated the road before them, its rectangular windows glowing like ghoulish eyes from the stoic brick facade. But no shadows moved beyond those misty panes. Indeed, it was as if the place was entirely deserted. Only when a huge cheer rose up from beyond an adjacent fence did Hawke understand. "That's the pit?" When Corissa nodded, he frowned. "Doesn't look like much."

"What were you expecting?"

He shrugged. In truth, he had once read an article in the Manchester Mercury relating the many and various curiosities of England's capital. The piece featured tales from Hockley-in-the-Hole's heyday, describing in great detail the high-sided terracing that climbed out of the muck like a Roman amphitheatre, erected in obvious homage to the grandest bear gardens of Tudor Bankside. Hawke recalled the lurid passages telling of a polygonal killing ground, into which were thrown bears and lions, some antagonised by dogs, others strapped with fireworks to madden them. "I heard it was a grand place."

"Not no more," Corissa said, leading him across the road. "They tore it down years back." She gave a quick snort of amusement. "Hoped it would clean up the community."

They entered the tavern, nodding to a couple of bored looking toss-pots and weaving between empty tables and vacant chairs. Corissa showed Hawke to the rear of the building, where a thick door, jammed open to the elements, yawned onto a yard where the establishment's patrons had gathered.

Hawke hesitated as the icy breeze chilled his face. "What's to be achieved here?"

She grinned, exposing neat, white teeth that seemed to glow against her bronzed complexion. "You scared?"

"Aye," he said truthfully. "Turn over a few rocks, Szekely said. That was all. Do you intend to walk up to the Giltspur lads and ask if they killed Lucas?"

"That miserable bastard at *The Bell* said they were fighting dogs tonight. They'll be here hours, gambling and whoring and drinking. Let us linger. Let us listen."

Hawke swallowed hard as another cheer came from outside, reaching an ear-splintering crescendo that told of an animal shredded and wagers won. "God damn it all," he said, and followed her through the door.

The yard was packed. They were able to advance little more than two yards before the way was barred by bodies. All eyes faced inward, towards the pit that marked the arena's core, and they chatted and laughed as preparations were made for the next bout. A mist of mingling tobacco smoke and breathy vapour clung to the air, smudging the soft light from a phalanx of hook-dangled lanterns. Hawke's view was blocked by shoulders and the backs of steaming heads, perhaps half-a-dozen deep, but he could only presume that a ruined carcass was being dragged clear of the space. If it was a bull, its savagely tenderised meat would be supplied to Boris Milne and his ilk at Smithfield.

"There," Corissa hissed close to his left ear. Somehow she had spotted one of the Giltspur clan amongst the melee. "And another over there."

Hawke saw that she had identified two more members of the gang. One was tall and skinny, with high cheekbones and a hooked nose, while his companion, with whom the first shared a deep, muttered conversation, was stocky and ruddy-faced. Both sported the distinctive red hair that was the mark of the Giltspur Boys. Corissa was already moving through the crowd towards the first man, so Hawke supposed he should approach the other two. He eased his way into the dense hedge of spectators, elbowing a route that was bruising but pliable enough to allow progress to a man of his slim build. The din was almost painful now that he had been enveloped by the crowd. He could glimpse the pit now, albeit fleetingly between the shifting onlookers. The footprint of the fighting ring was roughly the same, Hawke suspected, as it had been at its zenith a century earlier. It lacked the towering stanchions, of course, from which seating for scores would have been suspended, and he could readily imagine the old spectacle might have been garnished with bright bunting, bellowing pie-sellers and a good deal more pomp, but still the brutal pit was deep and wide, large enough to accommodate an impressive array of exotic beasts, its surface made of compacted earth and dusted in blood-spattered wood shavings.

Hawke inveigled himself between a pair of burly fellows, construction labourers or stevedores perhaps, who stood close to the Giltspur men, but did not appear to be associating with them. He used them as screens behind which he hoped he could remain inconspicuous as he tried his best to eavesdrop. He could hear only fragments of the conversation, for their voices ebbed and flowed with the animation of the crowd, but nothing was said of note, and he found himself cursing Colan Szekely for dispatching him on so futile an errand. His private diatribe was cut short almost immediately by a great yowl lifting from within the pit. The crowd joined with one voice, and in the cacophony the Giltspurs ceased their hushed discussion, choosing to watch the spectacle like everyone else. Hawke's own gaze was inexorably drawn back to the bear garden's epicentre.

Around a dozen dogs had poured into the pit, circling the edge, cocking legs and sniffing at the bloody ground. They yapped and snarled at one another, sensing the excitement of the feverish throng and anticipating what was to come. They had doubtless been isolated and starved in recent days so that, when the time came, they would be angry and famished, and their collective frenzy was immediately evident. The crowd cheered and chattered as stakes and odds were called and a small fortune wagered. Men roared encouragement to particular animals as serving wenches weaved their way through the hazy arena with slopping jugs of ale and saucy retorts.

The dogs were howling now, gathering in excitement. Most of them were small creatures - terriers of all descriptions - more accustomed to challenging rodents than bullocks. But in their midst were a brawny trio of fully fledged bulldogs, their massive shoulder muscles rippling as they moved, lower jaws protruding to expose huge teeth that could rip flesh and shatter bone. One was pure white, another brindle and a third, taller than the others, possessed the mask of deep black that betrayed a lineage strengthened by mastiff blood. They were the real killers. Ugly and vicious, panting madly with clouds of slobber foaming like pricked ulcers at their glistening jowls, and they swaggered across the sawdust, kicked it up with scraping claws and stared truculently at the little enclosure set at the opposite side of the pit, eyes flashing black and red in the torchlight. Within that pen, brown flanks a blur between the timber slats, moved the object of their slavering attention. The bull was small, but compact and powerful looking, with short, sharp horns that were upturned to form a trident of sorts with the tufted crest of its skull. It was roped about the neck and tethered to its prison, and it turned tight circles, desperate to find a route to freedom. A young fellow clambered up the enclosure's side, leaning precariously over the top slat, and in an expert show of skill, at once released the rope and blew a sharp gust of dark powder directly into the animal's face.

The bull jerked back its head as if it had been cudgelled, the pepper cloud searing its nostrils. It brayed loudly, a deep, guttural sound that was accompanied by a blast of mucus and vapour, and immediately the dogs responded with a discordant chorus of their own. Its tormentor gave a triumphal cry and waved an arm as he swung back to the safe side of the railing.

"Let's be on wi' it!" a man with a raw, diseased face and one clubbed fist shouted over the din from the side of the pit. A relative hush descended at his word, and he grinned, exposing a mouth of black gums. "At 'im, hounds!"

The enclosure's gate was hauled open by men holding ropes at a safe distance. The bull, duly enraged, broke into an immediate charge, careening headlong into the dogs' lair. The smaller hounds went first to the fray, flitting beneath the furious beast with high-pitched snarls and snapping jaws that were comical, so utterly mismatched were they. But they distracted the bullock, which was their unwitting duty, and as it stamped at them and swept its muscular head low to the sawdust in a vain attempt to snag one on a horn-tip, the real fighters sauntered in. The first bulldog, the brindle, which, Hawke now noticed, was missing an eye and an ear, leapt at the bull's exposed flank. It had aimed to land its bite near the shoulder, but the larger creature had wheeled instinctively away so that the dog's jaws affixed nearer the rear. The bull bellowed, the wretched sound reverberating through Hawke's guts, and, though blood immediately spouted, it began to fight back. The dog was dangling, like a nightmarish leech, refusing to release the huge teeth that had skewered deep into the shifting slab of the bull's hip, but it was precariously close to a powerful hoof, and that impromptu weapon was up in a trice, flailing wildly, stabbing the air once, twice, thrice. When it connected on the fourth attempt, the brindle might have been fired from a cannon, so far was its carcass flung. The hoof caught it in the chest, tearing its jaws free and sending it cartwheeling out of the arena to land amongst a crowd that cheered and guffawed, celebrating the beleaguered bull's small victory.

If the crowd were impressed by the bull's fight, the white bulldog and the one with a mastiff's muzzle were not. They acted with one mind, circling quickly, confusing their prey as the terriers buzzed like a swarm of hackled flies, and when the black-faced hound pounced, tiger-like, onto its snorting foe's back, its white confederate lunged in tandem, going for the throat. Both dogs clamped down hard with teeth and claws, hooking the living meat in grotesque parody of its shambles future, and Hawke found himself unable to look away as the dazed and bleeding bullock staggered like a gin-shop drunk. It still fought, still thrashed, still tried to gore with those lethal horns, but its life blood was seeping away with each passing moment. The white bulldog was red now, dyed from wrinkling snout to docked tail by the gushing, steaming fountain that cascaded from its victim's punctured neck, and it did not simply hang there, but jerked in short, sharp movements designed to wrench the arteries clean out through the thick layers of skin and muscle.

The bull dropped onto its fore-knees, strength sapped, the weight of the mastiff-cross sprawled over its back becoming too much to bear. And then it was down, listing, keeling to the side, and the dogs rolled nimbly clear as a huge, endless sigh escaped from the bull's vast lungs. The pack howled its victory, and then they were upon it in an instant, even the smallest ratters, barking at one another as they ripped at the exposed underbelly that was so soft and inviting.

The crowd erupted with delight and dismay as money began to change hands. And at last Joshua Hawke managed to look away. Straight into a pair of malevolent brown eyes that glittered above an aquiline nose.

"Some kind of Mary-Ann are you, friend?"

Hawke swallowed thickly as he stared up at the thinner of the two Giltspur Boys. "What?"

The skinny fellow sniffed hard through his hooked nose and licked narrow, chapped lips. "After a buttock banquet?" he asked with a gentle Irish lilt. "We saw you staring, so we did." The man's companion - broad, fleshy cheeks almost as red as his hair - stood in grim silence at his shoulder, but he nodded agreement slowly.

"You are mistaken, sir," Hawke said, struggling to peel a suddenly parched tongue from the roof of his mouth. "I was not looking at you, but at the baiting."

"Ah, but you were," the Giltspur said. "Thought we'd wander over, so we did. See what it is you find so intriguing, Nancy-lad."

Hawke shook his head, furious with himself for having let his attention slip so catastrophically. He decided to ride out the danger with bluff belligerence. "Begone, sir, I would place a tanner on the next bout."

With an ostentatious gasp, the Giltspur planted a hand on his own chest. "Ah! Jesus, Mary and Joseph! Then I must be mistook after all!" He made to turn, then paused, clicking his fingers as if struck by sudden epiphany. "But now that I think on it. I do believe we've met before."

Hawke felt vomit rise through his gullet. He swallowed it back with difficulty, throat burning. "Oh?"

The Giltspur winked. "At *The Bell.*" Now the brown eyes flickered away from Hawke, scanning the crowd of bodies that ebbed and flowed around them. "I think you've been a-spyin', boy, so you have. Naughty, that. Very naughty. You and your lovely lady."

"Lady?"

"Don't play the dullard, boy. Saw you together, so we did."

"I do not..."

"I said don't bother yourself. We saw the two of you back at Smithfield. You were in the tavern swillin' gin. What is she? Blackamoor?"

"No, sir, I..." Hawke persisted, though he knew his denials were mere wasted breath.

The bigger Giltspur pulled club-like fists from the pockets of a thick overcoat. Something glinted bright and sharp in one. His confederate said, "The girl was watching us, so she was." He tapped his nose with a bony finger. "Don't think we didn't spot yous. So you followed us here. By my reckoning, that makes you worth killing. Who'd you work for?"

Hawke backed off a step, giving himself room so that he could pat the knife at his waist. “Fuck yourself, friend.”

Both Irishmen apparently found that comical. “No, boy,” the thin one replied. “I don’t think I will. Your lady, on the other hand.” He licked his lips. “Cunny’s cunny when all’s said and done, eh? Black, white, brown or yellow, tis all the same to me.” He flashed a nasty grin, displaying all three teeth left in his skull. “I’ll swive her raw while you’re scooping your own guts off the floor.” He grunted and the man with the blade shifted forwards. “I’ll tell him to do it quick if you point us in the right direction, so I will. Now, where is she?”

“She’s here,” replied Corissa Lott. And then she stabbed the skinny Giltspur in the side of the neck.

Her victim reeled away in horror, hand pressed hard over the wound, steam-wreathed blood seeping freely between bone-white fingers. His hulking companion lumbered forwards, stepping round the injured man who was bending low, curling and clenching around the sudden pain. The big fellow snarled like one of the bulldogs, knocking

Hawke clear as he lunged for Corissa, whose own forearm was stained with blood, the slender knife still in her grip. She was backing away, staring at the man she had hurt, and for a second she failed to react. The Giltspur grabbed her wrist with a meaty paw, twisted it savagely so that the blade dropped away, and then hauled her into him, enveloping her slim frame within his bear's embrace.

Joshua Hawke fell. He heard Corissa's desperate pleas, muffled by the fat fingers of a captor preparing to tear her limb from limb, and knew she must think he swooned. All to the good, he thought, for if she considered him pathetically feeble, then so would the huge Irishman. He rolled forwards quickly, pleased that his agility had not gone the same way as his strength, and Corissa's blade was in his hand. The Giltspur Boy seemed not to flinch as the wicked tip punctured his skin. Indeed, as Hawke threw himself clear, sprawling amongst the legs of stunned onlookers, he wondered whether the bovine brawler would notice at all. But then the big man howled. Not because of the pain, but because he was crumpling like an undermined building, sloping inexorably to one side as his leg began to fail. His face was bright red, creased in a grimace of confusion, and he put his hands to the collapsing limb like a pair of buttresses.

Θ

It was chaos.

Hawke and Corissa sprang free, allowing themselves to be swallowed by the pulsating melee of a crowd thrown into panic. They stumbled pell-mell through the human gauntlet, shouldering a ragged path, hauling one another along as a hue and cry rose up in their wake. Corissa, smaller and more nimble, took a natural lead, not looking back, ducking and weaving along her improvised route like a twinkle-toed pugilist. It was impossible to tell how lethal her blow had been, for things had happened so quickly, but as they crossed the threshold into the tavern, her victim could still be heard shrieking above the din like a gelded hog.

They ran through the building, kicking open the doors and emerging onto the wide, empty road.

“Christ on His cross,” Hawke panted through a surge of relief that stole the air from his chest.

“How did you do that?”

He looked down at the woman. Her brown eyes shone in the moonlight. “Do?”

“You are a sot, by your own admission,” Corissa said, not taking her gaze from his. “The way you moved.” She shook her head slowly, reflecting on all she had seen, weighing its implication.

“I slit the tendon at his heel,” Hawke said. “Clean through. He’ll not be walking again for a long while.” He shrugged. “If ever.”

Shouts from inside the tavern made them move again. They crossed the road, moving into the shadows of the narrower alleys. “I would not have thought you capable, Joshua,” Corissa said after a long while.

“Come,” Hawke spoke in the blackness. “Let us be gone from this damnable place.”

Θ

It must have been approaching midnight when Hawke returned to the overcrowded rookery that was his home. The street lamps disappeared as alleyways became constricted, and his senses sharpened instantly with the gathering gloom. The rookery was a place of unfettered danger, where lawmen feared to tread and visiting strangers might vanish into thin air. A labyrinth of rotten hovels, gin shops, brew-houses and brothels. Respectable homes had lined the roads once, but they had long since fallen to ruin, their door-less entrances gaping like black mouths, poised to devour any who dared enter. Within, separated by crumbling stairways and mouldering corridors, each squalid space would be let out by avaricious landlords to as many desperate souls as possible. The area was a hub for Irish immigrants especially, and their large, vulnerable families might find themselves squeezed twenty or thirty to a single room. Men and women, young and old, crammed cheek-by-jowl; lice-infested, disease-ridden and desperate, sleeping head-to-toe on floorboards that stank of piss and shit.

The very nature of St Giles, its pervasive odour of decay and its oppressive air, put Hawke in a dark malady that had but a single cure, and, upon entering Buckbridge Street, he skirted past his lodgings and continued instead to the nearest of the area's countless gin palaces. The building had once been a modest terrace house, two windows wide and three main storeys high, topped by a garret storey in the roof. He had often thought it would, in its pomp, have been a pleasant enough structure to behold, erected in soft yellow brick, with clever arches to the upper windows and a pair of large, imposing chimney-stacks bearing a level of workmanship that spoke of care and pride. But those high windows were covered now in nailed boards, the crests of the stacks were clogged with birds nests, and the roof was patchy, like corrupted skin, where its tiles had long been stolen. Only the ground floor managed to rekindle something of the building's former self, for it had always been intended as a shop front, with huge, rectangular windows facing the street. Those windows had been put through, and the big timber door was marked with a long, pale scar where some kind of ram had battered it open, but its function remained the same.

Hawke pulled his knife and went inside. Even at this time of night, the gin shop was open for custom. It was murky, lit only by a single flickering lamp, and the whole place smelled strongly of tobacco and damp. The shop, taking up almost the entire ground floor space, was a sparse affair, the decor uniformly miserable. There were only a half-dozen chairs and a single table that appeared to have been split straight down the middle, while bundles of rags lay against the walls, the snores coming from within those stinking piles betraying the sleeping folk within. But, crucially, there was a long counter at one end, against which a lone patron perched, swaying precariously on his high stool. Seeing no immediate danger, Hawke sheathed his blade and crossed the sticky floor.

"Gin," he said, unnecessarily, to the pock-scarred man who emerged from an anteroom.

The bar tender pulled a bottle from somewhere behind the counter and filled a glass, sliding it into Hawke's eager hands when a couple of coins had passed the other way. Hawke realised he was still shaking, still reliving the bloody skirmish at Hockley-in-the-Hole, and he gripped the vessel hard. He sank the gin without pause. The impassive bar tender took the cup with tattooed fingers and replenished it. Hawke drained it again. The warmth was luxurious within his chest and guts. He realised, too, that the shaking was beginning to subside. He felt suddenly exhausted.

"Leave the bottle," he said, producing more money. The bar tender gathered the coins deftly and made himself scarce, slipping down a steep flight of stairs that presumably led to his cellar. Hawke fished within the lining of his coat, laying fingers upon a small glass container, which he thumbed open without delay. He tilted it carefully, letting two drops of its dark liquid tumble into the pale gin, before returning it to its secret home. He swirled the bottle, making sure the tincture was well mixed, then drank deeply, satisfied that his face was beginning to feel numb. Gradually he turned his mind away from the baiting and the fight and the breathless chase that followed. It was harder to push the image of Corissa Lott from his mind. Her bright eyes, the smell of her hair, the mildly amused smirk she seemed to preserve for him alone. Yet to dwell on her was to court unimaginable danger. He had left Corissa on Great Russell Street, within spitting distance of Szekely's home, and now, he knew, she was best forgotten. Instead he reflected upon the task set by George Ruthven. A dead sewer scavenger and a mutilated girl. Who had killed them? Why? Hawke still possessed the stalks that had been taken from Betsy Milne's ruined corpse, and he took them from his coat, placing them either side of the gin glass. He stared blearily at them. If he had hoped for a flash of inspiration, nothing came. He knew he needed to discover their significance. One was a section of a fennel stem, but the other was still a mystery. Identifying that second stalk would need to take priority, he told himself.

And what else did he know? He lifted the gin glass and stared down onto the surface of the liquid. "The girl's father," he muttered quietly, "promises vengeance in his grief-stricken fury. Lucas, a resurrectionist, murdered."

"Eh?" the other man at the counter said, looking up from his drink. His eyes were blood-shot and entirely vacant, and the movement of lifting his head almost toppled him from the stool.

"Nothing, friend," Hawke replied. "That is to say, I have enlisted your help in my investigations."

"Quite... so..." the inebriated fellow managed to utter, before slumping forwards, head in hands.

"Ruthven considers the crimes related," Hawke went on. "An eye for an eye. But Szekely believes the death of Lucas is a symptom of gang-warfare, nothing more." Hawke waited as his unwitting sounding board coughed up a thin stream of vomit that streaked his coat sleeves. "I had presumed Ruthven was right, but now that I have encountered the raging Butcher Milne, I discover a man not basking in promised retribution, but seeking it still." He paused to drink deeply, setting down the cup and taking up the fennel. If he did not think Milne had killed Lucas, then was it the Giltspur Boys as Szekely believed? "No," he said to the stupefied man at his side, "it was not them. Maybe." He laughed bitterly at the web in which he had found himself entangled. “A girl, a tosher and a resurrectionist, and I cannot fathom who did away with any of them.”

“Come again, sir?”

Hawke looked up, startled, chiding himself for the lack of discretion. It was the bar tender who spoke, returning with a crate of gin bottles that clinked as he set them on the counter. Hawke smiled, nodding at the vomit-covered sot at his side. “My friend and I set the world to rights.”

“Just as you should.” The patchy skin of the barman’s brow creased further as he frowned suddenly. “I got some dried beef out back if your belly growls. Good an’ tasty.”

Hawke followed the man’s gaze and realised that he was looking at the plant stems. “This is no meal, I assure you.” He fished for another coin. “But I’ll take some of that meat.”

The bar tender grunted. “As you wish.” He glanced at the fennel again. “That stuff’s good only for animal fodder. Pig an’ rabbits.” As he turned away he added, “Or ground up by god-damned quacks.”

CHAPTER THREE

FRIDAY

It was almost noon the following day when Hawke reached the premises of, as the gin palace barman had put it, the god-damned quack. The journey had not been a long one, for the shop of Ansell Brommett was located in the same disreputable neighbourhood as Hawke's own lodgings but the morning had been one of swimming senses, burning eyes and a skull that felt as though it were a blacksmith's anvil. Eventually Hawke had clambered out of his bile-stained bed and crawled across floorboards still bearing the dark reminders of Lucas's murder. He had hauled on his breeches and fumbled to get into his shirt, and then he had collapsed for a little nap that had, he later realised, stretched to several hours. Now, with a pounding head, churning guts and hands that trembled like candle flames in a draught, Hawke was struggling to keep his precarious perch upon an uneven three-legged stool as the subject of his visit bustled around him like a bee at a flowerbed.

"Sage, vinegar and a dash of betony."

Hawke wrinkled his nose as the bundled cloth wafted past. "Stinks."

The man carrying the poultice rolled his small, chestnut eyes. "It will ease her bruising."

"The stench will have me revisiting my breakfast."

"Do not blame me for your gin habit, young man." Ansell Brommett, a man perhaps just into his forties, with delicate features, a willowy frame and a gait made awkward by childhood rickets, tutted his way across the large chamber. He added, "And your red eyes condemn you for the abuse of laudanum." The space was more cluttered maze than orderly workshop, crammed with boxes, bushels and overladen tables, with tall racks of potions and shelves that bulged haphazardly with books, scrolls and powder pots. There were glass jars everywhere, each coloured by strange liquids or piled to their stoppers with all manner of pills and lozenges, and where the shelves ceased, hooks began, from which there hung all manner of tools, from curved blades that reminded Hawke of gelding knives, to tiny saws and long tweezers. In the room's corner, bathed in the glow of one of three oil lamps, a little girl, evidently Brommett's daughter, was seated on an iron-bound chest. She looked to be eight or nine, Hawke reckoned, with a face full of freckles and loose, straight hair that had the same flame-red colour as her father's. She had hurt her knee after a fall during a game with the other local snipes, and now Brommett crouched before her, pressing the poultice against her injury. The girl, wincing, hissed her displeasure.

"Then have a care, my poppet," Brommett admonished. "Consider the placement of your feet *before* you place them."

In amongst the musty chaos, shadows shifted to the lilting tune of youthful laughter. Hawke had the distinct feeling that they were being watched.

Brommett clapped his hands. "Go. Be gone, I say."

The girl jumped up, gave her father a peck on his neatly bearded cheek, and ran out of the room. More laughter. The shadows moved again, skittering out from their hiding places to reveal the gleeful faces of children. The trio, two girls and a boy, squealed with delight as their father shooed them through the low doorway and down the rickety staircase in pursuit of their sister. When he turned back it was clear he had failed in the mastery of a stern aspect, and instead shook his head amid his own rueful chuckle.

Smiling, Hawke said, “It is a wonder you have time to study your potions, sir.”

Brommett simply shrugged. “That it is, Mister Hawke, that it is, though I’d not have it any other way.” They were in the attic of a tap-house, and the boards creaked loudly beneath his feet as he sidled to one of the low tables. “When I brought the family here, I had a burning ambition to be London’s greatest apothecary. But you can see my attention finds itself drawn away all too often.” He laughed again, spreading his palms. “We are helpless before fate, are we not?”

“Indeed. One might argue it is fate brought me here.” Or, Hawke thought, the vague, gin-soaked memory of the previous night’s brief conversation. He had made contact with a couple of reliable acquaintances after leaving Buckbridge Street, asked discreet questions, and the consensus had been unanimous; find Ansell Brommett. In the event, Hawke was content that he had followed the advice, for Brommett appeared to be a jovial enough fellow, with intelligence dancing behind a permanently amused gaze.

“Ah yes,” Brommett said as soon as the clattering footsteps of his offspring had faded into the floors below. The table in front of him was full of glass jars, and he inspected each one in turn. “You say you are making enquiries about the death of a child?”

Hawke nodded. “A girl. Found murdered in a sewer. Mutilated. Her face cut away most cruelly.”

Brommett looked up, keen eyes crinkling. “Curious.”

“How so?”

"You told my wife," the apothecary said, glancing in the direction of the doorway through which Mrs Brommett had earlier departed, "that you were a hospital porter."

Hawke read the glint of challenge in Brommett's gaze, and met it with his own hard stare. "I am." At least that had been true a couple of months back.

Brommett licked his lips, pausing for thought. He regarded Hawke closely for a few seconds, evidently considering what risk this unexpected visitor might pose. Suddenly, he said, "And you believe I might in some way prove helpful? I am not a physician, you understand. Nor an anatomist."

"I do not ask you to look at the body, Mister Brommett, for it is already under ground."

"Then you are here because?"

"She was wrapped in vines. Or, rather, plant stems."

Brommett picked up one of the jars. It appeared to be moving independently, its black contents a writhing swirl. "Wrapped?"

“As if it were a death shroud,” Hawke said, realising the jar was full of leeches. He snaked his arms around his own midriff. “Like so.”

“What kind of plant?”

Hawke reached inside his coat. “These cuttings were taken from the corpse.” He held out the stalks for Brommett to inspect. “I hoped you might answer your own question.”

The apothecary set down the vessel of glistening leeches and took the two items, sniffing them in turn. Then he made his way across the rickety boards to one of his lopsided shelves. He took up a lamp, squinting in its warm light as he began to peruse the books lined before him, tracing a finger over their spines to score a trail through the dust.

Hawke stood, feeling his back crunch as he arched a touch, then went to the only window in the stuffy loft. It was small and unglazed, and the cold breeze wafted through to stir cobwebs in the dark rafters. Adjacent to it, benefiting from the weak daylight, was a trestle table so wide it set Hawke’s mind to wondering how on earth it had ever been brought to this high, slanted chamber. Its surface was littered with objects, from what looked to be a rodent's skull, to a bell jar that seemed to contain a desiccated toad, and a chalky long-bone that Hawke supposed had come from a cow or horse. At the far side of the table, arranged in line against the wall, was a phalanx of delicate glass vials, each containing measures of dark liquid that looked ominously akin to blood, and at intervals there were stacks of papers weighted down with grey pebbles. On the floor, beneath and beside the table, were piles of what looked to be body parts, and Hawke had a moment of horror as his mind caught up with his eyes. In a breathless couple of seconds, he realised, with a gush of relief, that the objects, limbs mostly, but a few ears and noses too, were possessed of an unnatural smoothness, free of the blemishes of real flesh. They were hewn from wood in the main, some hammered out of plate metal, and all finely sanded and polished.

"A passion of mine," Brommett said, looking up from the book.

Hawke arched his brows. "Whittling an occasional leg from an oaken bough?"

Brommett frowned. "Oak would not be practicable, Mister Hawke. Goodness me, no. Fruit-wood is best, I find, though I am ever searching for the perfect material, as I'm sure you can imagine."

Hawke stooped to pick up a leg. It was long and pale, surprisingly light, the toes rendered in exquisite detail, the ankle hinged so that the foot would move. He grasped the limb at thigh and shin, bending it at the knee, for that joint was articulated as well, a robust metal pin allowing the parts to shift up and down. He looked at Brommett. "A peg leg."

"A prosthesis," Brommett corrected irritably. "More than a simple peg, I think you can allow."

Hawke nodded, still working the hinged knee, and feeling certain his awe was etched over his face. "You are skilled, sir."

"Were you in the Peninsula, Mister Hawke?"

"No."

“Too young, I suppose. Lucky for you. That cruel conflict was a blight upon the human race. An outpouring of evil.” Brommett paused, apparently needing to steady himself against the memory. Hawke sympathised.

“You fought?”

Brommett shook his head. “Tended the wounded.” He smiled sadly. “Lopped off arms and legs mostly. Stitched up wounds, only for the flesh to fester and turn bad.” He blinked hard, dragged himself back to the waiting book. “Gave me an interest in artificial limbs. I could not help those poor bastards in Spain, but I can help them at home.”

Hawke put the leg back and went to the dusty windowsill to stare down at the street. The tavern was not a single structure, but a large cluster of buildings around a fan-shaped courtyard that nestled at the corner of High Holborn and Drury Lane. The spire of the parish church dominated the skyline to the west, and all around were the narrow, twisting alleys that formed the arteries of the sprawling rookery. Those ominous passageways stretched like the tentacles of some malevolent kraken, enveloping vagabonds, wastrels and refugees alike. Good people, Hawke thought - people like Brommett - came to St Giles, but they rarely left. Their respectable lives and their honest intentions corrupted by the very place they called home. He felt suddenly sorry for the apothecary and his young family.

He looked up, noticing dried herbs tied in bundles and hanging from the rafters. It gave his memory a jolt. "What do you think to the plants?"

Brommett had plucked a thick, leather-bound tome from the shelf, carefully placing the stems in its stead, and now seemed deeply engrossed within its yellowish pages. He did not look up as he said, "One of these plants is fennel. If you are to make a good intelligencer, Mister Hawke, then you should have known the scent."

"I am not an intelligencer," Hawke said, trying to remain impassive before the shrewd thrust, "but I did identify one as fennel." He ignored Brommett's wry smirk. "The other, though, eludes me."

"It is sorghum. A kind of grass. Yields good grain. The ancient Egyptians were partial to it, I believe."

"Is it grown here?"

Brommett shook his head. "Requires more warmth than the British climate will allow." He turned back to the book. "Here we are. Italy."

"Italy?" an exasperated Hawke echoed.

Brommett jammed a forefinger at a particular place within the book, and he trained his eyes on the handwritten text. "Curious. Most curious indeed."

"What, Mister Brommett, is curious?"

"Have you heard of the *Benandanti*, Mister Hawke?" Hawke indicated that he had not, prompting Brommett to return to the inky scrawl, scanning a paragraph or two with impressive speed. "Now then. The *Benandanti*; a pagan cult, most often encountered within agrarian communities, driven to extinction by the Inquisition. It was claimed they fought nocturnal battles with Malandanti; evil witches."

"Fought?"

"Indeed. For the success, or otherwise, of their crops. The *Benandanti*were armed with stalks of fennel. In their night battles, if they won, there would be abundance, but if the witches prevailed, there would be famine."

"And the sor...?"

"Sorghum," Brommett repeated. "The weapon of choice for the evil doers."

Hawke glanced incredulously at the dry stalks on the shelf. "You jest."

The apothecary closed and replaced the book, handing the fennel and sorghum back to Hawke. "Did you, or did you not, discover a corpse wrapped in fennel and sorghum?" He waited for Hawke to nod slowly. "Then witchcraft is your first consideration."

"I came to you for your knowledge of remedies," Hawke said, unable to disguise his incredulity. "That you might identify the mysterious plant."

Brommett grinned. "My reading is, as they say, fairly broad." Colour climbed through his cheeks. "Fairly deep."

"Then..."

"Then why am I a penniless potion-pusher?" He gave a mirthless laugh. "I was rusticated from Trinity College, for reasons that shall remain my own."

"Rusticated?"

"Shown the door, Mister Hawke."

"Trinity College, Cambridge?"

"Oxford. Returned, albeit fleetingly, to my native Kent, but war turned fortune's wheel, as it did for so many. Portugal, Spain and France became my destiny. After Bonaparte's defeat, we came here." The pleasant odour of hearty cooking filled the room. The apothecary looked at the open door, through which the smell wafted. "Mrs Brommett's famous stew calls to me, sir. Alas, I must take your leave."

Hawke tried to conceal his lingering intake of breath, swallowing back the saliva that was relentlessly filling his mouth. "I thank you for your time."

Brommett essayed a quick bow. "I will investigate." He nodded towards his packed shelves. "I may have been slung to the wolves by Oxford University, but still I have many books. Visit us again and I will tell you what more I've learnt. If a warlock prowls my city, I should like to assist in its demise. While I read, perhaps you would be well served by speaking with our Latin friends, Mister Hawke. The *Benandanti* were a sect from the northerly territories of Italy, after all."

"I am not a native of London," Hawke said, suddenly embarrassed.

"Lancashire, by your accent."

Hawke nodded. "Aye. My understanding of this city is not as it should be. Where would I begin to look?"

Θ

When Hawke returned to his lodgings, mind swirling with images of cackling witches and supernatural warfare, there was a boy waiting for him. The lad leaned casually against the damp wall at the top of the echoing stairwell, sucking on a briar pipe that looked bizarrely over-sized in his hand, and he stepped into Hawke's path, blocking the way.

He was snub-nosed and bright-eyed, smartly dressed for a rookery snipe and bearing a belligerent haughtiness that instantly betrayed the identity of his employer.

"What does he want?" Hawke asked.

"You."

"Why?"

The boy blew a trio of immaculate smoke rings, peering up at Hawke through the last as though it were a port hole. "Couldn't say. You're to attend upon Mister Szekely forthwith."

The message - or, rather, summons - was not something to ignore, and Hawke turned on his heels without bothering to enter his home. The boy had vanished before he reached the foot of the stairwell, which was a merciful thing, he reflected, for he did not much fancy a journey in the company of one of Szekely's puffed up brats. Such imps were the very strands by which the gang master had woven his web. They were his loyal acolytes, his mouthpiece, his eyes and his ears. The cogs in a vast, lucrative machine. And they knew it, right enough, which made them objectionable in the extreme.

A thin, bitter rain saturated everything as he strove northward, heading for Bloomsbury, St Giles's more respectable neighbour. Turning up his collar to give some protection to his ears, he pulled the brim of the topper down so that the biting wind would not send it twirling down the road. He was forced to run across Great Russell Street to avoid a stagecoach that raced in a cacophony of jangling traces and cracking whips, its quartet of horses whinnying madly as diluted muck sprayed their fetlocks. Pale faces peered from the windows, eyeing Hawke suspiciously from within the bouncing coop. Funny, he thought, how the sight of such folk made him feel like he was the one in a cage. There were smaller hackney carriages too, now that he was out of the rookery and into London's wider civilisation, and between their trundling progress and the scores of people on horseback, the dung-filled road was quickly becoming a mire.

Once he was on the north side of Great Russell Street, he turned right, heading east, towards the imposing façade of Montagu House. In a city not his own, Hawke had learnt that navigation by landmark was the most expedient means of making one's way through the metropolis. The tactic was not foolproof, of course, for, in the poorer districts, one sprawling row of tenements was often identical to the next. Indeed, it was this homogeneity that made London's slums so dangerous to outsiders. But its grander areas, its traffic-clogged thoroughfares, shopping arcades, great mansions and smart parks, were beacons to a man like Hawke. Montagu House was one such place, a lighthouse by which a traveller might make his way.

The building itself was huge. A century and a half old, it was no longer a private residence, having been home to the British Museum since the 1750s, but it remained one of the capital's grandest piles, dominating the Bloomsbury area. Its plot was expansive, a boundary wall surrounding immaculate lawns and fountains, while the house itself had two main storeys, sectioned into seventeen bays, and was flanked by spacious servants' wings. Hawke walked to the west of the house as he made his way up Charlotte Street, twisting back a touch to marvel at the mansion's large domed roof. Once he had crossed beyond the wide expanse of Bedford Square, he checked briefly for prying eyes, then hooked a left into Great Store Street.

There was a haberdashery situated roughly fifty yards in, and Hawke ducked under the lintel.

“Ladies,” he said, acknowledging the manageress and her assistant with a perfunctory doff of his hat as he made for a narrow side door that was almost invisible in the gap between a pair of sentry-like dressers. There was no need to conceal his action, for the shop was empty of patrons, and he pushed open the door without delay.

“Where have you been?” Colan Szekely said.

The chamber beyond the secret entrance was well appointed, panelled in dark wood, with soft skins on the floor and furniture of high workmanship and vigorous polishing. The rooms above, Hawke knew, were a deal more opulent, being Szekely’s private lodgings, the king’s privy chamber, but this was his office, his day-to-day headquarters, and an expensively functional theme prevailed. The space had aways reminded Hawke of a lawyer’s apartments, and the irony was not lost on him as he offered his employer a respectful bow. “Having a tooth pulled.”

The Hungarian was seated in a high-backed, luxuriously upholstered chair, and he crossed his thin legs, resting his chin on his knuckles. "Where?"

Hawke glanced at the faces he knew so well. Blackbird was here, as ever, with Goaty, Gilroy Penley and Corissa. He tapped his jaw. The rotten molar smarted at his touch. "Very back."

Szekely's expression tightened, the white scar arcing to a crescent shape between mouth and eyelid. "Not which tooth."

"Down on Clements Lane, Mister Szekely," Hawke lied. Blackbird was standing closest, so he moved towards the glowering man, opening his mouth wide. "Want to see?"

Blackbird recoiled. "Christ, you stink!"

"You wanted to see me, Mister Szekely?" Hawke said, content that further interrogation would not be forthcoming.

"My mother would wear a chain about her neck," Szekely said in his soft, strange voice. "She hung a pair of mole's feet from it as a charm against toothache." He yawned suddenly. "The baiting. What did you learn?"

Corissa was perched on the edge of a desk hewn from gorgeous walnut. Hawke looked quizzically at her, but she failed to return his gaze. "Has not Miss Lott relayed all that transpired?"

Szekely's face was impassive. "May I not hear it from you, *Sólyom?*"

"We went to *The Bell*, like you said. The Giltspur Boys were there. But then Butcher Milne walks in, making threats against the resurrectionists."

"And?" Szekely prompted.

"The Giltspurs made themselves scarce."

"After that?"

"We followed them to Hockley beargarden." Hawke's pulse quickened as he relived the night. The fury of the dogs clamoured again in his ears, the stench of the blood and the horror of the moment the Giltspurs had challenged him. He met the cold blue eyes, his own anger spurring him to ill-considered impertinence. "Where we almost got ourselves killed."

The scar quivered like a plucked harp string, betraying a barely perceptible twitch at Szekely's thin mouth. "Oh?"

"Careful now, Hawke," Blackbird growled at his flank.

Szekely made a steeple of his fingers, propping his delicate chin on the manicured point. "And still you went. Still you walked into the lion's den like Daniel. But you did not do it for God, *Sólyom*. I am honoured."

Hawke stared resentfully down at the gang master. "You're welcome."

Szekely's mouth creased in a smile that did not reveal his teeth. "Saved my Corissa's life, so she tells me. She also tells me you fought as though you were born to it."

"You know I can fight." Hawke spared a glance for Goaty, for it was always worth reminding him of the fact.

Szekely licked his lips. "This was particularly impressive, by Corissa's account."

Hawke looked at her, feeling a pang of longing when this time she met his eyes. "She flatters me."

"I was not certain of your loyalty after Lucas's untimely demise," Szekely's voice sliced through his wistfulness. "Now, I confess, I am more unsettled than ever."

"How so?" Hawke asked, nervous, suddenly horrified that he might have been spotted with Ruthven or Brommett. "You said I proved myself."

Szekely regarded him coolly, letting out a long, lingering breath. After a few moments he said, "Harlowe is dead." He traced a line across his own neck with a pearly white finger, then took a pair of cream coloured gloves from his pocket, pulling them on as he spoke. "Throat slit, ear to ear."

Θ

There was a yard behind the building, ankle-deep with mud. It was almost empty, save a gaggle of scrawny hens performing a gamut of peculiar dances to charm worms to the surface. The whole space was bounded by a high brick wall, and, some thirty yards from the haberdashery's rear, a row of wooden sheds marked the very end of the plot.

"When?" Hawke asked. "Where?" They were all standing in one of the sheds, rain hissing on the roof. Harlowe's body was there too, face up, lying flat on the filthy floor beneath a sheet that had been tugged back as far as his sternum. The blood had been wiped clean away, so that the destruction made by the blade was plain to see, the exposed tissue ragged and pink.

"During the night," Szekely said. "At his rooms down on Little Compton Street. Penley found him and brought him here." He pursed his lips, pondering something. "First Lucas, then Harlowe. No coincidence, I'd wager."

Hawke tore his gaze away from the corpse, jolted by the pointedness of the words. "You think I did it?"

"His lodgings are pissing distance from yours," Goaty sneered through his dog-chewed jaw, relishing the opportunity to implicate his rival.

Szekely looked at Hawke and Corissa in turn. "No one has seen you, *Sólyom,* since the two of you parted."

"I've been drinking," Hawke said, which was, at least, not wholly untrue.

Szekely smiled. "Now *that* I believe." He turned to Corissa. "What say you, my love?"

Her coffee-brown eyes seemed to gleam in the murk as they shifted from Szekely to Hawke and back again. "He did not do it."

Hawke should have been relieved to have her support, for Corissa's word carried more weight than most, but his mind was turning cartwheels. Not so much because of the suspicion he found himself under, but, rather, because he was innocent. All the while the others stared accusingly at him, he found himself peering into their faces, wondering which of them might be the real killer. The shed walls seemed to be getting closer. The fetid air hotter.

"The Giltspurs have declared war," Blackbird growled, deep voice echoing. "Did I not tell you? They're picking us off, one by one."

Hawke ignored him. He crouched instead beside the dead man, whose face had taken on a bluish marbled effect, but twisted to look back up at Gilroy Penley. The hospital porter returned his gaze quizzically. He was the Szekely gang's connection to London's anatomist community. Had something gone awry in that relationship? Was one of Doctor Vine's competitors attempting to undermine his business? Perhaps they had some kind of leverage over Gilroy, or they could afford to pay him enough for his betrayal. Beside him, Goaty's ruined face leered down in open challenge. The man hated Hawke, made no bones about it, but did his enmity run deep enough to attempt to frame him for murder? Especially as such a plan appeared to involve the whittling and weakening of his own comrades? It did not make much sense. Hawke glanced at the others, realising that none could be trusted in truth. Was Blackbird ambitious enough to destroy Szekely in an attempt to rebuild the organisation in his own image? Could Szekely himself be engineering a war with the Giltspur Boys for some complex purpose? And Corissa Lott. What had she to gain in all this? Hawke realised that he could be sure of no one.

That was why, when he looked quickly away, he knew that Harlowe might just hold the answer. When he had worked in Manchester, under Joseph Nadin, a man generally disliked for his brutal methods but universally respected for his results, he had learnt to look upon the scene of a crime through the lens of scepticism. So much could be detected when one saw beyond the obvious. The respect might have leaked out of Nadin's reputation after the massacre in St Peter's Square, but the memory of his investigations remained indelibly inked upon Hawke's mind.

So he focussed. For the first time in such a long time, he tried to remember his old life, to recall his old skills. Tried to sharpen his senses and his wits. What would Nadin have done? The corpse, Hawke thought. The murder had not taken place here, so Harlowe himself was the only evidence. He studied his erstwhile friend. The neck had been slashed wide open, so violently that bone shone white at the base of the wound. The flesh, gaping at either side like escarpments over a crimson creek, was torn and frayed. Not the clean line he would expect from a butcher's cleaver. He whispered, "Jesus wept."

"No doubt what killed him," Gilroy Penley said. "Not a drop left in his body, poor bastard."

It was those words that stirred something within Hawke. He agreed, of course, for a torn throat had obviously made certain the murder. But the mention of doubt lit a spark somehow. Was that what the killer wanted, for there to be no shred of uncertainty? He leaned in, even as Goaty and Gilroy embarked upon a fatuous conversation about which type of blade was best suited to severing a windpipe. Checking the upper torso, he found nothing of importance. No unusual bruising, no broken ribs, no stab wounds. He revisited the neck, which, though ruined, showed no other signs of struggle. No ligature or finger marks. The skull, too, seemed robust and undamaged. Gently, he placed his fingers on Harlowe's stone-cold jaw and eased the head to the side. He could not shift it far, so rigid were the muscles, but he did not require a great deal of movement before he saw what he had been looking for. A pair of tiny freckles, set just above the collar bone on the right-hand side. He squinted in the feeble light while the others talked and the rain came down. The marks were not as closely positioned as those he had found on Lucas, the distance between being more like three inches, but the zig-zagging pattern, albeit patchier and more faded this time, was unmistakable upon the skin. He pressed thumb and forefinger to the flesh either side of the almost anonymous lesions, pulling the openings apart. They would have been lost amongst the blood had the body not been cleaned. Yet now, against waxen skin, they were plain to see.

A dull thud sounded through the shed wall. Hawke looked up, startled. "What was that?"

Szekely was apparently unmoved. "While you have been drowning yourself in gin, dear *Sólyom*, I have conducted my own investigation." He left the shed, beckoning the others to follow.

Hawke hung back, taking the coil of wire from his pocket and quickly unravelling it. He inserted it into one of the strange puncture wounds, pushing and teasing the shaft so that it found a route into Harlowe's neck. It went remarkably deep. Two-thirds of an index finger, maybe fractionally more. Someone called to Hawke, startling him, and he whipped the wire free, stuffing it back into the pocket and making for the door.

Θ

"Who is he?" Hawke asked. The noise had come through the thin timber wall, and Szekely had led the group to the shed adjacent to Harlowe's temporary resting place. Now the six of them gathered around a figure who was very much alive, but whose feeble mewling spoke of someone who would rather that was not the case.

"Seamus O'Neill," Szekely said, the Irish note in his accent becoming prominent as he uttered the name. "Of Giltspur Street."

Hawke gaped. The captive was bound to a chair with thick rope. He was gagged, bloody and naked from the waist up. His face was almost devoid of discernible features, so battered was it, the lips split to shreds and the eyes almost entirely swollen shut. "You've started a war." He looked round at Szekely. "You said you wanted to know for certain."

Szekely sucked at his teeth. "As you have witnessed, *Sólyom*, matters have moved on a pace. They fired the opening salvo when they murdered Lucas." He brushed dust from his immaculate collar with gloved knuckles. "And by your own account, you and Corissa have done little to build new bridges."

"They did not make us at the baiting. Harlowe's death cannot be blamed upon what happened." Hawke pointed to O'Neill, to the ragged strip of flesh where, until very recently, his right ear had been. "But this? How can you hide this? There is no going back."

"They started the war. I will finish it."

"I do not think it was the Giltspurs, Mister Szekely."

The Hungarian rounded on him, that steely glint inflecting his blue eyes. "Why? Was it you after all?"

"No." Hawke thought back to the night at Hockley-in-the-Hole. He had no evidence for the Giltspurs' innocence, but years of practice had taught him how to gauge a person. He did not know how to articulate such a notion without inspiring a raft of further questions, so in the end he simply shrugged. "Their demeanour."

"Demeanour?" Blackbird echoed incredulously. He spat a gobbet of phlegm that landed in O'Neill's lap. "Horse shit."

Szekely's gaze was still locked onto Hawke, like a cat eyeing a mouse. "How is it that you are able to read guilt - or innocence - on a man's face?"

"They were at leisure," Hawke tried to explain as evasively as possible. To his side, he could feel Corissa's intensely curious gaze. "At the baiting, I mean. Relaxed. I would be on my guard if I had recently murdered one of Colan Szekely's soldiers."

"Let us say you are right, just for a moment," Szekely said. He paused briefly, for O'Neill was mumbling something through the filthy rag that blocked his mouth. Blackbird's hulking frame lurched forwards with surprising speed, his huge fist darting out like a spear to crack upon the helpless man's chin. O'Neill's already battered head snapped back with sickening force, then lolled loosely to the side. Szekely politely thanked Blackbird, then looked back to Hawke. "You think it Milne?"

"In truth," replied Hawke, "I have my doubts."

"You said he made threats."

"Wouldn't you, were you in his position?"

"If I were in Milne's position," Szekely replied coolly, "every man and woman under the merest hint of suspicion would have been flayed alive by now."

Hawke spread his palms. "You have proved my point better than I ever could."

Szekely considered that for a few moments. As he did so, he plucked the exquisite gloves from his fingers, handing them to Corissa. "So you are saying," he said, removing his coat as well, "our persecutor is a third party?"

"I am saying we cannot be certain." In his mind Hawke saw the marks. The little wheels imprinted on the skin of both Lucas and Harlowe, encircling what looked to be stab wounds of unknowable depth. Did they link the murders?

Szekely nodded. "I must think on it. And you are in the right of it, dear *Sólyom*. We must attempt to avoid confrontation if at all possible." When he moved it was like the strike of an adder, all speed and efficiency. There was no discussion, no struggle and no remorse. Szekely, thin as a reed and delicate and pale as porcelain, had covered the few paces between himself and Seamus O'Neill before Hawke even realised what was going on. The knife that somehow found its way into Szekely's hand was long and slender, and it slipped easily through the Giltspur Boy's left eye, not stopping until its ivory hilt met the solid socket. Szekely stepped back, clicking his fingers, and Goaty was immediately on hand to take the blade for cleaning. The Hungarian yawned, as if the murder had tired and bored him in equal measure. He looked at Hawke again. "In the mean time, let us bend our minds to business. There was a burial this afternoon, out at Angel." He took his coat and gloves from Corissa and got dressed. "The night watchmen assure me they will doze just after midnight. You'll go with Blackbird and Goaty. Pay your respects. When you sell Doctor Vine the corpse, offer him this one as well." He nodded towards the twitching body of Seamus O'Neill. "Give him a discount for the damaged product."

"It's wet out," Blackbird protested.

"The soil will be cold enough," Szekely said, slipping his fingers into the smooth kidskin. "Get it done."

Θ

"Eat up, Jemima, there's a good girl." Reggie McDow spoke gently, lovingly, as he hand-fed scraps of dried fish to the little grey cat that perched on the edge of a well-used woodworking bench. "A smidgen more, ma' beaut?" he muttered, his vowels coloured by the rhotic influence of the South Western counties. He offered the meat for the purring cat to take. "Aye, you're a greedy girl, aren't you, eh? Aren't you, ma' beaut?"

Joshua Hawke, leaning against a glass-doored cabinet that held an extensive collection of chisels, mallets and planes, thrust his fists into the deep pockets of his greatcoat, lest he smash something in frustration. "Spit it out, Reggie, for Christ's sake."

McDow's spine was permanently distorted, compelling him into a perpetual hunch, but indignation allowed him to straighten a fraction as he shot his unexpected visitor a hard glance. "No need for rudeness, chum. You'll give her tummy ache." He stroked the cat's chin with a finger. "Won't he, Jemima?"

Hawke sucked at his rotten molar, the pulsating pain a welcome distraction. He had always found McDow, an ashen-faced man in his mid fifties, to be a frustratingly opaque figure, whose bumbling obfuscation was a touch too convincing to be accidental, but, he told himself, the man's broad knowledge was worth suffering. There were a few hours to spare before Hawke's grim night's work would begin, so he had resolved to see the patternmaker, whose premises were on Coal Yard, about the strange, narrow stab wounds he had discovered on the bodies of Lucas and Harlowe. The interview could, if necessary, be expedited by furnishing McDow's calloused palm with one of Ruthven's thick coins, but the expert patternmaker had been in Szekely's pay for a decade. A bribe would be at once both wasteful and dangerous. That was why, after a slow ten-count and a lingering breath that was ripe with the smell of wood-shavings, Hawke said patiently, "I need your advice, Reggie, please. Do not force me to relay that you were unaccommodating."

It was risky, invoking the spectre of their mutual master, for it heightened the possibility of word getting back to the haberdashery on Great Store Street, but Hawke doubted whether McDow would tell tales when his assumption would surely be that the interview had been ordered by Szekely himself. In short, let the coy bugger believe Hawke had been sent by Szekely, and dare him to call the bluff.

Hawke, in truth, did not fully understand why he had kept the knowledge of Harlowe's curious neck damage to himself. Or that it was almost identical to injuries present on Lucas. The decision had been borne out of instinct. At the very moment when he was gauging his colleagues, wondering which, if any, of the resurrectionists he could trust, the notion of revealing his discovery seemed at odds with every fibre of his being. Thus, he had kept his mouth shut, a choice made simpler by the distraction of Seamus O'Neill's untimely demise.

He was pleased to see the hint at Szekely's displeasure had apparently done the trick, for the patternmaker grimaced. "Worrisome, is all. I worries, chum, really I does." McDow winced, perhaps at a passing fragment of memory. "I pass on what I hears to Mister

Szekely. Happy to. And I pays him my rents, on time and ne'er a penny short." The cat had been forgotten now, left to paw the air at his back. "But injuries? Violence? To be embroiled in such doings, chum. Gives me the shivers."

"Then answer me and I will leave you in peace," Hawke replied. He gazed around the workshop, at the tools and the piles of paper that were marked with intricate scale drawings. Nodding at one such stack, he said, "You work with those?"

"From which I makes wooden patterns of machine parts."

"They are sent to a foundry for casting?"

McDow nodded. "All manner o' thing, chum, I can tells you."

"Without your expertise," Hawke said, "the factories would soon grind to a halt. You are the best in your field."

McDow managed to puff himself up proudly, flashing a smile as crooked as his back. "So they do say!" He glanced at the cat. "Do they not, ma' beaut?"

Hawke looked out of the workshop's large window onto Coal Yard. Outside, the rain had stopped, giving way to a fog that thickened by the minute. On the sill, amongst bits of discarded wood and dog-eared sketches, lay the latest editions of several crime broadsides, tatty now and crumpled. One in particular caught his eye and he picked it up. "And you make use of many different hand tools to achieve such marvellous workmanship?"

"Very many indeed," McDow answered. "Right devil's breath, this one," he added as he took note of the fog outside.

Hawke stared at the broadside in his hand. It was a single printed sheet, dominated by the title *Horror Beneath the Streets,* below which was an engraving of a corpse wrapped in thick coils that looked to Hawke like serpents. He did not need to read the fine text to know what the story was about. Silently he swore. If the tale of Betsy Milne spread beyond the cruder publications and into the more respectable newspapers, hysteria would soon take hold. He pushed it from his mind. "Then I'll ask you again, Reggie. Which tool would be thin, little wider than wire, but sturdy and sharp enough to pierce a man's flesh? Long enough that, upon entering the body here," he jabbed a finger at his own collarbone, "it might reach a vessel, thereby incapacitating the victim." The last comment was a deal of guesswork, for he had no proof as to the final depth of the wounds, so fleeting had his glimpse been, but a theory had already begun to take form in his mind.

McDow went to an ornately carved cupboard, swirling oak-sprigs rendered around the doors by a remarkably gifted hand. "Here," he said, taking a box from within. He set it on the bench, causing Jemima to leap clear, and fiddled with the lid's catch. "These are your most likely culprits."

Hawke inspected the contents of the box. "Awls?"

"Bradawls and scratching awls," McDow said. He ran a hand over the tools, a dozen in all, each with a wooden handle and straight, thin blade. "For puncturing and marking respectively. Nowt else comes close to what you're describing."

And not a single one narrow enough, thought Hawke, "You've been a great help," he said, trying hard to hide his disappointment. "Thank you for your indulgence."

“Ghouls and goblins,” McDow said. He was looking at the broadside in Hawke’s hand. “What will they come up with next?”

Hawke tossed it back on the windowsill. “Quite.”

“Plenty o’ murders in these streets, I’m sad to say, but that?” The patternmaker laughed, shaking his head. “They’ve gone too far, if you ask me. The printers, that is. B’ain’t no chance such a thing be true.”

Hawke looked at him levelly. “If it were?”

“The rioters would return, sure as eggs is eggs. And London, like as not, would burn.”

CHAPTER FOUR

SATURDAY

"Well?" Hawke said curtly as the tall figure approached through skeining dawn mist. He was ill-tempered already, having slept in a cramped and malodorous doss-house attached to Black Horse Yard, a large stable-block off Tottenham Court Road, too fearful was he to return to his proper lodgings, but clapping eyes on the new arrival stoked his ire yet further.

The man, who moved with a gallingly confident swagger, wore a long blue coat and black cravat. Red hair sprouted from beneath the brim of a black topper. "Mind your tone, little fellow."

Hawke spat bitterly, tugging his own, rather more threadbare, coat tighter. "God damn you, Runner."

Principal Patrol Officer George Ruthven pulled an expression of sheer disdain as he came close, gilt-topped tipstaff brandished like a club in his meaty fist. He glanced at Hawke's tall boots. "I see London's phantoms have been haunting the dearly departed."

Hawke looked down, realising mud from the cemetery at Angel had clung to the soles. "I do what I must."

"Still, you may count your blessings. Not many of your ilk are fortunate enough to posses cavalry issue boots."

"What do you want?" Hawke snapped irritably.

"I should like you to make your report, Mister Hawke. What have you discovered?" An unpleasant smile formed across his ruddy face. "Your edges appear a little... frayed."

Ruthven's summons had reached his unwilling operative, through the usual network of whispers, late the previous night, though fortunately before Hawke had imbibed himself into oblivion. The Newgate Street rendezvous, in the shadow of the nation's most infamous prison, was presumably intended as some kind of warning, a reminder to do Ruthven's bidding well, but there was logic, too, in selecting a thoroughfare bustling enough to render them near invisible. A pair of anonymous faces in a sea of anonymity.

Hawke, with scant choice but to obey, had been waiting for an hour now, nursing a gin-induced headache, the cold irking him as much as the delay, and now the sight of that smug face threatened to send him into a rage. “Frayed?” he hissed, as Ruthven ushered him away from the high grey fastness of Newgate’s outer wall. “Lucas and Harlowe are dead.”

They walked more than thirty paces in silence, until finally Ruthven appeared satisfied, steering Hawke into the doorway of a small bakery. “Lucas and Harlowe.” His brow furrowed as he mined the depths of his memory. “Szekely’s men?”

“And my friends,” Hawke said. He could feel the heat of anger rise up through his guts and into his chest. “My friends, Ruthven. You task me with investigating this girl’s death, and my group start dying. What in Christ’s name is going on?”

“That, Mister Hawke, is what I would ask of you.” Ruthven’s expression, for once, seemed devoid of amusement. London’s premier enforcer of law and order had long since cultivated a look that spoke of hidden nuance, as though he alone held the real truth in any situation. But now it was all gone. He was telling the truth.

The reality came as a shock to Hawke who had spent the night staring at his ceiling, wondering whether some deeper machination was playing out around him. He had told himself that the meeting with Ruthven, as inconvenient as it was, would, at least, provide a chance to confront the Bow Street Runner. Thus, he had left Buckbridge Street before dawn, expecting to discover some new morsel of information, but now his head simply swam with doubt. He scraped cold hands over cheeks made rough by stubble. "I know nothing. Have found nothing. The girl, the tosher, and now..."

"And now your grave-plundering confederates," Ruthven interjected archly. He paused, mulling over the news and breathing deeply of the air that blasted in sudden warmth from within the bakery, the aroma evidently as intoxicating for him as it was Hawke. "You find yourself looking into four murders? My my, but you appear to be taking on my duties as well as your own."

"I would rather have nought to do with any of it," Hawke said truthfully.

"Then why involve yourself?"

"Szekely commands me as you command me," Hawke answered bitterly. "A dead child, Butcher Milne rampaging about London and the prospect of war with the Giltspur Boys."

"The Holy Land," Ruthven said, using the nickname St Giles had earned on account of the high number of Irish immigrants to the area, "will verily run with blood."

"It already is," Hawke said.

Ruthven gnawed the inside of his mouth. "Go on."

"I was dispatched to follow the Giltspurs."

"Why?"

"To discover if it was they killed Lucas. In the event, they caught us."

"Us?"

"My associate and I."

"And?"

"My associate stabbed one of them in the neck. I hamstrung another."

Ruthven grinned wolfishly. "All that gin and opium," he crowed, tapping out a rapid tune on the bakery's door-frame with his tipstaff, "and the old thief-taker's still in there."

"When I made it to safety," Hawke went on, "I discovered that Harlowe had been sent the same way as Lucas. In the mean time, Szekely had abducted a Giltspur and attempted to torture the wretch into confessing to the murders of our men."

"And the hapless fellow failed to cough?"

Hawke shrugged. "What could he say?"

Ruthven frowned. "You do not think his gang were responsible?"

"Do you care what I think?"

"If Szekely and the Giltspurs chop one another to bits, all the better for me. But I'll indulge you."

"No, I do not think they killed Lucas or Harlowe, and I told Szekely so."

Ruthven chuckled. "Impertinent fellow. Did he heed your advice?"

"I think he did."

One of the officer's eyebrows arched. "In another life you'd have been called to the bar." He rubbed his chin thoughtfully. "But still he offed the fellow he had tortured?"

"Aye."

Ruthven made a clicking sound with his tongue. "Sensible. Can't have him scuttling back to Giltspur Street telling tales of woe, can he?"

"The Giltspurs will eventually discover it was Szekely," Hawke said, "and then we shall be at war regardless."

Ruthven waited for a trio of teenage boys to trundle past pushing barrows stacked high with flour sacks. "Was I right about the butcher, then? Is it Milne? You said he was... what was it... rampaging?"

Hawke said that he could not be sure. "I encountered him by chance at Smithfield. He did not seem like a man who had exacted revenge, but one who yet sought it." He thought about Betsy, the butcher's daughter. He had not seen her, but her injuries were easy enough to imagine. One thing that both men could agree upon was that her killer needed to be caught. The image shifted in his mind's eye so that her ruined face became the staring, pale visage of Lucas. He met Ruthven's stare. "Besides..."

"Speak plain," Ruthven pushed.

"The bodies bore strange marks."

Ruthven gave a mirthless grunt. "I would say young Betsy's injuries were not altogether run-of-the-mill."

Hawke shook his head, trying to find the right word. "Different, then. Unexpected."

"Go on."

"Two small holes at the base of the neck," Hawke said eventually. "Just above the collar."

"A cleaver will make holes," Ruthven said. He added a quick wink. "So will swords, as well you know."

The memories bubbled up then, as they always did, and Hawke instinctively turned to scan the row of shops.

Ruthven's smile broadened as he sensed his barb had snagged. "Plenty of gin palaces hereabouts. Need to service the crowds when they come to watch the hangings."

The fact that Ruthven had guessed correctly was enough to bring Hawke's mind back from the brink, and he shook the urges from his head. "The wounds were present upon the flesh of both Lucas and Harlowe," he said, forcing sharpness back into his mind if only because he would not give Ruthven the satisfaction of seeing him scrabble for the drink he so dearly wanted. "They were narrow. Almost invisible. But deep, I think. Not the kind of damage done by an edged weapon."

Ruthven seemed unimpressed. "Ask your Doctor Vine."

Hawke shook his head. "It would get back."

"To Szekely?" The corners of Ruthven's eyes wrinkled with interest. "You haven't told him of this matter? Of the deed done to his employee?"

“What if Szekely did the deed?”

Ruthven looked at him sceptically. “Why ever would he dispatch his own man in so strange and secretive a manner? It makes little sense.”

“What makes sense to me,” Hawke retorted hotly, “is the fewer people who know of it, the safer I am.” He gathered himself for a moment, then said, “Betsy’s body. Did you see it with your own eyes?”

Ruthven indicated that he had. “What of it?”

“Did it bear the same marks?”

“It had been mutilated,” Ruthven answered impatiently.

“You said the eyes were gouged out. Be specific, please.”

Ruthven’s small eyes narrowed further as he plucked detail from quarters of his memory necessarily locked tight. “Her face was removed. Eyes, lips, nose.”

“And she had been throttled?”

“Yes.”

“But no narrow holes?”

"None that I noticed," Ruthven said, "though I confess I was not looking at her god-damned neck." This time he waved a gloved hand, as if swatting any further questions away. "Enough of this! I am unconcerned with the tawdry happenings of you and your fellow gutter rats."

"Tawdry?" Hawke almost spat. "We are being murdered."

"And not a one of you will be mourned," Ruthven said in an iron tone, "but the Milne girl will see our good citizenry panic. Once that sluice is open, it will not be in my gift to shut it. Her death matters."

Matters to your career, Hawke thought, though he could hardly deny the truth of it. "Sorghum was the second plant used in her," he hesitated as he considered the state in which her body had been discovered, "cocoon."

"Sorghum?" Ruthven said. "Never heard of it. But that is commendable work, nevertheless. Does that lead you down any new paths?"

Hawke shook his head. There was no need to inform the officer of his discussion with Ansell Brommett until he had something more certain to report. "I will keep my ear to the ground."

"Both ears," Ruthven said, jabbing the tipstaff into Hawke's chest.

"And your men?" Hawke asked pointedly. "What have they discovered?"

"Inquiries continue to be made," Ruthven said, a little too primly, and Hawke knew that the great and good of Bow Street had blundered down a dead end. "I intend to scour Limehouse in due course. Strikes me as a case reeking of superstition, and where better to look than the Orientals who infest that part of the city? Whether they be Mussulman or Chinaman, they're all rotten at the root. They believe in pixies and jinns and all sorts of absurdities and perversions. My shilling's on Limehouse. That's where we'll find this vermin. But you must continue to keep that nose of yours to the breeze." The hero of Cato Street breathed on the end of the tipstaff and buffed it with his sleeve. "This matter is my sole concern. Therefore, it is your sole concern."

"Christ, Ruthven," Hawke hissed through gritted teeth, pushing the staff away. "Our group is whittled away through acts of supreme violence, and you would have me do nothing but your own bidding?"

"What Szekely and his rivals do to one another is their business. Indeed, it is a slice of good fortune for the Patrol, truth be told."

"I cannot look into Betsy Milne's death when I myself must fear daggers in the dark!"

Ruthven laughed at that, a sound dripping with scorn. "Oh, but you can."

"Spare your breath, you self-satisfied bastard. You'll inform Szekely of our association. I am well aware of the threat."

For answer, Ruthven unexpectedly lifted the tipstaff again, making Hawke flinch. This time he touched its tip to the door of the bakery. "I can be more creative if you'd like. After all, it doesn't pay to have folk blabbing your private affairs about town, not least when the knowledge of those affairs might get you torn to shreds by the unwashed masses." He paused for effect. "If you refuse to do as you're told, sirrah, then I shall whisper one little word that will spread around this great metropolis as a plague, and you will be hounded to your doom like the flea-bit rat you truly are."

Hawke felt horror climb the sinews of his neck like ivy vines. "You would not."

"Try me. I can see it now. A full page in The Times, recounting that dreadful day." He leaned closer. "A list of the names of those involved. The brave members of the Manchester and Salford Yeomanry Cavalry and the gallant Hussars that provided such stoic support."

Hawke swallowed thickly, he could feel his hands trembling at his sides. He feared the man standing before him, and yet he could not believe Ruthven would jeopardise a key informant so callously. "Fuck yourself, Runner."

The bigger man tutted, as if correcting an errant child, and pushed the tipstaff so that the door swung inward ajar. To Hawke's bafflement, he began to softly sing. "And the heroic host no more shall boast, the mighty deeds of Waterloo."

Incredulity turned to twisting horror in Hawke's guts. "Mister Ruthven, sir, stop." He spied with dread the folk on the other side of the door.

Ruthven went on, grinning, "But this henceforth shall be the toast," his voice built in volume, "the glorious feats of Peterloo!"

There were six or seven people within, the baker and his assistants, and their bustling work ceased, all eyes training on the doorway. "Sir?" one of them called.

Ruthven waited, letting the word hang there, an invisible but pungent ingredient mixing with the floury air. Then he looked down at Hawke, who could manage nothing but a weak nod. Ruthven looked back into the bakery. "Peter who? I was asking my friend, here, about a mutual associate. I cannot recall Peter's family name."

"Well close the door, if you please!" the baker bellowed. "It's too bleedin' cold out!"

"My apologies, of course," Ruthven said, "I do have a habit of leaning too heavily."

"I should fucking do you right now," Hawke snarled as the door thudded shut. His hand was clamped fast round the hilt of his knife.

Ruthven was unruffled, though he placed the staff between them as a precaution. "You are free to try, naturally. After all, it is eminently sensible to eliminate those privy to one's dirtiest secrets." With his free hand he patted a spot at the side of his long coat, eliciting the unmistakable clink of coinage. "Depends whether you can afford to do without me."

Hawke relented. He stared into those tiny eyes, wondering whether the lawman knew just how tempted he was to commit murder. "I will do my best with the Milne case."

"There's a good fellow," Ruthven said smoothly. "I want a report by dusk. Come to the safe house on Red Lion Square."

Θ

"*Che cosa vuoi da me*?"

The eye peering through the narrow slit was dark brown, the voice behind it nervous and accusing. A metallic click followed, the unmistakable speech of a cocking pistol.

Joshua Hawke let go of the dolphin-shaped knocker and took a step away from the door so that he could be easily seen. He held up his hands to show they were empty. "No need for that, friend."

The disembodied eye flickered rapidly left and right, up and down. "You are not here to buy."

"Who says?"

"You're a vagabond," the voice, obscured by thick timber and thicker accent, went on rapidly. "Tell me what you want or I blow a hole in you."

Hawke smiled, partly because of the brutal assessment, and partly because he would like to see how the fellow proposed to get a bullet all the way through the stout oak. "I would speak with you, sir."

"About?"

"The *Benandanti.*" Hawke waited now, letting the words sink in. Then he added, "Ansell Brommett sent me."

The interior of the building on Perceval Street was a place of wonder. A cavern of fine, strange tools, built for work of complexity and precision, of benches littered with objects in glass and metal, toothy cogs and intricate numbering scales rendered in carefully inscribed ink. The walls groaned with shelves displaying what appeared to be the completed products, though Hawke was unfamiliar with the exotic devices. They were things of great beauty that seemed both functional and fantastical in their design, inventions combining expertly carved wood, mesmerising dials, and slender tubes filled with liquid. They were boxes in the main, rectangular cases with no lids, so that their spectacular innards were displayed for the world to see. They reminded Hawke of the fine clock his father, a moderately successful brewer, had kept in the reception hall of the family home as a sign of his hard-earned status. Yet this curious machine had neither pendulum nor hands. He forced his eyes away from the walls to meet the suspicious gaze of the man who had confirmed himself to be Marco Totti. "Barometers?"

"To measure atmospheric pressure."

"You make them?"

Totti, around forty years old by the look of him, shook his head, glossy black-and-silver curls shimmering at his shoulders. "I create them."

"This is fine work, sir."

Totti still gripped the pistol. He shook it gently. "Who are you?"

"No one of importance," Hawke said. "I merely have some questions." Reading the scepticism in Totti's face, he added, "Brommett told me to come to Clerkenwell. Assured me you were a man with answers."

"Then Brommett should watch his mouth."

"Why so nervous, Mister Totti?"

The Italian blasted air through a red-tipped nose that was prominent at the bridge. "Have you read the broadsides and those," he tapped the side of his head, "*pazzo* little pamphlets? Murders on the streets. Murders committed by foreigners. And now you come to ask me about the *Benandanti*?" His gaze jumped to the door. "It will be a rabble soon, bringing more than questions."

"Information," Hawke said, trying to banish any impatience from his tone. "That is all I want from you. I give you my word." He smiled. "Though I suppose the word of a vagabond is not worth a great deal."

The Italian let the tiniest flicker of amusement cross his face. "You are a friend of Ansell's?" When Hawke nodded, he said, "Then I apologise for the insult."

"No matter," Hawke waved him away. "Can you assist?"

Totti seemed to consider the request for a few silent moments. He rubbed his free hand over a deeply lined brow, then massaged the large bridge of his nose with thumb and forefinger. In the end he took a slow breath and said, "Good Walkers. That is what they called them."

"That is what who called them?" Hawke pressed, nonplussed.

"The folk of Friuli, in the north."

"Of Italy?"

"*Sì.*" Totti leaned against a wooden pillar from which hung an array of tools. He was beginning to relax a touch, though he looked unlikely to relinquish the weapon.

"You hail from Friuli?" Hawke asked, recalling Brommett's surety in referring him to this row of unassuming businesses in the heart of London's burgeoning Italian community.

Totti confirmed that he did. "I have knowledge of my people. Of our shared past. It is a particular passion of mine." He gave a mirthless chuckle, showing teeth that were small and white. "You understand, our land has been dominated by others for generations. The Spanish, the Austrians and the French have all taken their turn. All fed from the trough. We, the common people, must remember our history if we are ever to forge a future." He moved to one of his workbenches, upon which perched a pewter goblet. He took it, sipped slowly, then said, "The Good Walkers are long dead."

Apparently not, Hawke thought. "So tell me about them."

"What do you want to know?"

"Everything."

"Let me see." Totti gnawed at the inside of his mouth as he dredged long-silted memories, then said, "They were strongest two - perhaps three - centuries ago. The Benandanti claimed to travel out of their bodies while sleeping."

"To do battle with Malandanti."

"Indeed," Totti said, clearly impressed. "They believed the witches would spoil the crop. The Walkers would fight them, wielding stalks of fennel, in order to ensure a successful harvest."

"And these witches carried sticks of sorghum?"

Totti nodded. "*Sì*."

"What did they look like, the Good Walkers?"

Totti laughed at that. "Look like? They did not have wings, if that is what you are asking. Nor horns, nor tails, nor cloven feet. *Benandanti* were believed to have been born with a caul on their head." He sketched a halo above his own skull. "The fluid in which a foetus resides while inside the womb. The presence of the caul at birth gave them their power. Their ability to take part in the night battles. To the eye of the man in the street, they are no different to the rest of us."

Then, Hawke thought, he was looking for a truly tiny needle in the largest haystack of all. Just another stranger lost within London's sprawling embrace. "You say they are extinct, Mister Totti. What became of them?"

Totti shrugged as though it were obvious. "The Inquisition. They hunted down the *Good Walkers*, tried them as heretics and Satanists. Exterminated the cult." He was probably an inch or two taller than the Englishman, and he peered intently down that crimsoned nose as if attempting to read Hawke's thoughts. "This is a strange interest indeed. Perverse, even. What brings you here?"

Hawke knew he should not risk offering any more detail. It would do him no good if Szekely got wind of his involvement in the case. And yet his formidable employer would get to hear far worse tales should Hawke return to Ruthven empty handed. He swallowed hard, throat feeling suddenly constricted, and made a decision. "The murder to which you referred."

The Italian frowned. "The story told in the penny bloods?"

"The corpse was discovered wrapped in fennel and sorghum."

Totti's dark eyes widened. He mouthed an oath in his native tongue. "And you believe the Good Walkers responsible? They fought malevolent witches, *Signore* Hawke. If this is the cult resurrected," he gave a sardonic smile, "then perhaps your victim is where they belong."

"You will recall that the victim was a child," Hawke said brusquely. "A little girl."

That gave Totti pause. A look of shame rippled over his strong features. "Of course. Fear makes a man speak without consideration."

"Fear?"

"I have always cause for fear in this city, S*ignore.* The summer riots had nothing to do with my people, and yet men of darker complexion were still made targets of the mob's fury. It is always thus." He rubbed thin fingers over his lips. "Now this murder may bring the wolf to our very door." He took another sip from the goblet, grunting softly as a thought evidently dawned. "If the *Benandanti* have truly returned then you have precious little time, for their activities were limited."

"To?" Hawke prompted. "By?"

"*Quattuor anni tempora*," Totti intoned. "Ember Days."

Hawke was suddenly back in church. A young lad, full of life, full of promise, learning scripture and revelling in each new day. "Ember?" he repeated slowly, the word echoing in his mind like a shout across a deep valley. "Set aside for fasting and prayer, yes?"

"You have it," Totti said. "Four separate occasions of three days within the same week, equidistant in the circuit of the year, reflecting the four seasons. These four times were the only opportunity for the night battles. The only time they could take place. If your killer is truly *Benandanta...*"

"He may only be active on Ember Days," Hawke completed the train of thought. "But when do they occur?"

"*Sant Crux, Lucia, Cineres, Charismata Dia,*" Totti intoned in barely a whisper. "*Ut sit in angariâ quarta sequens feria.*"

"I will require a little help, Mister Totti."

“Fasting days and Emberings,” the Italian switched to an English equivalent of the rhyme, “be Lent, Whitsun, Holyrood, and Lucy.” He gnawed a fingernail as he considered his own implication. “When was the child murdered?”

Hawke shrugged. “She was badly decomposed.”

“For the sake of argument, let us indulge your flight of fancy, and say it occurred in September, during the Holyrood Embertide.”

“That would work.”

“Then the next battle,” he arched an eyebrow, “if the *Benandanti* are really to blame...”

“Saint Lucy’s Day,” Hawke cut in. He frowned. “We did not make a great matter of it in my home town.”

Totti said, “Santa Lucia has just passed. Two days ago, in fact. Thus, the final Embertide for this year falls next week.”

A chill traced its icy progress along Hawke’s spine. “The Emberings are three days within the same week?” His mind tumbled now. “Which three days?”

"Always the Wednesday, the Friday and the Saturday," Totti said. "But wait, *Signore*, you are stumbling blindly into assumption."

"Four days. I have four days to fathom this affair."

Totti held up staying hands as if he calmed a skittish colt. "Consider the matter with care, *Signore*, I beg you. It is madness to suggest any cause for this deed beyond common wickedness."

"Fennel and sorghum," Hawke retorted tersely. "The torn body of a young girl entombed in their stalks. Tell me what is common in that." Totti held his gaze, inhaled, but his words never came. Hawke made to leave. He had to get back to Bow Street. Ruthven needed to be warned, to expect more carnage on the streets of the capital. The following Wednesday, to be exact. He was already walking towards the workshop door when he called over his shoulder. "Thank you for your help, Mister Totti, truly."

"Wait!" Totti called, pursuing him through the gauntlet of benches and tool chests. "You seek an Italian for this crime?"

"There are a great many of your compatriots in the city," Hawke answered as he reached the door, turning back.

"The wars of Napoleon ravaged our country," Totti said as he drew up before the Englishman, his voice desperate, pleading. "The north is a ruin. Como, Lucca, Friuli. We come here for a better life. Do not presume we are killers, I beg you."

"That is your concern?" Hawke snapped with sudden anger. "To save your own skin?"

"And the skins of those I love? *Sì*, *Signore*, and I do not regret it." Totti placed a staying hand on Hawke's elbow. "A mob stirred by fear is a terrible thing to behold. Once unleashed it cannot be recalled."

That made Hawke hesitate, though he could hardly tell the fellow why. He glanced at his elbow and Totti let go. "I harbour no wish for mob justice. But do you think me wrong?"

Totti offered a pained shrug. "Any man may study the Good Walkers, echo their exploits for an evil deed. Please, sir, do not raise a hue and cry on mere presumption. The people are fretful already, driven so by nothing more than rumour. If those rumours are confirmed, revenge will sweep like wildfire through this community.

Clerkenwell will be aflame before sunrise." He pressed his palms together, eyes glistening. "I beg you, *Signore*, do not throw us to the dogs."

Θ

Throw us to the dogs.

Christ, Hawke thought, as he made his way south on Little Northampton Street, but Totti had a knack for tugging heart strings. The fact that he had been so easily manipulated annoyed him, for he was fairly sure that, regardless of the barometer-maker's doe-eyed pleas, the killer seemed far more likely to hail from the *Benandanti* heartlands than Smithfield or Moorgate or any other place this side of the Alps. And yet, despite himself, he was reluctant to be the one to whip the mob into frenzy. He had seen what had happened when a spark was touched to the gunpowder of fear, and this powder was already bone dry. The crime broadsides and vulgar pamphlets would be circulating unchecked, spreading from ward to ward like an outbreak of plague, their salacious tales of sorcery and child-murder, probably only half true, serving to sow seeds of fear into fertile minds. London's Italians were a growing group, and with their businesses and influence gaining traction so soon after a war in which they were Britain's enemy, it made their entire community vulnerable.

The sheer pressure of it all felt like a millstone about Hawke's neck, and he decided to consider his next move over a well-earned drink, while waiting on his scheduled meeting with Ruthven. He hailed a hackney coach at the intersection of King Street and Compton Street, giving some of the Runner's coins to the driver, and clambered up.

The driver was an elderly man, with straggly hair the colour of yellowed snow and ill-fitting teeth that had probably once belonged to a horse. He glanced at Hawke dubiously, before making a clicking sound that inspired his pair of palfreys to pull away with a jolt. "Where to, young sir?"

Hawke called above the clatter of hooves, "*The Punchbowl* on Red Lion Square, if you please!"

Θ

Hawke sat at a low, wildly unbalanced table near the drinking den's open door. He stared out onto the street, the light already fading to grey, and eyed the neat but barren Red Lion Square beyond, occasionally tilting back his head to quaff gin straight from the bottle, gulping feverishly, desperately, so that the liquid might burn away the cold.

The Punchbowl nestled between a drapery and a brothel on the north side of the square. A large tobacconist that served as a front for the more clandestine of Bow Street's operations was situated immediately opposite, on the far side of the central garden, visible through a lattice of branches stripped bare by the bitter season. A carved and painted figure of a native of the Americas stood sentinel outside, his colourful skirts and headdress made from tobacco leaves, large tobacco rolls stuffed under both arms. Behind him, the building's expansive glass frontage boasted a gaudy array of colourful jars and pots. Hawke observed the busy shop's comings and goings as he cradled the gin, trying to guess which of the patrons brought genuine custom and which were Runners in disguise.

It was to the tobacconist that Hawke must ultimately report, as per Ruthven's instruction, yet now that he was here, he felt a gnawing undercurrent of reticence. Marco Totti's terrified warning had taken hold, like a leech latching onto his skin, and, despite the calming libation, he was finding it difficult to detach. Hawke had seen the fire of panic and retribution spread once before, and that conflagration had altered the course of his entire life. His actions that day had made him an object of hate for common folk, and his behaviour since had brought shame to his family. If he could avoid becoming the fan to that kind of flame this time, then he would. He needed time to think before planting a seed in Ruthven's mind. Bow Street needed the case resolved, publicly and decisively, regardless of the wider cost, and his information might very well lead to the vilification of an entire community. Besides, a warming tot or three would not go amiss.

He swilled the bottle, watching intently as the spirit clung to the inner face of the vessel, snaking its way back down the neck in thick rivulets. Perhaps he could divine the right course therein, like some street-corner fortune teller. He knew that at some point he would have to face Ruthven, regardless of whether he was ready to relay Totti's information. But what exactly was to be relaid? That Betsy Milne had been murdered by an Italian witch in some kind of pagan ritual? That the murderer was likely to strike again, but not until next Wednesday? He laughed blackly at that last thought. It seemed utterly preposterous. The ravings of a drunk. He regarded the bottle again, his hazy reflection peering back, though he barely recognised the creature he had become. "Fucking wastrel," he muttered, putting the gin to his lips. His skin was, at least, beginning to feel warmer, glowing from within. He shut his eyes, wallowing in the supreme sensation. The image of Harlowe came to him in the darkness, and that of the Giltspur Boy, Seamus O'Neill. What had he fathomed of that case? Someone was targeting Szekely's grave-robbing operation. Hardly an impressive display of detection. All in all, he had nothing but scraps to feed the ambitious Bow Street Patrol Officer.

At a nearby table a man with a palsied arm and a face that was a filigree of claret-coloured veins, sucked hungrily at a wooden pipe. When he coughed, loud and racking, it disturbed Hawke's stream of thought, and he snapped open his eyes and slumped back in the chair. He reflected upon his meeting in the fantastical Clerkenwell workshop, pictured the Italian who had brought his exquisite technical skill to a new country, and feared losing it all at the hands of panic-stirred rioters. Hawke drank deeply. Absently he watched the tobacconist again, but his mind was no longer in Red Lion Square. It meandered almost two hundred miles northward, to a place called St Peter's Square, where another crowd gathered in their Sunday best, dignified and quiet, waving banners daubed with slogans imploring peace and progress. Hawke was there too. He saw the faces, the massed bodies of men, women and children surrounding a cart where men would come to speak. Yet he was not amongst them, but set apart. His vantage was high, rocking, obscured by the pricked ears of a huge bay mare. The faces were looking up at him, pale with terror as the bodies linked arms for protection. Hawke heard the slicing song of swords drawn in unison.

He sat bolt upright, blinking hard, and plunged a hand in his coat pocket. The bottle he pulled out was insignificant enough. Just a few ounces of transparent glass, four inches tall, slightly misshapen, hardly crystal in clarity and stoppered with an imperfectly fitted hunk of cork. Yet Hawke felt like genuflecting before it, as though it were holier than the rarest relic. The man smoking the pipe leered at him through the pungent cloud, sharing an amused wink that might have once appalled Hawke, but, in this moment, he did not care. All that mattered was ridding himself of the memories that buzzed like flies in his skull, for he knew they would not stop. Not until he was screaming and sobbing. It was always thus.

The label on the bottle had faded, the result of much handling, but the words remained, beckoning like a siren song. The printed block text read "OPIUM TINCTURE", but it was commonly known by another name. He thumbed free the stopper and lifted the tincture to his lips. There was hardly anything left of the reddish brown liquid, enough for a couple of drops, so he simply upended the bottle and let the last vestiges of the substance gather at the rim, battling gravity until the growing bead was too fat to cling on. It fell suddenly, one then another, dropping directly onto the tip of his tongue, tainting it with its deeply bitter taste, and he clamped shut his mouth as if the elixir might somehow escape. The deed was done and things, for a time at least, would be good. He washed it down with a generous helping of gin.

Laudanum. Harsh, pungent, beautiful laudanum.

It was Hawke's greatest ally and his most implacable foe. He loathed it with every fibre of his being, yet no saintly bones could have elicited greater reverence. When events at St Peter's Square had overtaken him, when he had found himself in the midst of horror as decent folk had bled and died beneath cold soldierly steel, he had been lost. Unable to face his peers, unwilling to endanger his family, all the while spiralling inexorably into a bottomless abyss. He had gone south, fled to the only city where he could be truly anonymous, but the ghosts had chased him. The horrors had refused to fade. Nothing would ease the pain or the guilt. Nothing except laudanum. He still remembered the first time, when the razor-sharp memories had been blunted in one fell swoop. A miracle, Hawke had thought. A bona fide intervention by God. It was only when the tincture's effects had worn off that he truly understood, and from that moment on, his very existence had skewed towards recapturing that feeling. A feeling of mindless, remorseless, exquisite oblivion. But the cost had been high. To exchange night terrors with euphoria the drug had enslaved him, as liquor had enslaved him. But the chains of laudanum were far longer, far thicker, far heavier than any to be found in a gin barrel.

As his body began to relax, he tipped the bottle over, a petulant gesture that sent the vessel rolling away to clatter upon the floor. He hated himself, hated laudanum. But at least he no longer cared about the day that had come to be known as Peterloo.

He drank more.

Turning his unshackled thoughts to the strange killings in London's sewer, he tried to imagine what kind of wickedness would inspire a man to wrap his victims in sorghum and fennel. Except that it was not both victims, just one. Was the tosher simply a bystander? A witness to the crime, in need of silencing? Perhaps he had been murdered elsewhere, by an entirely different perpetrator, and his corpse had floated on the city's subterranean river of effluvia to find a resting place near poor Betsy Milne. One thing was certain, beyond tall tales of Italian heresy, Hawke had little of value to add to the case. At best he would receive a tongue lashing from George Ruthven, laced with more mockery, as was the Patrol Officer's way. The most celebrated of Bow Street's enforcers despised Hawke as a prime example of wasted opportunity. A man toppled from a great height by his own self-loathing, kept languishing in the gutter by addiction and sin. He replayed Ruthven's jibes in his mind, imagining himself driving a dagger into the Runner's heart every time the bastard issued an insult or brayed that smug laugh.

Then Joshua Hawke sat up. Despite the effects of the laudanum, despite the gin in his veins and the tiredness in his limbs, something else Ruthven had said had struck a chord within him. The tune was distant, barely perceptible, but Hawke strained to hear it, to discern the notes. What *had* Ruthven said? It made sense. Suddenly, brilliantly. What was it?

“What was it?” he snarled aloud.

He noticed faces turning to regard him with the hostility of those disturbed from their own private wallowing. He stood, knocking over his chair. The clack of wood reverberated about the low ceiling. Someone growled angrily. The music in his mind faded, Ruthven’s words lost once more.

Hawke cursed. He stooped to retrieve the stool but fell, sprawling on the tacky floor. He could smell his own vomit, ripe and bitter as it swirled about his face and bubbled at his nostrils. He closed his eyes.

CHAPTER FIVE

SUNDAY

"Looks like shite warmed up, I can tells ye." Milky Mayhew, named for his right eye, which was entirely white, stood on the Thames foreshore in the shadow of Blackfriars Bridge, oblivious to the grubby tidewaters that lapped at his feet. He leaned against a long hoe, the principal tool of his trade, its butt-end driven deep into the sandy shingle. With his good eye, shot through with livid veins, he scrutinised Joshua Hawke, suspicion unconcealed.

Hawke, having tracked him down easily enough via the small community of toshers and mudlarks who had made their homes in hovels along this little stretch of the north bank, breathed deeply to ward off a wave of nausea. "I do not sleep well."

Mayhew grunted, rubbing leathery cheeks with fat, grimy fingers. "I must a earn a crust, Mister Hawke, so," he scrunched up his mouth in an expression of insincere apology, "say what you've come to say, if you please."

It was late morning already. Hawke had slept away the day's earlier hours, shaking off the heaviest effects of the laudanum, though he felt exhausted now, encumbered by a state of heavy-limbed torpor. It helped not a jot that he had made do with a supremely uncomfortable canvas hammock in the muggy, fetid doss-house at Black Horse Yard, the hours passing to the inharmonious comings and goings of drunks, whores, beggars and opium-fiends. The only thing that would fend off the impending shakes was another dose of the drug, but his supply had run dry, and he inwardly berated himself for not having made provision earlier. Today, he knew, would be one of suffering. He gripped his guts as they churned again. "My apologies." He stared into the mist that clung stubbornly to the surface of the river. "You work on a Sunday?"

Mayhew, who might have been anything from forty-five to sixty, effected a wry smile that suggested Hawke was stupid. "If I wish to eat." He winked the dead eye. "And I was at church for a dawn sermon, sir. Were you?" When Hawke did not answer, Mayhew kicked a small mound of pebbles into the water. "Now then. You asked to speak of my friend?"

When Hawke had been dashed from his stupor the night before by a painfully chill bucket of water, he had found himself out on Red Lion Square, swearing viciously at the gin palace landlord as he staggered towards the tobacconist's shop. But a shred of wit must have lingered, for, halfway across the immaculate gardens, he had swerved away, thinking better of attending a meeting that would, after all, provide Ruthven with precious little.

Instead, he had wandered the city as a biting, hoary dusk had taken hold and the lamplighters had set to work. He had thought of the murdered resurrectionists, Lucas and Harlowe, and of Seamus, the Giltspur Boy whose life had been snuffed out in revenge, and he asked himself who might have reason to exterminate the Szekely gang. The answer, naturally, was a great many folk. The proverbial needle in a haystack. So he had replayed the conversation with Ruthven in his mind, that which had given him cause to depart the gin shop in the first place. He smelled again the heady scents of baking bread and reminded himself of the Runner's smug superiority. Out of it all had grown a theory. A wisp of a thing, but one that had refused to diminish as the shadows lengthened. It was small but persistent, like a sapling's first, delicate shoots, to be nurtured and fed if it was to survive. He had mulled it over during the deepest, darkest hours, and it had begun to take root.

For now, though, he knew that he must ease it aside as he considered the fate of poor Betsy Milne. He needed to find out more. Discover her final steps. But there were no witnesses to question, no body to inspect, and her grieving father's proximity to the underworld of Szekely and his associates meant that Hawke could not so much as speak with him, let alone ask anything meaningful. Then he had remembered the tosher whose body had been found floating beside the mutilated girl, and he had decided to come here, to this community of ramshackle sheds and gaunt faces, in order to speak with those who had known Tapp personally. He did not know what was to be gained, but it would surely be a more productive use of his time than making empty reports to Ruthven or dodging Giltspur daggers in St Giles. "Varney Tapp, that's right. You discovered his body?"

Milky Mayhew's knuckles whitened as he gripped the hoe harder. "Aye. In the sewer 'neath Upper Thames Street."

"But he had been missing some weeks?"

Mayhew pursed lips that were cracked and red. He took a while to wet them with his tongue before he spoke. "Several. It stood to reason that he would turn up somewhere down there, but the tunnels stretch for miles."

Hawke blew warm air through his nostrils, making a roiling cloud of vapour in the cold. "Then he must have been badly decomposed. How did you recognise him?"

Mayhew hesitated, gnawed his chapped lower lip, then patted his own breast. "His clothes."

Hawke noted the tosher's long velveteen coat and canvas trousers. Together with the hoe it certainly painted a particular picture. "You are a distinct breed, granted."

"I knew he was one of ours immediately, and his bag, lanthorn and hoe were near too." Mayhew screwed up his face suddenly, as if tasting something rancid. "His skin was all dark and rotten. Body dreadful bloated, I can tells ye, but he'd taken a French sabre, just here," he traced a line along his jaw with a fingernail, "at Cacabelos back in '09. I could still see it, in spite of everything."

"Then it was you discovered the girl too?" Hawke suggested.

"God help me," Mayhew said. "Gave me a fright, I can tells ye."

"She was wrapped in vines, they say."

Mayhew frowned, worried by the revelation. "Who says? Who are you?"

"A friend."

The hoe tilted in Hawke's direction. "A liar. Them what knows about the vines, about what happened to the girl, they're few and far betwixt."

Hawke shook his head. "The story's found its way onto the crime broadsides."

"Shite on a stick. That'll shake the hornet's nest."

"Hence our urgent need to bring the killer to ground."

"Our?" Mayhew's face set hard. "You with the law? I told your lot everything already. You ain't pinning fack-all on me, I can tells ye."

Hawke stepped back, boots crunching on shingle, raising hands to placate. "I would search for the truth, that is all." The urge to vomit was sudden and strong, and he paused to allow it to subside. When it had released its cruel grip, he fished in a pocket for a coin, flicking it to Mayhew, who plucked it deftly out of the air. "The truth, sir. The girl deserves it. Varney Tapp deserves it."

Milky Mayhew's face became strained, as if invisible threads tugged from all directions. He stared out across the river, at the jetties and wharves on the south bank, the shallow-draughted barges criss-crossing the waterway between. He was seeing it all, but somehow bearing witness to another time and place entirely. At length, he said quietly, “She was wrapped in vines, aye, but her face, what was left of it, was something I shall ne’er forget.”

Hawke took a tentative pace towards the tosher. “But not Mister Tapp?”

“No,” Mayhew answered, still gazing sightlessly away. “Old Varn had been stabbed all right, but not like her.” He blinked suddenly, eyelids fluttering like moth wings, and he turned back to Hawke. “She was different.”

She was different. Ruthven had suggested as much, but he had shown such wilful disregard for Varney Tapp that the fellow’s fate barely warranted a mention. After all, the demise of a sewer dweller was hardly of interest to Bow Street. Mayhew’s confirmation was useful, nonetheless. He said as much to the tosher, adding, “Clarity is useful. Though the bodies were discovered together, the respective murders were not necessarily two halves of the same crime.”

Again that careworn expression emerged through the lines on Mayhew's face. "I am sorry I could not be a greater help." He pinned the sore lower lip between his teeth once more.

Hawke sensed something was out of kilter, and gave Mayhew a long look. The tosher immediately threw his gaze upon the Thames as if he had noticed a passing skiff rowed by chimps. That did it, and Hawke took a step inward, concealing himself from prying eyes up on the riverbank as he pressed the tip of his knife into Mayhew's soft stomach, gently, carefully, but hard enough to elicit a satisfying whimper. "I am not a cruel man, Mister Mayhew," he said quietly, "and I wish you no harm, but believe me when I say that cruelty is, on occasion, necessary."

"What do you want from me?" Mayhew stammered. "I told those fackin' Runners that..."

"Look at me," Hawke interrupted. "Look at me, Mister Mayhew, and speak plain. Do you believe me capable of using this blade?"

Mayhew did look at him, his milk-white eye reflecting Hawke's face like a mirror. Did the tosher see a cold-blooded killer or perhaps just the pathetic visage of a gin-soaked wastrel on the edge of desperation. It mattered not, Hawke thought to himself, so long as the fellow believed in the steel at his belly. Sure enough, Mayhew gave a mute, slightly tremulous nod.

"You did not give the Runners everything," Hawke said, keeping the knife steady and hidden. "I can tell, you see. I do not pretend to read men's minds, but I smell a lie well enough. You're holding something back, sir, and I intend to use any means at my disposal to draw it forth. I can bribe you. A reward for your assistance. Or I can take your good eye so that you never search another drain again. I will have candour, Mister Mayhew, one way or the other." Mayhew shifted his feet a little. Perhaps he had soiled himself. Hawke smothered the pang of guilt as he said, "Do you understand?"

"I do, sir," Mayhew replied in little more than a whisper. "I do."

"Then?"

"I was there."

Hawke frowned. "You were where?"

"In the tunnel with Varn." Mayhew swallowed audibly. "When he died." He must have heard the indirect incrimination in his own words, for he blurted, "But I didn't do nothin', sir, 'pon my honour!"

"You saw it?" Hawke asked. "The murder?"

Mayhew shook his head. "We were far apart, working different stretches. But I heard his cries."

"Tapp's?"

"Aye. Went to him as fast as I could, but I'm no spring chook, Mister Hawke, I can tells ye. Took me a while, wading as I was." He clamped shut his eyes, reliving it all. "When I reached him it was too late."

"Dead?"

"Almost." Mayhew shuddered. "I held him in my arms as he slipped away. There was no hope."

"Did he speak?" Hawke pressed. "Come, Mister Mayhew, the time for timidity is long gone." He removed the knife, sheathing it, but stayed close, his tone earnest. “Your testimony may yet catch a murderer.”

Mayhew gave a despondent sigh. “I have nothing more to testify. Varn gasped, he choked on blood. He told me to pray for his soul.”

“And the killer?”

The tosher shrugged meekly. “Varn never saw the devil’s face.”

Hawke cursed softly. “Nothing more was said of him?”

“Only that he was an Irisher.” Mayhew evidently noted Hawke’s nonplussed frown, for he added, placing a hand upon his own breast, “He wore a brooch, here. Shaped like a harp, it was. Varn was in Dublin in ‘98, putting down the rebellion. The bog-trotting bastards wore it as their symbol.”

The revelation threw Hawke utterly, and he stepped away, leaving Mayhew to shake himself down like a dog freed from a leash. An Irishman? Christ, but half of St Giles was Irish. It hardly narrowed the search down. But what of the *Benandanti* connection? Was he no longer searching for an Italian? The thought brought him round to the second of the sewer's corpses. "Mister Mayhew, did Varney mention the girl? Did he witness her death?"

"I've told you everything he said, and that's the Almighty's truth, I can tells ye."

"But you found Betsy Milne with Varney. Was her body rotten?"

"Nay," Mayhew answered, "not then. Only when I returned."

Then the deaths, Hawke mused, might truly be connected. He met Mayhew's single eye. "It was weeks before you reported any of this."

For the first time a glimmer of defiance animated Mayhew's face. "I was terrified." He tensed, standing slightly taller as his shoulders rounded, his jaw quivering with the clench of his teeth. "Facking terrified. I ran out of there like Satan's own hounds were at my heels. And who was I to report this to, without receiving a stretched neck for reward?"

Despite Hawke's annoyance, he could not refute the point. Blame would surely have been attached to Mayhew, a man with neither the friends nor resources to make a robust defence. Especially when this was the kind of case in which the authorities would seek a speedy conclusion, one way or another. Ruthven had implied as much. "So you waited until the coast was clear. Discovered them for a second time, once they had suitably decomposed."

"Aye," Mayhew confirmed, "that's about the size of it. I ain't proud, I can tells ye. Truth is, I'm downright ashamed. But I am alive."

Hawke nodded. He stepped away, looking back up the slope towards the city. "Thank you. I'll not betray your confidence."

Milky Mayhew gave a rueful grunt. "Yet I've given you nought that'll catch Varn's killer."

"Time will tell, Mister Mayhew. It is something to learn that they were murdered at around the same time, albeit in very different ways." He began the short walk up the shingle. "Still, perhaps your friend was simply robbed by other tosher-men, with young Miss Milne's corpse nearby as a matter of coincidence."

"Robbed?" Mayhew scoffed at his back. "No, sir, he weren't robbed, I can tells ye. His bag and pockets were well weighted with trinkets when I stumbled across him. Poor things, mind, but worthy of theft. I took them when I fled." He looked sheepish. "Not to steal, mind, but what use were they down there?"

That peaked Hawke's interest and he stopped. "What kinds of things?"

Mayhew shrugged. "Couple o' spoons, few coins, the chain from a pocket watch." He smiled, a little embarrassed. "We are mudlarks of the sewer, you understand. Magpies. We collect what we may." He snapped his fingers as something else dawned. "Old Varn was clutching one such item when he perished, God rest his soul."

"Oh?"

Using his hoe for support, Milky Mayhew rounded Hawke and led the way towards the ramshackle homes clinging to the edge of the bank. "See for yourself, sir, by all means. I have it still."

Θ

Hawke went back into the city after leaving Mayhew, heading north and west, the breeze beginning to sharpen at his back. At the end of Dorset Street he was waylaid by a small crowd where the road opened into Salisbury Square, and he slowed, curious as to the commotion.

The mob, collecting new members at an alarming rate, appeared to be focussed on a kneeling man who looked for all the world like a penitent, his head dipped, his hands clasped together. Except that it was not forgiveness he sought, but mercy. As Hawke drew closer, he could see the latticed fingers were raised in urgent plea, begging for those around him to relent. The man on his knees was dressed like a swell, a blue tailcoat and cravat complimenting saffron-coloured trousers and a fine, high-collared waistcoat, but all that was crumpled now, sullied by the muck from the road, and his tall hat had long since been kicked to the gutter. Above the shabby finery was a thatch of ink-black hair that looked matted above his left ear, and Hawke realised he bled substantially from the temple.

The crowd clamoured about him like hounds, calling each other on, encouraging further bloodshed. The man renewed his pleas for them to relent, and they laughed as one, like the onlookers at a baiting, though their numbers comprised women and children as well as men, from successful-looking gentle types to the lowest of the low, unified by nothing except a shared antipathy for the man on the floor.

Hawke reached the mob's periphery to see that the object of their wrath had mournful brown eyes and a dark complexion that he guessed might hail from the Ottoman lands or the Barbary Coast. He was murmuring something in a foreign tongue. Someone spat at him, earning an ominous cheer of approval.

"What is happening?" Hawke asked a thickset man in a woollen cap who was carrying a stack of pamphlets in the crook of his arm. "What is his offence?"

"Murderer," the man answered gruffly, not taking his gaze from the foreigner.

"Killed a wee bairn!" a woman squawked at Hawke's flank, spittle flecking the corners of her mouth. "Just a wee bairn!"

"Warlock!" another screeched.

"Devil-monger!"

"Kill him!"

The crowd cheered again. Missiles were lobbed. The well-dressed man wailed at the sky. Hawke was vaguely aware of the whinny of a horse somewhere over his left shoulder.

"There'll be no killing today!"

The impromptu assembly turned with one mind to see the rider rein in. He wore a long blue greatcoat above a waistcoat of rich scarlet, and in his hand he gripped a long, solid-looking staff. The people grudgingly parted as he dismounted. One anonymous voice yelled, "Piss off, Robin Redbreast! Leave him to us!"

Grumbles of agreement erupted in pockets, but the officer of the Bow Street Horse Patrol appeared unmoved as he strode to the felled man.

"She was from the people!" an unseen voice shrieked. "Tis the people what must avenge her!"

The Robin Redbreast, a Runner's mounted cousin, seemed to sigh as if dealing with a schoolroom full of errant children, though he held tight to the staff as he stood protectively over his new charge.

Hawke said to the thickset man, "Avenge what, exactly?"

"This." The man turned now to face him, plucking one of the pamphlets from his bunch and handing it to Hawke. "Did you not see?"

Hawke took the paper, scanning it quickly. The case of Betsy Milne, recounted - and tastelessly embellished - through several pages of lurid text, accompanied by graphic pictures of corpses, black-clad evil-doers and horned beasts. Clearly the cheaply-produced penny bloods, as Ruthven had warned, were leading the way in whipping the masses to frenzy, reaching London's streets in a way the broadsides and high-brow newspapers could not. He gave the publication back, nodding towards the man who still cowered behind the staff-wielding officer. "And what proves this man's guilt?"

The pamphlet seller scowled at the crowd's target. "They say the killer is of foreign stock. Brings witching from his heathen hole."

He spat. "This man is from Syria, so they say. He sells childish dolls to the chil'ens of the rich and mighty."

"Dolls?" Hawke almost laughed, though he thought better of it and bit his tongue.

"Dolls what are used in witchcraft. He fashions them in place of your enemy, see, if you pays him enough. Chants spells over them, and sticks them with pins. They say he is oft witnessed talking to young girls."

"Perhaps they like the dolls."

The pamphlet seller's jowls reddened. "He's a murderer, friend, and he'll hang."

"Disperse, I tell you!" the Robin Redbreast was commanding, emboldened now that two more horsemen had arrived. "We shall deal with the matter."

"String him up!" someone protested.

The officer raised the stick high. "If that is what the law demands, then so be it!" he called. "But you are not the law! He will see the inside of a cell, and nothing more, until his fate is decided!"

The Syrian was helped to his feet by the Bow Street men, thanking them profusely in a stream of words in his native language. Hawke glanced again at the penny bloods that were being passed about the disgruntled onlookers. With a creeping sense of trepidation, he slipped away.

Θ

The wind became bitter as Hawke reached Drury Lane. It numbed his face and stung his eyes and lips, and he was forced to clamp a hand upon the rim of his topper to keep it from whirling away with the last of the leaves. He stared hard at the ground, placing each foot carefully as he stepped, for his head still swam precariously. A coach rounded the junction with High Holborn, fifty yards up ahead, and thundered towards him. He was forced to scuttle to the opposite side of the road lest he be crushed beneath wheels and hooves. As the whip-wielding driver bellowed obscenities at him for good measure, he found himself skirting the frontage of a row of businesses. A cobbler first, a bonnet maker and a tailor. Then came the inevitable gin palace. An oasis.

Hawke's mouth filled with saliva and his skin pulsed hot in spite of the prevailing chill. He plunged a hand into his pocket, groping for the hard metal of Ruthven's coins as he peered through the small window. As he laid fingertips on the money, he found himself staring into the reflective glass, at the gaunt, pathetic face gawping back at him. He felt more sick than ever.

A figure, pale and diminutive, flashed in the reflection above his shoulder. He turned on his heels. Studied the far side of the road. Examined each doorway and the openings of every narrow alley that cut between shops and homes. Had he been followed? He could see nothing out of the ordinary, but something in the way the fleeting figure had moved - and how quickly it had vanished - seemed furtive, and made him uneasy. He rubbed his eyes. They ached, the pain lancing right out to his temples, and he supposed his stewed mind must be playing tricks. He walked twenty paces up the street, then, as another carriage rolled past, shrank under the porch of a tenement block. He waited and watched. Nothing moved.

Hawke cursed again, upbraiding his own senses for the deceit. The spell of the gin palace had broken, however, and he resolved to press on with his unwanted duties. He moved more swiftly now, hugging his coat tight as he came to the tavern at High Holborn that was his true destination. He went inside, stepping into a high-ceilinged foyer of dark-painted wood, and was immediately hit by the warmth from the main taproom's raging hearth. It was a welcome sensation, but he veered instead towards a wide staircase that led to the upper floor lodgings.

Hawke made hard work of it, scaling the worn steps as if they were the sheer face of a jagged cliff. He paused in the stairwell at the first-floor landing, gathering himself, clutching the alarmingly loose handrail as a wave of nausea surged through his stomach. There was a small window, unglazed, at his eye-line, and he peered through. The parish of St Giles spread out far below. The wind had swept away the morning mist, but the tenements and streets were yet wreathed in a thin skein of dirty smoke. The Lord's day of rest appeared to be scarcely adhered to here, the bustle of people and animals and vehicles as frenetic as ever. He wondered absently if somewhere down there, hidden in plain sight amongst all that life, there stalked the depraved killer of Betsy Milne. And how many more?

Pressing on, head pounding, he rasped musty air into his lungs no less desperately than had he been treading water in a storm. He had removed his topper to cool himself, but still sweat dripped freely from his bald pate, tumbling into his eyes and off the end of his nose. He rounded the summit of the final flight, feeling like he owed himself a triumphal jig if only he had the breath left to perform it. On the landing he encountered a group of children, all facing inwards around something unseen, clustered like so many flies at a carcass. They were jeering, shrill and cruel. They turned, almost as one, upon his approach.

Through the rabble, Hawke could not identify the object of their attention, but the scene brought the plight of the hapless Syrian doll-maker into sharp relief, and he called a challenge without thinking. His warning was dry and feeble, more croak than roar, but it did the trick all the same, and they scattered in all directions, vanishing into a nearby corridor or skirting him to flee down the staircase.

There was a girl left alone as the swarm departed. She was stooping forwards, arms clutched defensively about her head, but still she stood, defiant to the last. A curtain of straight hair, the colour of rich copper, had fallen across her face. Hawke replaced his hat and stretched out a hand. “How fare you, lass?”

She stood tall, sweeping the hair clear with a lily-white hand. “I’m well, mister. Ain’t afeared o’ them.”

Hawke smiled. “Good.” He found himself looking into a face he recognised. It was the girl who had hurt her knee when first he had visited the lodgings-cum-apothecary. “Your father home?”

Θ

“I am indebted to you, Mister Hawke,” Ansell Brommett said as he settled into a seat beside the fire, “for seeing her home safe. Especially on the Sabbath.” He looked up into his guest’s face, one eyebrow slightly raised. “I would have expected you to be at worship.”

Hawke was standing on a threadbare rug that was pock-marked with tiny black cinder-scars, hands clasped tight at his front to keep them from trembling. "A rare week off."

Brommett lifted a hand to smooth down his beard, but his thin, pale fingers failed to conceal the trace of a smirk. "Quite so." He canted his head, like a hound sniffing the wind. "You are an intriguing fellow, Mister Hawke. Forgive me..."

"Forgive you?"

"That is to say, you are of the streets, yet there is a certain nobility about you. A soul fallen from grace, perhaps."

"Is that a question or a statement?" Hawke countered icily.

"Whichever you'd prefer."

"I would suggest that falls from grace were your area of expertise, Mister Brommett."

"Touché!" Brommett barked. "Now *that* they are!" He glanced at the brick hearth, beside which stood a buxom lady with florid face and keen blue eyes. "Kitty, dearest, would you hand me that vial?"

Kitty Brommett stepped away from the black pot that she had been stirring, and picked a small glass container from the mantelpiece just below her eye-line. She passed it to her husband, though her gaze remained firmly on their visitor. "You shiver, Mister Hawke. Are you cold?"

Brommett opened the vial and held it up for Hawke to take. "He will be positively glacial to the touch, my dear, but he sweats as though he arrived in this room by way of the chimney."

Hawke regarded the transparent tube, smelled the dark liquid within, identifying it instantly. A solution of alcohol, infused with the juice of the poppy. His breath became ragged, though he tried to hide it. "I have an ague, sir. Do not concern yourself."

"An ague," Brommett scoffed. "You come here for my assistance, my intellect, yet you treat me like a child. Take some and be done with it."

"I do not..." Hawke resisted weakly.

"You most certainly do," Brommett cut him off. "Your body suffers, not because of the laudanum, but because you are overdue the next dose. Take a drop. Just one, mind. It will put you at ease."

Hawke did as he was told, lifting the vial to his lips. His fingers fluttered as they fought for grip. They were already beginning to steady by the time he gave it back. The sense of slackening, of well-being, bubbled through him and he had to part his stance a touch to keep from keeling over entirely. He blinked slowly, thanked Brommett for the act of kindness, and heard Kitty demand a chair be brought for him. It appeared, by magic to Hawke, and he poured himself into it with a guttural groan, hanging his head, breathing deep, revelling in the warmth that rose through his chest and neck and face.

When he sat up, rubbing his eyes, he had no idea of the time. Hours might have slipped by. Panicking, he made to stand, but Ansell Brommett, still seated on the chair opposite, waved him back down. "Calm, Mister Hawke," he said, seeing Hawke's evident distress. "Minutes only, be assured." He fiddled again with his beard. "And now we can speak with candour and clarity, yes?"

Hawke stared dumbly about the chamber. He remembered the encounter with the red-headed girl out on the landing. Recalled her showing him in. This room, the family's living quarters, was adjacent to her father's workshop. It was humble, as one would expect from lodgings above a tavern of the rougher kind, but, even with a pair of beds taking up one end, spacious enough to be acceptable. He pressed the heels of his palms into sore eyes, kneading them like fresh dough. The pungent tang of laudanum still tainted his mouth. He thought, but what a miraculous potion it was. He noticed the young girl now, as she came to perch on the end of one of the beds, muttering to the trio of smaller children who had gathered at her feet in the throes of some game that seemed empty of rules and full of laughter.

"Forgive me," Hawke said, his voice cracking. He cleared his throat. "I am ashamed. They should not see such things."

Brommett had lit a pipe and spoke while managing to keep it clamped in the corner of his mouth. "I administer my tinctures and poultices to the folk of this great parish. They have witnessed plenty."

Hawke's stomach griped, the smell of the broth forcing its way through now that the haze of addiction was thinning. He glanced again at the girl, dropping his voice. "They were taunting her outside."

Kitty grunted angrily as she stirred the bubbling pot. "The boys around the way. Despicable creatures, all."

Hawke remembered how, upon his first encounter with the Brommetts, it had been claimed the girl had hurt her knee roughhousing with her siblings. He saw again the look of dignified stubbornness she gave him when the mocking children had scattered. "She has a courageous heart."

Brommett said, "Oftentimes too courageous." He stared sadly into the roiling smoke cloud. "It is my doing, this trouble. My fault."

His wife adjusted the woollen shawl about her shoulders. "Of course it is your fault." As Brommett pulled a hurt expression, she let her thin lips ease back in the beginnings of a fond smile that he immediately returned.

Brommett placed a hand over his chest. "Dearest Kitty, you are the mistress of my heart."

"Go on with you," Kitty Brommett snapped, though her smile broadened. She looked at Hawke with an expression full of interest but, he was pleased to see, not hostility. "You're from the north west, sir?"

"Droylsden," he said, feeling stronger and sharper with every passing moment. "And you, perchance, would be a Yorkshire lass?"

She beamed, revealing neat white teeth. "Skipton and proud, sir! 'Course, I departed those green dales many moons ago. Exotic promises of far-away lands got the better of me, I confess." She lifted the ladle to slurp noisily at the stew, then plunged it home as her free hand rummaged in a wicker basket for whatever spice she deemed required.

Hawke remembered what the apothecary had said during their first meeting, of how he had taken the King's shilling after his ignominious departure from Oxford. "You went on campaign, madam?"

She nodded. "I was following my first husband's regiment. Dear Frederick. He bought it at Rolica, God rest his soul. Pistol ball in the ear." She spoke distantly, stared hard into the bubbling pot. "I was left with nothing." She half turned, lifting her gaze to regard Hawke. "You know what a woman must do to survive, sir, in a place like that?"

Brommett clapped his hands, tearing the cloak of melancholy that seemed to have settled across his wife. "But we found one another, Mister Hawke, and God be praised for it! Married before Vimiero. Together we did battle the tyrant Napoleon and all his minions, did we not, my love?"

"That we did, husband," Kitty declared, chasing away the old grief and turning to Hawke. "Made a life for ourselves here after the war, as so many wandering souls have sought to do. London is the kind of place where everyone is from somewhere else, do you not think?"

"I do, Mrs Brommett."

"But our children will put down roots here." She gave a wry smile. "Perhaps not within earshot of the bells of St Giles, God willing."

Ansell Brommett chuckled bleakly. "The Holy Land is not wholly conducive to the raising of civilised young people." He pushed up from the chair, wincing at the effort, and walked in his lop-sided manner to the bed, playfully prodding the four children until they rolled away laughing, before stooping to fetch an object from the floor beneath.

As he sidled back to the fire, Hawke asked him, "Why do they taunt your daughter so?"

"They say I am a warlock." Brommett tossed the object to his guest, who caught it despite obvious surprise, then took up the seat again, glancing at ceiling beams that, like those of his workshop, were adorned with various dried plants and other curiosities. "A difficult accusation to refute."

"Particularly in a parish such as this," Hawke said, "where folk are like to blame sickly babes and balding heads upon the local crone, should she own a black cat." As he spoke, he inspected what he now realised was an artificial hand. It was large, made for a man, and fashioned from small steel plates, riveted together like polished dragon scales. The knuckles were articulated to give them movement. He waved it, the fingers jangling as they flapped. “And this kind of thing cannot help matters.”

Kitty guffawed at that. “You are quite right, Mister Hawke, and I have told him so, time and again!”

“This kind of thing,” Brommett, undeterred, echoed Hawke’s words in a poor parody of his accent, “is what will get us out of St Giles.” He took a long drag on the pipe. “What think you to that, sir? A fine piece, is it not?”

Hawke turned the prosthesis slowly, admiring the detail and workmanship. Fingernails had even been added, the work of one with keen powers of observation and a steady hand. “Fine indeed, Mister Brommett.” He looked up. “You must have seen a great many in need of such adornments.”

Brommett nodded. “In the Peninsula, hundreds. But here in London you cannot cross the street without laying eyes on a poor wretch in need of a foot or an arm. I will provide them. Better, more practicable pieces than those doled out by the hospitals. A hand like that," he jabbed the pipe at the metallic creation, "will not only replace the missing part, but allow the wearer to conduct his daily affairs with little or no limitation. It has become my life's work." He sat back, returning to the pipe fog. "Strange, I know."

"Admirable."

"You are too kind. It will change lives, and make my fortune. That is my hope." Brommett leaned across his chair to catch his wife's attention. "Kitty, dearest, would you fetch our guest some sustenance? And perhaps remind the bairns that papa has business to attend."

Hawke opened his mouth to refuse, but his stomach griped again and he thought better of it. He took the bowl Mrs Brommett offered, revelling in the smell and the heat. As he blew on the thick, steaming contents, he noticed her usher the children to a far corner to eat.

"Did you manage to contact my associate up at Clerkenwell?" Brommett asked, now that his offspring were occupied elsewhere.

Hawke swallowed down the first spoon-full. It scalded the roof of his mouth, but he ignored the pain and went for more. "He spoke of

Benandanti, as you suggested he might. The Friuli region of Italy, more specifically. In truth, he seemed much opposed to the notion."

"Of an Italian witch stalking London?" Brommett said, amused. "Does this surprise you?"

"No."

"It is the strongest scent in the room," the apothecary said, rising from his chair, "and it is logical that you should follow it. But for Signore Totti it may just represent a community torn to pieces by a frightened multitude. This place is a tinderbox, Mister Hawke, as well you know." He went to the hearth, tapping the pipe against the chimney breast and collecting his own bowl from Kitty. "It takes but a tiny spark for flames to lick high." He took his seat again, sighing deeply as he eased into it. "The streets have only recently been cleared since the last trouble."

Hawke nodded. There had been major rioting in August when the crowd awaiting Queen Caroline's funeral procession had learnt that the bier was to be rerouted. Chaos had reigned, people had died, and the memory of it certainly gave texture to the picture Brommett painted. Hawke said, "Then does it soothe or disturb you to hear that the waters are rather muddier since last we met?"

Brommett set to his meal with vigour, perhaps stalling as he weighed the question. Swallowing, he glanced up. "How so?"

"There was a second body, discovered with the girl."

Kitty Brommett, still at the hearth, shifted round to look at him. "She of the vines?"

Hawke regarded her, vexed. "Indeed."

Kitty shrugged. "Come now, Mister Hawke, you are surprised that a man divulges detail of an intriguing conversation to his wife?" She flapped a hand at him. "Tell us of this second poor mite, do."

"Not a mite," Hawke replied, admonishing her with a prim tone, "but an adult. A tosher-man."

Ansell Brommett snorted scornfully. "Might you not have enlightened me of this the last time we met?"

"It did not matter then," Hawke explained defensively.

The apothecary frowned beyond the fragrant steam. “Two bodies in the same location might be attributed to the natural flow of the sewer.”

“Possible,” Hawke said, and the theory certainly had credence. The normal movement of effluent through the miles of subterranean highways may well have thrust the cadavers together, caught up in a common kink with so much other detritus.

“But you are not convinced,” Brommett asserted perceptively. “Were they dispatched in the same manner?” When he received a shake of the head for reply, he asked, “Then are they in fact linked?”

“I cannot be sure.”

“Why?”

“The tosher was killed after he came across the girl wrapped in vines.”

“A substantial leap,” Brommett cautioned, “would you not concede?”

“There was a witness, of sorts,” Hawke said to the obvious surprise of the others. “Another tosher-man. He did not see either murder enacted, but came upon the final moments of his colleague, who had been stabbed right through the body."

"Did he glimpse the murderer?" asked Kitty.

"Alas, no. But he tells of a swift and savage attack, with no sign of theft. The tosher-man was carrying a significant haul of trinkets he had recovered from the sewers."

Brommett sucked his teeth, then nodded. "A logical assessment, all told. Why, then, are the waters muddied?"

"Because on his dying breath, the tosher-man spoke of an Irish harp, worn by the perpetrator." Hawke set the bowl, scraped clean, on the floor and rubbed his eyes again. "So you see, I have another line of enquiry. Do I seek an Italian magician, an Irish rebel or one who would lay the blame at the door of such folk?"

"Line of enquiry?" Brommett echoed incredulously. To Hawke's surprise, and not a little chagrin, the apothecary laughed. "A strange phrase for a hospital porter." He called over his shoulder, "Wouldn't you say, my love?"

It was a challenge, pure and simple. Delivered with typical bonhomie, undeniably, but Brommett's gaze twinkled with intrigue. His wife came up to stand at his flank, placing a hand protectively on the back of the chair. Her own face was impassive enough, but the stance alone made her seem like a sentinel. She said to Hawke, "What are we getting ourselves into, sir?"

Silence hung between them, as heavy and ripe as Brommett's tobacco smoke. Hawke regarded them both in turn. They were kindly folk, but patently bright, as shrewed as they were convivial. It was etched on their expressions, in stares now glistening with steel. He shook his head. "I like you, Mister Brommett, Mrs Brommett, truly. I can never express my gratitude for your hospitality. I cannot repay the hot meal, the..." he let his eyes flicker briefly to the dark vial on the mantelpiece, "the treatment."

"Oh, but you can repay us, Mister Hawke," Kitty cut in, "with the truth."

"I cannot elaborate on my work," Hawke resisted firmly.

Brommett had set the bowl down and rubbed his beard with those delicate fingers. "You deal in danger, my friend. It oozes from every pore. I can help you. I want to help you, for this is my city too. But you owe me honesty." He shrugged, smiling. "Besides, a little sharing of context might prove invaluable."

Hawke hesitated, for Brommett was more right than he knew, yet where else was he to turn? He was stuck fast between the twin boulders of Szekely and Ruthven, bad men both in their own worlds, and, without a breakthrough in either case, one would surely crush him. He licked dry lips. "I am here on behalf of Bow Street."

The Brommetts shared a glance. Kitty broke the silence. "You're a Runner?"

"Not as such. I work directly for Principal Patrol Officer George Ruthven. A matter of utmost secrecy."

Brommett breathed deep through his nose. "Then let us reflect." He leaned forwards, placing elbows on knees and joining palms beneath his chin. "We have a possible Irish connection in this harp. What else did my Italian friend tell you?"

Taking the question as tacit permission to proceed, Hawke said, "The night battles took place on Ember Days."

"Ember Days?"

Kitty tapped her husband gently. "Fasting days and Emberings," she recited, echoing exactly the memory verse given by Totti, "be Lent, Whitsun, Holyrood, and Lucy."

"And there you have the enquiry," Hawke said. "I believe the girl was murdered during the Embertide following Holyrood, given the extent of her decomposition."

"Have there been others, then?" Brommett asked. "What of Lent or Whitsun? Why are bodies wrapped in fennel and sorghum not piling up around our ears?"

Hawke screwed up his face in a weak grimace. "I know not."

"Runners," Kitty interjected, "tend to deal with cases brought to the magistrates at Bow Street. Who's to say there weren't more, but those poor victims simply had no-one to seek justice on their behalf? There could be dozens for all we know, dragged out of ditches and slung in pauper pits, with none to mourn them. Nobody to care."

"Mayhap," Brommett concurred softly, chewing the inside of his mouth as he gave the matter thought, "yet that is hardly high upon our agenda for now. Saint Lucy has only recently come and gone."

"Then the final Embertide of the year is upon us," Kitty said.

Hawke nodded. "It begins this coming Wednesday."

"God help us," whispered Kitty. Her blue eyes pierced Hawke like twin lances. "You think the killer will strike then?"

"Or on the Friday, or the Saturday. Assuming he is, indeed, an insane Italian or Irishman with a penchant for medieval witchcraft."

Brommett rubbed his face hard. "When you put it like that..."

"Precisely," Hawke said. "It is madness, and yet I have almost nothing else to consider. You warn me against inciting a riot, but you offer no alternative."

"Almost?" Kitty said.

Hawke looked up at her. "Beg pardon, madam?"

"Almost nothing to consider, you said."

"The second body in the sewer," Hawke answered. He groped in the pocket of his coat until his fingers fell upon cold metal. It was the object Milky Mayhew had given him. He tossed it to Brommett. "The very thing the dead tosher-man was clutching when he was found."

Brommett held it out on a flat palm so that his wife might see. Kitty said, "A button?"

"Brass," Brommett confirmed. "From a military garment." He traced the numbers that were embossed on its surface with a fingernail. "One and seven, surrounded by twin fronds. It denotes the 17th Regiment."

Kitty craned to look at it. "Perhaps he took it from his killer."

"Or perhaps," Hawke said glumly, "he had just picked it out of the water. Discovering such things was, of course, his reason for being down there in the first place."

Ansell Brommett made a sucking sound with his teeth. When he looked up, his eyes were glinting in the firelight. "And yet one does not often find this kind of thing, Mister Hawke."

"The button from a veteran's coat?" Hawke replied testily. "I should imagine such a thing would be common place."

"In Paris, perhaps," said Brommett with a slight smile.

"The 17th Regiment, you said."

"Aye," replied Brommett. He studied the tiny object again. "17th Regiment *d'Infanterie de Ligne*. This button is French."

Θ

When he left the Brommetts' lodgings the light was bleeding away. The tavern's broad yard was a treacherous scape of deep wheel ruts, hardening by the minute, so that he was forced to pick his way carefully out onto the street like a twinkle-toed dancer, avoiding a rooting piglet and a dog lapping a pool of its own vomit. Always his mind turned circles, rotating about the twin axles of the cases he had been charged with investigating. And now there was the added complication of a connection with France. There were plenty of French emigres in England now that the wars were over. Artisans and artistes, fugitives, tradesmen and many more. Any number of those might have marched in Napoleon's army in a former life, but to travel to the capital city of your most recent and bitter foe, still donning the coat that betrays your service? It seemed an unlikely decision to make. The kind of decision, indeed, taken by one who did not possess the funds to easily discard clothing of quality. But why would such a person travel to London in the first place? An impoverished French soldier would surely seek work or charity in Paris. It made no sense, which was why Hawke was relieved to know that Ansell and Kitty Brommett would now shoulder some of the burden. They had arranged to meet in the morning, and he hoped that they would have with them some further information.

Out on High Holborn it smelled of acrid coal smoke but the starry sky was clear and crisp, free of the earlier oppressive mist. The temperature had duly plummeted with the sinking of the sun, and Hawke's face began to sting as he made his way westward onto Broad Street, passing under the soaring Palladian bulk of St Giles-in-the-Fields, the black gaze of its high windows peering censoriously into his soul. On the opposite side of the road was a row of semi-derelict but overpopulated houses, backing onto a timber yard guarded by a vicious pack of deliberately underfed dogs whose snarls and howls carried up into the night like the call of tormented spirits. Ordinarily Hawke would have hooked a right into an alley that ran flush against the yard, a conduit into the heart of the rookery, but he was determined not to return home until he could be sure of his safety. As sure as was possible in a place like this. He therefore kept to the main thoroughfare as it skirted the slum and swung north to become Tottenham Court Road. His temporary doss-house at Black Horse Yard was the better part of a mile up ahead.

Somewhere a scream rent the new night, a female or young boy, abruptly silenced. He halted to pull a gin bottle from the waistband at his hip, taking a mighty pull of the fiery liquid to combat the cold, and thrust it home, pressing on. Gaslight showed the way over slippery cobbles. A carriage chundered past, springs groaning low beneath the clatter of iron-bound wheels, and he instinctively placed a protective palm over his chest, feeling the hardness of glass within the inner-lining pocket. Having been impressed with the efficacy of Ansell Brommett's home-made tincture, he had purchased a new bottle using Ruthven's bribe money. The thought gave him perverse amusement.

Hawke tilted down his topper to shield the upper portion of his face from the cutting air. Much good it did. He turned up the collar of his greatcoat, fastening the uppermost button beneath his chin so that the wool was snug about his cheeks. A fox, small and skinny, with half a tail and a scabrous flank, shot across his path, making him start. He snarled a curse as the creature slunk into the shadows. Breathed deeply to still his hammering heart.

"You should be dead," the voice whispered at his back.

Hawke spun, freed the knife from his belt, then gaped. "Corissa?"

She was holding a pistol with both hands, which she pointed at his chest. "Can be dead, still."

Hawke remembered seeing someone in the reflection of the tavern window on Drury Lane. He thought, it had not been a figment of his imagination after all. He looked down the pistol barrel. Its octagonal casing gave it a brutish, heavy appearance that was at odds with the delicate fingers curled about its stock. "You'd kill me? Why?"

The deep brown eyes flickered to his feet and back. “Nice boots.”

“What?”

“I’ve always admired your boots, Joshua. They’re very smart.” She shifted her stance. Perhaps she was nervous, he thought, or maybe just cold. Either way, the pistol stayed steady, despite its obvious weight. “Bit too smart, really, for a gin-soaked opium eater, less still for one what makes his money digging up the dead.”

“You babble, woman,” Hawke answered. “Are you drunk?” He tried to search for help in his peripheral vision, but the street was empty as a plundered grave.

“I followed you. Have been for days.”

“I was...”

“Spare me,” she hissed. Her face was taut in the gloom. The black eyebrows furrowed deeply. “I’ve been following you, because Colan is suspicious. And he’s always right. You met that big bastard with the tipstaff yesterday. Took me a while to place him, but I got there. I got there. Then Red Lion Square.”

"I do not know the place."

Corissa blew a sharp blast of air from her snub nose. "You sat supping gin. Alone. I reckoned you were just whiling away the time. Then I recognised someone else. A young lad. Went into the tobacconist opposite." Her full lips glistened as she licked them. "The lad is one of ours." She added pointedly, "He also runs messages for Bow Street."

Hawke returned the knife to his belt and raised both hands. "It is not what you think."

"I watched a while longer," she went on undeterred. "The tobacconist's shop was busy. Lot of comings and goings. Too much, one might say." She squared her shoulders in challenge. "And you barely took your peepers off it." She cast her eyes downward again. "Them boots, Joshua."

"I took them off a corpse," Hawke protested.

"Capital offence, that. Resurrect a body and you'll do time. Steal a pair of shoes from one and you'll swing." She shook her head slowly. "Those are army boots. So's your voice." Her tone was rising with her ire. "So's the way you handle a weapon. I got to asking myself, do we have a cuckoo in the nest?"

"No, Corissa. Please, I..."

"You know what cuckoo chicks do when they hatch, Joshua? They kill all the other - the rightful - chicks. Push them out, off their high boughs. If a cuckoo's egg is discovered in a nest, it must be thrown asunder." She cocked the pistol, its metallic clunk sounding unnaturally loud in the empty street. "Smashed."

Hawke let his gaze drift beyond her. "Where are they? The others?"

"I ain't told Colan. Not yet."

"Why?"

A pause, then, "You saved my life, back at Hockley."

Hawke, desperate, saw the chink in her armour. "Then you owe me a debt. Let us settle it now."

"A life for a life?" Corissa said, scathingly. "That ain't how it works round here, and you know it. Colan won't snuff you out quick.

He'll tease it out of you. I have not delivered you to him. If I kill you here, now, then you may count yourself fortunate."

"What do you want from me?" Hawke asked, stepping forwards but retreating as she twitched the octagonal muzzle. "What can I say?"

Corissa's white teeth glowed as she chewed her bottom lip in consideration. "Start with the boots and go from there."

Θ

"A soldier?" Corissa said as they walked, her captive in front, at the shadow-cloaked edge of Tottenham Court Road. "I s'pose that accounts for some things."

"I deserted," Hawke lied. Some truths were meant only for the grave. "Threw my uniform in a ditch." He looked down at his feet as they negotiated the precariously uneven cobbles. "But good boots are expensive."

"Down there," Corissa ordered, reaching past him to point to a black-mouthed channel between two buildings. She walked close to his back, her pistol pressed firmly into his spine.

Hawke turned hard left, as bidden. "Came to London," he said. "Found work at the hospital. Found gin too."

"And laudanum," she remarked sardonically.

"And laudanum."

They travelled another twenty-or-so paces, the tenements on either side leaning so severely that the upper floors almost touched. Corissa ordered him to stop. "Here'll do. Now talk."

Hawke duly halted, feeling the hard push of the muzzle. "To fund the habit I took extra work with Mister Szekely."

"And," she growled, "with the fucking Runners."

"Aye," he said. "I am not proud of it, Corissa, believe me." He raised his hands again so that she would not think he attempted escape, and made a slow, deliberate turn, coming about to face her in the dark. "I hate Ruthven, despise him."

"Ruthven?" she echoed, voice incredulous. "*The* Ruthven? That was him I saw?" When confirmation came by way of a nod, she seemed genuinely pleased to have laid eyes on a bona-fide celebrity. "He of Cato Street and all that?"

"The same. And the man who has me bent double over a barrel. If I do not feed him information, he will expose my duplicity to Szekely and..."

"You will be skinned alive," she said in the haunted voice of one who had witnessed such deeds first hand. "What kind of information?"

Hawke shrugged. "The comings and goings of the underworld. The world he spends every waking moment attempting to infiltrate, but in which he cannot ever walk. Thieves and fences and murderers." He stepped a little closer, his voice hushed. "Our world. He does not work to destroy Szekely, Corissa. In truth, he is hardly interested at all. Ruthven is an ambitious man. A pickpocket here, a resurrectionist there. Not his concern. The hero of Cato Street seeks only more repute. More fortune." He paused, trying to read her expression in the gloom.

"I report on the things I hear, but not in order to destroy Szekely. Rather so that Ruthven can be prepared for the next Cato Street. I am an informant, Corissa. I take money from Bow Street. But I am no traitor."

Her chuckle was contemptuous, but she seemed to take his point. He heard her swallow. "What were you doing at Red Lion Square?"

Hawke searched their new surroundings as a matter of instinct, but he saw that Corissa's choice had been sound. The alleyway was bisected here by another, and the junction they formed was a wider, more open patch of muddy ground, not overlooked by doors and windows. "I was supposed to report on an investigation in which I am involved, for my sins. The murder of Betsy Milne."

"Boris Milne's girl?" she asked, surprised. "It's all over the crime broadsides. The butcher blames us, the resurrectionists. Colan says we might even have to get rid of him."

"I do not believe he killed our men. I told Mister Szekely so."

“I remember. But the butcher makes nuisance of himself, nevertheless.”

“He is grieving,” Hawke said. “Angry. But he has taken the case to Bow Street, which suggests he is willing to give the Runners a chance to bring the murderer to justice. Besides, the injuries to our men were too ragged to be caused by a cleaver’s chop.”

“Where do you come in?” she asked.

“Solving such a crime would be a large feather in Ruthven’s cap, but he can hardly question Szekely or the Giltspurs. Not in any meaningful way.”

“So he asks you,” Corissa said.

“Commands me,” Hawke corrected.

“And what have you found?”

“She was not killed by resurrection men.”

“How can you be sure?” The gun twitched in her grip as she shuddered. “She was anatomised. Says so in the papers.”

“She was stabbed and cut,” Hawke conceded, “but it was ferociously done. Not the work of an anatomist.”

"You've seen her?"

Hawke shook his head. "But I know what occurred, and I've seen enough anatomised corpses to know the difference."

Her eyes gleamed and she swallowed again. "Then?"

"Then we have a murderer at large," Hawke rasped. He tapped his temple with a fingertip. "One with some sickness of the mind. Depraved."

Corissa held his gaze for a second, then drew breath, blinking, as if shaking off the effects of a spell. "You telling me this so I'll give you sympathy?" She reset her stance, straightened the arm bearing her weapon. "Let you carry on stabbing us in the back?"

"I'm telling you because you asked," Hawke said, making a show of putting up his hands again. But this time he could see that she was not going to kill him. Not tonight, at least. The spectre of a crazed child-killer loomed in her mind. He could see it in the tightening of her face. She might despise Hawke, but she understood that greater threats than an opium-addled double-dealer stalked the city.

"Did you kill Lucas?" she asked now. "Harlowe? Is that what happened? Found you out, did they?"

"No," Hawke said. "I swear it."

"Colan ordered you to discover who did."

"I am investigating."

"Investigating," she mimicked. Then she sighed heavily. "Busy boy, ain't you?"

"Am I? If you shoot me now, neither killer may face justice."

She stared at him, weighing the night's possible conclusions, all of them in her gift. "If he ever finds out..."

"We'll both be dead."

"Dead I can cope with," Corissa said darkly, and lowered the gun.

CHAPTER SIX

MONDAY

The morning rang with the rhythmic chime of hammer on anvil, the aggressive hiss of evaporating water, and the coarse bark of a blacksmith berating his apprentices. The sun had not long risen to preside over a brooding purple sky, but Joshua Hawke, with the help of his precious tincture, had managed to drag himself from Black Horse Yard to Fleet Street in order to keep the appointment. Now he hunched within his big collar as he peered into the bustling smithy, revelling in the blast of heat that bathed his face each time the stout furnace of grey stone and red brick flared bright at the workshop's heart. Other folk, he noticed, threadbare and gaunt as ghosts, were already close by, huddled at the flanks of the long frontage, desperate to bask in the warmth without drawing the attention of those wielding the hammers.

"There you are!" a familiar voice made Hawke look round. Ansell Brommett, carrying a bulging leather satchel and wrapped in an ankle-length coat, doffed his top hat as he bowed. "Mrs Brommett sends her regards, naturally, and," he added archly, "hopes that you are taking the appropriate care."

Instinctively Hawke's thumb brushed the glass vessel that nestled safely against his ribs. "I am, thank you." Embarrassed, he cast his gaze beyond Brommett's shoulder and was relieved to see another familiar face. "This is Miss Corissa Lott," he said quickly, keen to steer matters away from opium. "She is assisting me. You may speak frankly in her presence."

The apothecary turned to see Corissa, still ten yards off, who cut a well-heeled figure in a dark green, fur-trimmed pelisse, with braiding and frog fastenings in the military style. Brommett regarded her carefully, the intrigue clear upon his lean face. "You have an assistant, now?"

“Is that such a surprise?”

Brommett gave a wry smile. “Everything about you is surprising, Mister Hawke.”

Corissa drew up. “Ain’t that the truth?”

Brommett had asked Hawke to meet him here, and Hawke, in turn, had asked Corissa, because, at her own insistence, she was now involved. She skirted Brommett, placing a hand on Hawke’s shoulder as she whispered in his ear. He felt heat come into his face at the physical contact, and at the gentle aroma of lavender that accompanied her movement. He thought of Szekely, of how so brutal, so cruel a creature came to possess this woman, and a surge of jealousy blazed like the smith’s forge.

“Charmed, Mistress Lott, I am sure,” Brommett was saying. “Ansell Brommett, apothecary, at your service.”

Corissa acknowledged his greeting with a brief bob of the knees. “You aid Mister Hawke’s investigation. He told me so.” She seemed abrupt, even nervous. She addressed Hawke, “Well? I’m here, as instructed.”

Hawke, trying in vain to collect his thoughts, indicated the apothecary. "And I was instructed by Mister Brommett, so we await his explanation."

Brommett, clearly sensing the tension, looked warily from one to the other. "We had need to convene, regardless of the location, for I have the information, as promised. But I freely admit that your coming here has done me something of a favour, for I had prior business with the smith." He moved, at the perpetual mercy of his lurching gait, into the entrance of the premises, the huge double doors thrown wide and pinned back on massive iron hooks. Here, just over the threshold, had been placed two small baskets of soot-blackened wicker. Brommett gestured at someone within the building, who appeared to give a positive response, for he delved into the first basket, bringing up a handful of slender lengths of metal. He twirled one deftly in his fingers. "Messrs Babcock and Bull make the very best London has to offer."

Hawke moved into the doorway. The intensity of the heat was quite profound, for he felt sweat prickle at his forehead immediately. “What are they?”

Corissa, at Hawke’s left side, said, “Pins.”

“You have it!” Brommett chirped happily. “For the articulation of artificial limbs.” Seeing the look on Corissa’s face, he said, “A particular hobby of mine, Mistress Lott. To provide new limbs for those poor souls who find themselves sadly lacking in that department.” He let the pins tumble from his palm, fetching instead one of the curved objects in the second basket. He tossed it to Hawke. “Not only arms and legs, mind. Try it on. Indulge me, do.”

Hawke stared down at the piece, made entirely of metal and polished to a high sheen. It was hollow, roughly the size and shape of a man’s nose, and so, as bidden, he placed it over his own. It smelled surprisingly fragrant.

“My latest endeavour,” Brommett said with a broad grin. “Many a musket ball did deprive a man of his nose. I aim to rectify matters, in my own small way. Of course, it lacks the detail of nostrils or septum, which Mrs Brommett and I will add with our own fair hands, but the smiths, here, do me a grand service in the initial production."

Corissa gaped, her taciturn mask slipping just a tad as she regarded Hawke and his fake nose. "They make these for you?"

Brommett nodded proudly. "And the pins, as you saw, and various other accoutrements. There is a great need for such things in our war-ravaged society, Mistress Lott." He snorted with laughter suddenly, mumbling through a smothering hand, "Fetching, wouldn't you say?"

Hawke, who had tossed the nose back into its basket, felt increasingly uneasy, because Corissa was smiling too. He frowned at them, looked over his shoulder to see some previously hidden amusement, but noticed nothing. "Tell me."

"When you're dancing with your honey," Brommett broke into song, in an exaggerated Scots accent, "and her nose is rather runny, you may think that it is funny; but it's snot!"

Hawke put fingers to his nose, his real nose, and felt the beeswax polish that had evidently been present on the inner surface of the prosthesis. It was smeared now across his upper lip, slime amongst his stubble. "Christ, man," he snarled, wiping the wax away with his sleeve, though it was through a grudging smile, "but I have earned my information."

"That you have, Mister Hawke," Brommett said, still chortling, and beckoned them further into the workshop, "so let us speak away from the road."

They threaded a route beneath high beams, black as tar, that were adorned with a variety of horse shoes. They skirted workbenches of differing heights and functions, bushels of coal, vats of water, and deep counters cluttered with hooks and tongs and hammers, vices with gaping jaws and wickedly sharp chisels. There were eight or nine men and young lads working furiously at the forge and associated stations, all broad-shouldered and clothed in long, filthy aprons. It was searingly hot now that they were deep inside the smithy. Sparks flew continuously and the great pair of double bellows heaved alternately at the furnace.

Brommett found a corner away from prying eyes, ensconced amongst stacked trays of punches, swages and pliers. He appeared to exchange a brief gesture with one of the senior blacksmiths, a short, burly man with silver hair, howitzer forearms and a glass eye, then said to Hawke, “To business.”

Hawke felt Corissa’s hand on his elbow. He knew it was a warning, and said to Brommett, “Folk will eavesdrop, whether you trust them or not.”

Brommett raised his forefinger, as if waiting for direction from heaven. Sure enough, the stocky smith brayed an order, and an apprentice swung the largest sledgehammer Hawke had ever seen. It careened over the lad’s head in a massive arc to smash down upon a length of glowing iron that Hawke saw was positioned, in the grip of large tongs, upon an anvil. The noise was deafening. Brommett said, “The smith, Babcock, owes me a debt.” He touched a slender finger to his cheek. “For his false eyeball was one of my best pieces. He and his striker will be fashioning that iron for as long as we wish." He waited for the striker to resume the din, then said, "The button." He fished in a pocket and held out the item in question. "I have pondered its provenance, and consulted what records I could access in so short a time."

Corissa leaned in to look. The glow from the forge gave her skin a dark amber hue. "Taken from the tosher-man's body?"

"Aye," Hawke said. He had regaled her the previous evening with everything he knew of the case, before inviting her to meet him here, as per Brommett's request.

She turned her head to the side, examining the embossed numbers. "Army?"

Hawke nodded. "But not ours."

"How to tell such a thing?" she said. "Is there not a British regiment of the name?"

"The Leicestershires," Brommett confirmed. "Serving in India, at present." He held up the button so that they could observe more closely. "See here. The colour. French brass has a greater proportion of copper in the alloy. You note this reddish tint?" He turned the button over. "And the bigger shank, here, is more robust than its British counterpart. Ergo, the coat to which this button belonged was once issued to the 17th Regiment *d'Infanterie de Ligne*." He looked at Corissa. "I served in the Peninsula. The French 17th was a renowned unit at one time. Served all over. Right through Europe and back to Waterloo. Though by then it was a shadow of its former glory. They were part of the *La Grande Armée* that invaded Russia. Needless to say, the venture did not go well for the French. Were it not for that ill-considered campaign, Lord Wellington may never have had his final triumph. Russia destroyed *La Grande Armée*. Those proud battalions disintegrated in the snow."

"What has this to do with Italy?" Hawke asked, more baffled than ever. "Or Ireland? Or with goddamned witchcraft?"

"Nothing," Brommett said bluntly. He handed the button to Hawke and put a fist out to lean on a trough full of pig-iron ingots. "I will look further. Discover more. But a French military button is not commonplace in London. It is a thread to tug, do you not think?"

Corissa made a scornful grunt. “Commonplace? You don’t know where to look, Mister Brommett. There’s a multitude o’ the buggers. Started coming when I was small. Priests, mostly. Running from Madame Guillotine. Plenty more since.”

“This is from the coat of a common soldier,” Brommett said, eyeing the pocket into which Hawke had dropped the button. “It was the gentlemen came to London. Vestiges of the Ancien Régime.”

“Why would a commoner,” Hawke agreed, “an old French plodder, come here?”

“Work,” Corissa said. “Their soldiers are destitute as ours, I’d bet.”

Brommett shook his head. “A peculiarity of the war is that England, as victor, finds herself in dire financial straits, while France prospers.”

“Prospers?” Corissa echoed incredulously. “All them dead young fellas, and they prosper? So speaks a gent, an’ no mistake.”

“I do not deny their hardships, Mistress Lott,” Brommett answered testily, “only the assumption that in France there is no work for the common man. Firstly," he counted his point off by raising a thumb, "the revolution bankrupted our old adversary, causing them to entirely wipe clear the national debt. Secondly, the war Bonaparte waged, as I may testify with my own eyes, was one of pillage. They plundered every yard conquered, stole and raped, extracted and exported, like Pharaoh's plague of locusts. They made the war pay, Mistress Lott, and it made France rich. Thirdly," he raised another finger, "one would suppose that our dear leaders at Westminster squeezed *le coq gaulois* until it crowed. In truth, for matters of political expediency, they barely tickled its feathers. Thus we are the proverbial cripple, along with those who bore the brunt of Bonaparte's legions, while France finds herself in relative comfort."

"With a deal fewer men returning to their old employment," Hawke added.

"Plenty of work and no folk to take it up," Brommett said. "It is we who should be crossing the Channel, not them."

"Then if a French infantryman had occasion to seek work in England," Hawke surmised, "it would be of a particular variety."

Brommett nodded. "He is not in London to beg on the streets. He has a purpose. Something to offer. Perhaps he is skilled."

"Muscle," Corissa said. "He'd be on the ships, or at the wharves, or guarding some rich bastard's house."

Hawke swore in exasperation. "There might be hundreds by that token."

"Former soldiers?" said Brommett. "Who served on the ill-fated Russian campaign? There cannot be many of those in this city."

"But we must put the question to every possible candidate. How can I achieve such a thing?"

"The Runners?" Brommett suggested. "They have their ways and means, as we all know."

Hawke ignored the jibe. "Not even Bow Street has this kind of influence." But even as the words left his mouth, he knew he had the answer. It was a solution too good to pass up, yet too dangerous to contemplate. He swallowed thickly as he turned to Corissa. "Will you ask your... friends?"

Corissa held his gaze for a moment, her face becoming taut. She shook her head mutely.

Brommett cleared his throat. “Friends?”

Hawke was still staring at Corissa. “Colan has a web. You said so yourself. He can put the word out. You said you’d help. That’s why I asked you to meet us here.”

“I cannot, Joshua,” she said quietly. “You know what he’d do if...”

“And you know he has the ability, the reach, to find needles in haystacks.”

Corissa’s jaw quivered as she gritted her teeth. “Then you bloody-well ask him.”

“You know I can’t do that. He doesn’t trust me.”

“Nor should he,” she hissed bitterly.

“Say you’ve heard there is a rival group,” Hawke said, picking his words carefully, “over from France. Former soldiers, looking to establish their business in London.” He stepped forward earnestly, for the more he considered it, the more he realised that it was the only viable path, despite also being the one most fraught with risk. "Do not mention buttons, or Betsy Milne or Bow Street, or even me."

She laughed derisively. "Oh, that would suit you down to your swanky boots, wouldn't it?"

"That isn't what I meant," Hawke said. He rubbed his eyes with balled fists, racking his brain for an alternative.

"And what of my... *our*... friends, eh? Lucas and Harlowe." She jabbed a finger at the bewildered Brommett. "You enlist this fellow for his wit, so let him help us with our other problem."

Hawke tried to meet her fierce gaze, failing abjectly. Moreover, he knew there would be a heavy pistol concealed within her stylish pelisse, and probably at least one blade. She was not to be antagonised, so he let his eyes slip down to her dark lips, where they lingered for longer than he intended. "I would not bring the Brommetts into this."

"Brommetts?" Corissa echoed, nonplussed.

"My wife, Kitty, is a woman of keen intellect," Brommett offered, tentatively now, for he was nervous of Corissa's quick temper. "She lends me her mind in all things."

"How nice for you," she said witheringly, before shifting her focus back to Hawke. "Husband and wife, their dog and its fleas. I don't give a rat's turd, so long as they help us."

Hawke hesitated, looking from one to the other. He knew the point she made was logical, and that his refusal to embroil the apothecary in the affairs of Colan Szekely smacked of hypocrisy, but he feared it would compel the kindly couple along a dark path from which they could never turn back.

Corissa edged closer, more intense now than angry. "He knows matters of the anatomy, does he not? Of wounds and weapons. You said you could not fathom those strange holes inflicted upon Lucas and Harlowe."

Hawke nodded, for he had indeed described the curious injuries to her before they had parted the previous night. "But the

Brommetts are not from our world, Corissa," he said, trying to be firm, and suspecting it sounded feeble. "It is not for us to burden them."

"So we die in our beds?" She flicked her slender neck with a finger. "Jabbed to death with knitting needles?"

"Knitting needles?" Brommett asked, interest well and truly piqued.

"No matter," Hawke waved him down. "It is best you do not ask."

"I will strike a bargain," Corissa said, trying a conciliatory tone. "If we may put the quandary of Lucas and Harlowe to Mister Brommett, I will agree to ask Colan for help in finding our Frenchie."

Hawke muttered a filthy oath.

Brommett spread his palms. "Might one of you enlighten me?"

Corissa said, "We have another case to consider, Mister Hawke and I."

Brommett's dark brows climbed high. "The magistrates at Bow Street fill your days well." If he noticed her frown, he did not acknowledge it. "More murder?"

"Of a different kind," Hawke said. He took a deep breath, for the dye had been cast. "Men, not children. Slashed at the throat."

Brommett sucked at his bottom lip. "And what would you ask of me in this regard?" He clicked his fingers, remembering something. "Needles!"

Hawke nodded. "You worked with the surgeons during the war. What do you make of wounds that are deep but narrow? Very deep, perhaps many inches, but the smallest fraction in breadth." He held up thumb and forefinger, leaving an almost imperceptible chink between. "Like so. Boreholes, almost. Could they be fatal, inserted towards the neck from above the collar bone?"

Brommett thought for a couple of seconds. "The dimensions of the weapon are less significant than the precise angle of the thrust." He put fingertips to his own throat, swallowing thickly as he privately played out Hawke's scenario. "The neck is problematic. It is highly vascular, full of blood vessels, major ones, the puncturing of any of which might lead to a swift death. Then there's the trachea - the windpipe - which brings its own risk."

“There was a pattern,” Hawke went on. “A zig-zag, made in the skin around the wound.”

“Presumably marked by the strike of the hilt,” Brommett said, “as it impacted upon the flesh of the victim.”

Hawke nodded. “Help me, Mister Brommett. What manner of weapon do I seek?”

Θ

The cemetery was busier than Hawke had expected, and he had been forced, upon arriving at the dilapidated entrance arch, to veer wide and scale the wall. Now he loitered near the foot of the low, crumbling perimeter, propped on aching knees behind a severely lopsided gravestone, watching from afar as black-clad mourners gathered like a murder of crows. He supposed the deceased, the wife of a farrier, whose brains had been dashed by the kick of a horse, had belonged to a burial club, her husband’s weekly pennies ensuring this grim procession would have respectability as well as a healthy attendance. The mourners were silent in the main, save the occasional sob and whimper, as the hook-nosed rector delivered the service in a deep, resonant voice, battling the caw of gulls perched like vultures on the nearest rooftops. Hawke, far enough away to remain concealed beyond the grave-markers, could just about hear the words, though he paid them no heed. His duty here today was to note the layout of the burying ground, the entrances and exits, the arrangement of surrounding streets, the wooden huts that would house the night watchmen, and what extra precautions, if any, had been taken against the feared theft of the dearly departed. He was here because when Corissa had whispered into his ear upon her arrival at the forge, she had been imparting the latest instruction from their employer, Colan Szekely. It was Hawke's turn for reconnaissance duty, as the Irish-Hungarian liked to put it, as if his acolytes were soldiers in his army of the damned. What Hawke discovered in the afternoon would be put into practice when the funeral was done, and the assembly vanished, and when the grave and moon were both full.

The church bells rang out three after noon. Already the sky was the colour of day-old bruises. Fingers of mist crept silently between the slanting, moss-clothed stones, slinking low as if to deliberately defy the vagarious breeze. A black cat sat on one of the more ancient markers, yawning as it scratched an ear, tail lolling languorously. Hawke wondered if its presence was some kind of omen. He took a mental note of the scene as the plain pine coffin descended into its final resting place. The salient points were that security appeared to be light, and that the burial itself was relatively shallow. The cemetery, like many in the rapidly growing metropolis, was full - literally to bursting point - and the consecrated ground was crammed with the dead of generations past, each new corpse laid immediately above the last, so that many ended up no deeper than the topsoil, putrefying amongst the grass. This plot, in comparison with some, was positively gorge-like, but still it looked to be no more than a couple of feet. Ideal when it came to any nocturnal excavation.

The rector droned on. The grieving widower played his dutiful part, teetering at the edge of the pit as though he might fling himself in, held steady by the comforting arm of a stoic looking woman at his side. Hawke wondered if they were already planning a wedding, immediately chiding himself for his lack of charity, and took the bottle of gin from his hip, swigging hard. As the warmth cascaded through his neck and into his chest and belly, his mind ran to Betsy Milne. He imagined her funeral. How her father, so frightening in his lust for revenge, must have blubbed like a baby when he laid her to rest. And her murderer was out there still. Laughing, most likely. Taunting those who would see him brought to heel. At liberty to pick another victim. Inexorably, his mind turned to Lucas and Harlowe, slain at random or for their dubious employment? The work of vigilantes, stoked by rage against those who would cruelly exhume their loved-ones for profit? Was it, as Blackbird so firmly believed, a power-play by a rival gang? Or, worse still, one of their own? A fellow gang member, like an aggressive canker, eradicating Szekely's organisation from within?

Hawke had brought Ansell Brommett into his confidence - partially, at least - in order to hasten that investigation to a conclusion, but even the sharp-witted apothecary had not been able to explain the strange wounds Hawke's friends had suffered. Brommett had taken the task home with him, there to ponder further, on the agreement that they would meet again near the disused Bedlam site the following day. That rendezvous notwithstanding, Hawke suspected he would soon be forced to admit his impotence in the matter to Szekely, a man whose disappointment could well prove deadly. It made him feel queasy, so he revisited the bottle, taking a lingering draught in the hope of banishing the sensation.

"Don't get drunk," Corissa Lott said. "You're working tonight."

Hawke turned to watch her slide down the wall and come to crouch next to him behind the crooked tomb marker. "I can hardly forget."

Corissa stretched out gloved fingers for the drink, which he reluctantly handed over. "No Frenchies."

Hawke watched her press the bottle to her mouth. She might have been turning the gravestone to solid gold, so spellbound was he. "None?" he said thickly.

She swallowed. Licked her lips so that they glistened. "Well, a few, here and there." She gave back the bottle and counted her efforts on her fingers. “Squinty Francois with the wooden peg, down in Lambeth. There’s Claude the Bastard, cooking for the high and mighty at some club over at St James. And Jean of Cherbourg runs a gin palace up near Highgate. A motley crew, all told, but old and infirm to a man.”

“The docks?”

“More Frogs work the wharves than priests fiddle choirboys. You can question them all if you like.” She gave an amused grunt. “Damn sight fewer of them than Irish, at least, but you’ll still be there till Christmas next.”

“Jesus wept,” Hawke hissed. “What about the stews?”

She gave a slight shrug. “Some old soaks guarding the girls, but they’re in Colan’s pay. I doubt they’d take the risk.”

“Take the risk?” he scoffed. “Of committing murder when in the pay of such a man? It must be second nature to them.”

“Have a care, Joshua,” she warned, glancing over both shoulders.

“The wall has ears?”

"It is what lurks beyond the wall that bothers me, as it should you."

"You were followed?"

"Always a chance."

Hawke relented, bringing himself back to the funeral, which was reaching its conclusion. "I would speak with the men on Bankside. If they work for Szekely then they are hardly paragons of virtue."

"Suit yourself," replied Corissa, tucking ringlets of glossy black hair under the edge of her bonnet, "but do not reveal your association with Colan. It will get back to him."

He nodded. "How many does he employ?"

"Two, I think. Place called the Red Petal, near the foundry. The bawd's named Madam Yvette. With the big church at your back, head west, past the Anchor Brewery." She rummaged about her person for a moment, finding a hunk of bread wrapped in brown paper. "What about the killer closer to home?"

"None the wiser."

She had carefully unwrapped the bread, and was hungrily devouring it. With words muffled through a full mouth, she said, "Let us hope your 'pothecary friend brings us something to work with."

"You should not have pushed me to ask him," Hawke protested bitterly.

"And you should not have pushed me to ask Colan."

She was right, he knew. Szekely was a naturally suspicious man. To compel Corissa to bring him into their search, however peripheral the involvement, was inherently risky. "What did you tell him?"

"That I'd heard a parcel o' Froggies, veterans of Bonaparte's march into Russia, were looking to open a soup shop close by our territory."

"Clever," Hawke acknowledged. An illicit forge for the purpose of melting stolen plate into untraceable chunks was not the kind of move Szekely would tolerate from his rivals.

"Told him I'd heard they was making grand plans." She paused to brush flakes of crust from her pelisse. Her tongue searched her lips for crumbs. "Said it was just a rumour, that I'd look into it for him, quietly, if he named some names. Could have sworn he knew I was lying, Joshua. Nearly pissed myself."

"Thank you," Hawke said, feeling suddenly wretched. "All the same," he added, attempting to stifle the pang of guilt, "Ansell Brommett is a good man. I had hoped to avoid bringing him into this."

She nodded. "He seemed a bright fellow."

"And now he is a fellow in grave danger. All because I have needlessly embroiled him in our business."

"Wouldn't say it was needless. We need to know. *You* need to give Colan something." She backhanded his shoulder gently, indicating the funeral procession that now shuffled back towards the church, filing solemnly and silently onto the narrow cinder path that bisected the cemetery. "It's done. We can go. What do you reckon?"

"Tonight?" Hawke answered. "Simple enough. Deceased wasn't a big woman and she's lying shallow."

"Heard her skull's a mess. That'll affect the price."

"Plenty of her left for Doctor Vine to explore," Hawke said bleakly.

"Is she protected?" Corissa asked.

Hawke pointed towards a little wooden shack that leaned precariously against the wall at the opposite corner of the burying ground. "In there. I've seen two guards this afternoon. Both armed. They set goodly supplies in their hut."

"So they're in for the night."

"Aye," Hawke said. He watched her as she observed the guard hut with an expert eye. One of her eyelashes had fallen, sticking to her cheek, and he desperately wanted to reach out and brush it free.

She caught him looking, raised a brow inquisitively. "Yes?"

He flushed with embarrassment, feeling like an errant schoolboy as he searched for something to say. "Thank you," he muttered eventually, "for not betraying me."

"As you have betrayed us?" she said harshly.

The heat in his cheeks cooled at once. "I had no choice, Corissa."

"You're a treacherous weasel," she said, but her voice had softened.

"And yet?" he ventured.

She smiled grudgingly. "And yet I like you." It was Corissa's turn to look self-conscious. "I think you're kind."

"Kind?" Hawke echoed incredulously.

She frowned. "What?"

"Kindness," he spoke tentatively, not wishing to offend, but unable to quantify the sentiment with the lover of Colan Szekely, "is not something I'd expect you to value in a man."

"You think me a heartless sow, Joshua?"

He grinned. "Not a sow."

She punched him playfully. When he fell back, she clambered to her feet with a final glance in the direction of the church, ensuring the area was now empty. "I'll tell Colan the lift is to go ahead as planned?" When Hawke nodded, she tugged the pelisse tighter around her neck. "I'll go, then." Shivering theatrically, she said, "Christ, but it's getting cold now." She stepped closer to Hawke, who was still kneeling on the grass, and plucked off a glove, pressing her hand against his cheek. "See?"

Hawke felt the skin. Smelled it. He leaned into her, just a fraction, but it made her pull away. Furious at his own stupidity, he scrambled to his feet.

Corissa, putting on the glove, was saying, "That Ruthven seems a proper bastard, the way he's got you trapped."

"He is."

"I understand why you work for him. I'd do the same in your shoes." She looked down. "Boots." When he smiled, she said, "But how did he find you in the first place? And why not simply tell him to fuck himself?"

Hawke looked down at her. How could he tell her that he had been a broken shell of a man when he had arrived in London? A fugitive from the massacre that had shaken the nation to its core. A perpetrator. How could he describe the shame that had driven him to destroy himself with liquor and opium? "Laudanum," he said, which was partly true. "Ruthven offered to fund my habit."

Her sigh was disdainful. "Why'd you start with that poison, Joshua? You deserted the army. Plenty do. Don't mean they choose to broil their brains."

Slashing sabres, thundering hooves, snarled orders, swirling banners, massed bodies, screaming children, screaming women, screaming men. Blood. So much blood. "I can hardly recall." He smiled wryly. "My brain has been broiled, after all."

She flashed a white grin in the failing half-light. "Just as well I'm helping you, then, eh?"

"It is a great risk you take."

She nodded enthusiastically. "Aye, it bloody well is." Her expression hardened and she pointed to the ground beneath her feet. "But then I think of that poor girl, down there, floating in all that shit."

"Betsy Milne?"

Corissa nodded. "And I feel bound to find the animal that would do that to her." She thumped a fist at her own chest. "I'm a girl of these streets, just like Betsy. Lot of bad apples, everywhere you look. Twisted scum on every corner. Rob you, fuck you and stab you, given half the chance." She screwed up her mouth in a look of deep distaste. "Or wrap you up in strange twigs, 'cause that's what gets their member hard. London's full of madmen. Violent men. Ones who'll slice you up soon as look at you."

"Like Szekely," Hawke said, knowing jealousy pushed him perilously close to the edge.

To his relief, she did not become angry. "Colan looked after me. I know what you're thinking. There's a multitude of thieves and killers in this city and he's no better than any other." Her look seemed almost apologetic. "But he's the only reason I made it this far. Life ain't easy if you look like me."

Beautiful? Hawke's inner voice chimed. *Radiant*? "It isn't easy for most of us."

"Most of us," she echoed his words with an affected - and quite ridiculous - northern accent, "aren't the half-caste daughter of a lascar sailor."

"Lascar? From India?"

She nodded. "My grandfur. Came back on HMS Resolution in '80."

"*The* Resolution?" Hawke repeated incredulously. "Cook's ship?"

She wrinkled her snub nose dismissively. "He was dead by then. Along with most of his crew. That's why they had to take on more hands for the homeward journey." She shrugged. "Lascars are cheap and reliable."

"So he came to England?"

"Promptly had a tryst with a white woman and was murdered for it. But not before he'd put my mother in her belly." She shrugged. "That's what mammy told me."

"What happened to them?"

"Grandmother died pushing mammy out. Mammy went whoring over at Deptford, servicing the crews. They liked her dark skin, so she used to say." She gave an almost imperceptible shiver. "Liked mine too. One morning she was found under a jetty, ill used and battered to bits." She blinked rapidly, her long eyelashes fluttering like coal-black butterflies. "I came to the city. Colan found me."

Hawke's mouth was parched. He swallowed, falteringly, and braced himself. "Do you love him?"

Her eyes found his. "I do, in a way." A look of resignation ghosted across her face. "He keeps me safe."

Hawke watched Corissa in the gathering gloom, trying to gauge her. She was a hard woman, raised by the streets and wise to them in a way he could never be, and yet sometimes, just sometimes, he saw a flash of vulnerability that made him want simply to protect her. It was a wasted sentiment, he told himself, for she was Szekely's possession. Besides, between himself and Corissa, he was not certain that she was the vulnerable one. "But you fear him," he said eventually.

"Doesn't everyone?" Corissa went back to the wall, with Hawke in tow. There was no need to scale it, now that the congregation had gone, and they followed its crumbling brick face towards an empty arch that had once held an iron gate. She slowed.

“Without Colan, where would I be?” Her voice was stronger now, more defiant. “Getting ploughed by poxed old pervs down in Southwark, or caged in some workhouse.”

Words bubbled up from deep within Hawke. Chivalric words, declaring devotion, pledging loyalty and protection. Challenging her to flee London with him. Board ship to lands exotic and a new life. Those words were stillborn on his lips. “Not necessarily,” he managed to say, hating himself for a craven wastrel.

She made to reply, but footsteps crunched on the cinder path, shockingly close. They both turned to see a figure pacing through the graveyard, perhaps twenty yards off. A man, certainly, though his features could not be discerned in the weak light, he held a large pistol in one hand, the barrel resting on his shoulder. One of the men employed by the farrier to watch over his wife’s grave.

Hawke acted without thinking. He took Corissa by the wrist, hauling her away, and she yelped at the sudden roughness, but knew better than to demur. He dragged her beneath the arch, leaning back against the rusted hinge that once held the gate, and pulled her towards him so that their bodies pressed together. He held her there, close as they had ever been. Closer than he had ever dared. He could feel the swell of her breasts against his ribs. Her gin-laced breath felt warm on his face. Her scent, the hint of lavender he knew so well, drifted off her honeyed skin. He wanted so desperately to kiss her, for this would be the perfect excuse, but his courage failed him at the last.

The footsteps on the path faltered. The pistol-toting man had seen them, was observing them. Hawke's pulse roared in his ears. He held his breath.

Then the guard turned away. They did not watch him, could not take the risk, but the sound of his steps gradually diminished until there was only silence. Hawke let out the air that burned like fire in his chest. He released her. She stepped back, adjusting her bonnet and coat, smoothing them down as though she had suffered some violation. Suddenly uncomfortable, Hawke stammered, "I apologise, Miss Lott."

She shook her head. "No need, Mister Hawke. None at all. I should go."

Θ

Hawke fastened his greatcoat all the way up, the rough wool of his collar catching at the stubble of his chin. He hunched, tilting his topper forward like a plough against the biting air. It was less than a twenty minute walk to Covent Garden, so Hawke had decided to make for the wide, flat piazza, there to clear his head after the encounter with Corissa. He wanted to believe something had occurred between them. Some mutual understanding. Appreciation, even. But he could not allow himself the luxury. It was delusion, he knew. Dangerous at that. So he walked, and he let his mind wander, and, above all, he sought diversion. Covent Garden was the place.

The huge portico of the local parish church glowed in the encroaching gloom, its columns and piers, bathed in lamplight, looked to Hawke like the maw of some fantastical beast, sent to devour the sinful souls that would be drawn to this place as night fell. And what a place it was. In sunlight, six days a week, the rectangular space, hemmed by low railings, was home to the purveyors of fruits and vegetables. Pens, tables and sheds clustered at the edges, the cries of the sellers battling with one another above the chatter of customers from all strata of London society. But after dark, the theatres awoke, attracting a different kind of crowd that would be seeking a very different kind of entertainment.

Hawke crossed the piazza, dodging a club-footed peddler selling ribbon and breaking stride long enough to take a drop of Brommett's potent tincture on the tip of his tongue. Carts rumbled at the edges of the marketplace, drivers and horses bellowing alike, while a group of children ran and laughed and bickered in the wake of a ball that ricocheted haphazardly off walls and splashed in water-filled cart ruts. A haggardly street vendor, swaddled in a filthy shawl, sat on a stool beside a steaming pot of spiced salop that she stirred with a long wooden ladle. The smell made his stomach grumble, and the woman must have noticed, for she beckoned to him, but he waved her calls away. He had only one venue in mind.

Up ahead, close by the church, there was a small, muggy establishment he often frequented called the *Swan and Cygnet*. It was as he began to relax, salivating a little at the prospect of what lay beneath the tavern's crudely painted sign, that the shiver traced its way down his neck. A response, unsolicited, but keen as a razor-edge, to something he had glimpsed at the very periphery of his vision, half obscured by the brim of his hat and confused by the gloom of a narrow alley. It was a feeling from the old days, he knew. A sensation that instilled fear within his guts but had saved his life more than once.

A brewer's dray, packed with barrels bound for the *Swan and Cygnet's* cellar, rumbled slowly past. Hawke let it cross between himself and the alley, then kept pace with the vehicle, using it as a screen as he stared through a chink between the huge kegs. There they were, loitering at the mouth of the passage. Half a dozen men, hats angled to hide faces, some chatting and smoking, others keeping steady eyes on the piazza. One of them, the foremost, was a ruddy-faced fellow with a flattened nose, and he seemed to be overtly studying folk as they passed, as if searching for someone. Just behind him, chatting over billowing briar pipes, were a tall man with a bandaged neck and a broad fellow who was missing his left hand, a vicious-looking hook protruding from the sleeve in its stead.

Hawke kept moving, ducking lower until the dray had completed its ponderous journey, drawing up at the front of the tavern as the horses lifted tails to shit on the cobbles. He ran, then. Dived, almost, through the *Swan and Cygnet's* doorway as if his life depended on it. Indeed, it probably did, for he had recognised the men in the alley's mouth and a reunion was to be avoided like the flux.

The wave of heat immediately stung Hawke's eyes as he slipped between bodies into the tavern's heart, breathing deeply of the tobacco fug that swirled in bilious clouds, floor to ceiling. He liked it here, for the smoke gave concealment, and the drink was cheap, and there was a particular pot-girl that, baffling to Hawke though it was, had apparently taken something of a shine to him. He went to the very rear of the establishment, where it was darkest, and settled into a bench, slumping with a deep groan as he let relief wash over him. The Giltspurs had not followed him in, which was a mercy, but they had been watching. If not for Hawke in particular, then for someone. Perhaps, he thought, they were searching for Szekely's people. Any of his people. Which again raised the question of their involvement in the murders of Lucas and Harlowe.

He gave a short, high-pitched whistle to hail a young lad. The fellow - skinny, spotty, and with a peculiar droop to the side of his face - scurried off and returned in a matter of seconds, bringing with him a mug of frothing ale that he exchanged for Hawke's coin. He clutched the mug, waiting for his breathing and pulse to calm. Maybe the Giltspurs were simply at work, he told himself. Waiting to meet a contact for some clandestine job. And yet, there was something in the eyes of the red-faced lookout that had disturbed him, rang bells in his mind, though he could not fathom why.

Hawke supped thirstily. It was rich and punchy stuff, and he felt himself sink into it, the tension beginning to ease. He wanted gin. Strong, harsh spirits were the only blanket that would smother the deeper pain that dwelt in his heart and guts. Yet he knew he must keep his wits at least moderately sharp for the work that would come later, lest he wanted his own corpse to be the one gracing Doctor Vine's anatomy table. He drank more, picturing again the gang out on the fringe of the piazza, and thanking Joseph Nadin, a man generally reviled by common folk, for instilling within him a sense for danger that had preserved his life more than once. He bade the pot-boy linger a moment, drained the brew and demanded another with a slice of the day's pie.

When the lad disappeared, Hawke closed his eyes and tried to imagine himself how he had once been. Headstrong and vital. Handsome, even. The young Joshua Hawke had gleefully shed his obligations to the family trade as though it were a lice-infested cloak, embracing Nadin's way of life as if the man were the messiah, rather than Deputy-Constable of Manchester. Hawke had revelled in the danger that went hand-in-glove with the business of thief-taking. Bathed in the glory a successful snare would bring. Indulged in the material rewards that had been placed before him. And Nadin had taught him to trust instinct before anything else. He hated the man for what his influence had done, but he owed him a debt too.

When the fresh mug and warm food arrived he set to it ravenously, devouring all but a few pastry flakes and quaffing half the ale. Sated, he sat back, belching, and stared into the drink's dark remains, swilling them as if answers might be found in the seething swirls and ripples. He considered French soldiers and Irish republicans. Italian witches flying above fields ripe with fennel and sorghum, cackling madly at his failures. He thought of Ruthven's slab-like face, leering down at him, and of Szekely's wiry stealth. And always he thought of Corissa Lott. Tried to re-imagine how her skin had felt as she had put her hand to his. He closed his eyes and saw her more vividly. Saw her bright gaze and her raven hair. Her fierceness behind the barrel of her pistol. Recalled the way she had licked crumbs from her lips. Imagined that lambent tongue licking other things.

When he opened his eyes he noticed the serving girl, with whom he had previously dallied, collecting pots from one of the tables. She had none of Corissa's beauty, nor her anger or wit, but he went to her anyway, and she smiled. He took her arm and led her, unspeaking, outside to the nearest alley. She murmured something that he did not catch, and her breath smelt of tobacco and apples, but there was a hint of lavender too, Corissa's scent. Hawke felt himself stiffen.

The girl gathered up her skirts as he swept the hem of his coat aside and fumbled at the buttons that fastened his fall front. Eventually it dropped away and he sprung free. She kissed his neck as he pressed against her, pushing between her thighs and clasping his fingers into her cold rump. He kept his eyes clamped tight, seeing Corissa only, lifting her up as though she weighed nothing, staggering forwards until she yelped as her back met the wall.

The girl evidently sensed when it was almost done, for she pushed back at his shoulders, forcing him to look at her. "Not inside," she hissed, pleading. "Please, sir, not inside."

Hawke lifted her down as he shuddered, thumping his forehead against the rough brick, knees buckling. He could hear her through it all, thanking him for the consideration, and muttering something about a friend who had been afflicted with a disease that was rotting her from the inside. He nodded absently as he buttoned his breeches.

"Don't want to be poked and prodded by no quack, like them other girls," she was saying. Then she scuttled away like a hound-harried vixen, melting into the shadows.

Hawke leaned back against the wall, wreathed in the vapour from his own mouth, and swore aloud. Because she had given him an idea.

Θ

The job began around midnight. It was particularly dark, dense banks of cloud snuffing out the stars. Thankfully it did not look like it would rain. The men bearing shovels crept single-file through the arch, careful not to snag clothes or clang metal against the empty hinges where once a gate had swung. They stayed low, followed the dim light of a shuttered lamp, ears pricked to danger. There were five of them to begin with, but one, tall and broad, with fair hair and mutton-chop side whiskers, split off from the group, tracing the line of the cinder path that looked like an inky brook in the darkness. He cradled a blunderbuss in the crook of his arm, and his role was to ensure that the cemetery guards, ensconced in their hut, thought better than to brave the cold.

Joshua Hawke watched the man's large frame dissolve into the night. "He's done this work before?"

"Berg?" It was Blackbird who answered, his bulk reduced to a silhouette as he came to stand before the grave of the farrier's wife, a huge sack draped flaccidly over his shoulder. "Since you was sucking your mammy's tit, *Solly-yom.*"

The last word was said with its usual contempt. Hawke, on digging duty, shouldered the shovel as though it were a rifle. He considered spitting a foul retort at the gang leader, but quickly reconsidered, remembering well the splash as their previous chief had plummeted, trussed and weighted with chains, into the Thames. Instead he bit his lip and squinted into the dark, trying to make out what was happening in the soft light of the guard hut. "How long do we give?"

Blackbird was studying the hut too. Berg was his man, an old associate from his naval days, and it had been on his word that Szekely had brought the imposing Norwegian into the group, compelled by recent losses. If things went awry, it would be Blackbird's head to roll. "Give him time. He knows what he's about."

Hawke glanced at the second newcomer. A diminutive Irishman with a rampant tick, whose head reached no higher than a typical man's sternum. "And you?"

"Must o' lifted a hundred bodies, lad." The little man flashed a wolfish grin in the tremulous light. "Like the devil's midwife, so I am."

Blackbird sniffed wetly and spat. "Big Bill used to be with McGowan's men, till Szekely ousted them."

Ousted, Hawke reflected as he watched the hut, was a delicate term for what had been a markedly indelicate exercise. The glow was suddenly extinguished. His first thought was of trouble, but then he realised the huge Scandinavian had simply stepped across the doorway, evidently taking the matter in hand. Hawke could well imagine Berg clad in armour and toting a spear at a Viking ship's dragon prow.

"On," Blackbird growled.

Hawke stepped up to the rectangle of freshly disturbed soil, hoping he did not stink too strongly of alcohol, and rammed the shovel's sharp edge into the frozen earth. It only went in an inch, and he scraped it back, then repeated the action, taking off another shallow layer. His wrists and lower back ached already, and he was glad of the meat pie and ale that warmed his belly. At his chest was the laudanum tincture, knocking a rib as if in deliberate reminder. He looked forward to revisiting it, but only when the work was done. It was not worth risking Blackbird's fearsome ire by using it now, despite the bitter cold.

He hit the coffin's wooden lid in a matter of moments. Goaty, Gilroy and Big Bill moved closer, kneeling over the hole as they took smaller trowels to the task of clearing the last vestiges of loose dirt. Blackbird placed his lamp at ground level so that they could see. It was a tense job. The assignments set by Szekely were never jovial affairs, made grim by their macabre nature and inherent risk, but now the resurrectionists acted under an impermeable cloud of suspicion, the strange deaths of two of their number eroding what little trust had hitherto bound them. Now they worked with one eye on the prize, the other on their colleagues, never quite certain that a hidden hatchet would not find its way between the shoulder blades.

"Why's he call you that?" Big Bill murmured as he shored up the hole with deft pats of the trowel, like a builder laying mortar.

"*Sólyom*?" Hawke panted. The shallow excavation was clear enough now, and he held up the shovel like a poised guillotine blade, pausing for the others to get out of the way. "It means hawk."

"Latin or summink," Goaty said. His mutilated face, lit on one side by the wan glow of the lantern, looked like something conjured from hellish nightmare.

Blackbird cuffed their dog-chewed confederate. "Hungario, you doltish bastard."

Goaty rubbed his boxed ear, then glanced sideways at Hawke. "Corissa likes you, *Sólyom*, did you know?"

Now Hawke paused. He straightened. Heat came to his neck and cheeks in waves, though he was not certain whether it was borne of excitement or terror. "Oh?"

Goaty grinned salaciously. "Says you ain't normal."

"I'd stay clear of that slattern if you value your stones," Blackbird warned, the low volume emphasising his already languorous accent. He nodded at the hole, indicating for Hawke to get back to work, and swung another backhand at Goaty.

Goaty ducked this time, still grinning. "Says you ain't who you say you are."

Curses filled Hawke's mind now, a chorus of taunting alarms. The heat in his face turned ice cool. "I was not always a resurrectionist, that's true," he managed to say, despite a rapidly parching tongue. *Christ*, he thought, but she had given him away. What a fool he had been. He had opened his heart to her, betrayed himself, and all for what? Begrudging and ultimately worthless assistance in a case with which he had never sought to be involved. He would be strung up, or worse, for his stupidity. And for unrequited lust.

"Before this?" Goaty persisted. "What you do *oop* north?"

Hawke wondered if he should attack now. Swing the spade for all he was worth. But what could he hope to achieve? He might take Goaty, the nearest man, out of the fight, but the rest would tear him limb from limb. It was all futile. He gripped the wooden handle till his nails dug into the flesh of his fingers, bracing himself for a blow from cudgel or knife, and jammed the tool downward, splintering the coffin's pine lid with the first thrust. No strike came from behind, no one moved at all, so he repeated the action thrice more, even as he expected death, until the lamplight flooded the upper section of the corpse.

Hawke breathed hard, peering down at the pale shroud that concealed the woman's face, hoping no one could tell that it was fear rather than exertion that had overwhelmed him. Still none of the gang produced a weapon or spoke a challenge. He looked at Goaty. "What I did up north," he said, stressing his accent, "is none of your fucking business." He moved out of the way, arching his agonised back until it gave a dull clunk, then dropped the spade. He glanced at Blackbird. "She's all yours."

The West Indian produced a long coil of rope from the sack and rounded on the others. "Pull her up, you lazy bastards."

It took only moments for men expert in their trade to loop the rope about the cadaver. Goaty, Gilroy and Big Bill took up position along the length of the thick braid, with Blackbird at the back, the tail looped about his waist. They dug heels into the short grass and hauled, each man doing his best to stifle a grunt.

Hawke was excused the task because he had dug. By rights he should have slunk into the darkness to play lookout, but all he could do was stand and stare, because he was numb. Had Corissa betrayed him? It still seemed likely. And Szekely was not the kind of man who would delegate so personal a revenge to his lackeys. A swift dagger between the shoulder-blades would be a fate too clean for a traitor. Yet still Hawke lived when he had expected to take the place of the farrier's wife, and he could not help but tremble with relief.

The operation was executed swiftly, for the prize was skinny as a rake and light as a sack of feathers. She was already quite stiff, but she slid up and out of the shattered coffin with minimal resistance, hissing over the frosty earth. The men shifted four or five steps backwards as though victorious in a tug of war, then, upon Blackbird's grunted command, halted and dropped the line.

Gilroy Penley took up the small lamp and moved one of its shutters to direct a soft light by which they might work, while Goaty and Big Bill set to unwinding the shroud that had already begun to work loose, threatening to entangle them and waylay their task. They tossed it back into the grave. In the dim illumination, the farrier's wife glowed like an alabaster statue. The right side of her skull had collapsed completely, cracked like an egg shell by the horse's hoof.

Big Bill swore softly, screwing up his face in disgust. "Made a mess of her, right enough."

Goaty sniffed. "Vine'll do worse." He knelt beside the corpse, sliding gloved hands up and down her naked torso to ensure she had not been laid to rest with any item of value. His fingers lingered on her small breasts, kneading the pale flesh for a few seconds, and then he stood. "Clean."

"Sack her up," Blackbird said, before shooting Hawke a quick glance.

The rest of the gang unfurled the large bag that was to be the woman's temporary tomb. Hawke fetched up his shovel and went to fill the grave.

CHAPTER SEVEN

TUESDAY

It was during the night's smallest hours, pitch dark and oppressively cold, that they reached the anatomy school on Stanhope Street, stealing in through the side entrance like thieves. Except that they were not thieves, not by the letter of the law, which was what made the business of the sack-'em-up men so attractive. The building was as quiet as the graveyard had been, positively sepulchral once they were out of the watery moonlight, but Blackbird led the way with the lamp while the others hefted the bulging sack between them, grunting and scraping through corridors and doorways, their shadows climbing and morphing on the whitewashed walls like dancing ghouls until eventually they came to the school's inner sanctum. The Anatomy Theatre had presumably been the main reception room in what had once been a spacious townhouse, but now the benches around the outside gave it the feel of an auditorium, the focus placed upon the trio of empty tables at the room's centre.

It was to the middle table that Blackbird directed them. With a collective groan, they unceremoniously placed the sack upon it, shaking one end so that the corpse gradually emerged, a waxy moth from a grotesque chrysalis.

"As agreed," Blackbird intoned, seemingly addressing himself.

"She is in poor health," came a reply from the murky abyss of a far corner.

Hawke and the others turned to see a small figure emerge. Doctor Theophilus Vine lifted the candle to illuminate his face, the light making his sharp nose look incongruous in his little round face, reflecting bright from the thick lenses he wore, and from the polished surgical instruments that were arrayed all around.

Blackbird shot Vine a sour look. "Horse did that," he waved a big hand at the crumpled skull, "not us. You were forewarned of the condition."

"Even so," Doctor Vine said, his nasal tone more grating than usual in the silence of the hour, "I had intended to unlock the secrets of the brain."

"Then you're a fool," Blackbird replied.

Vine looked upon each of the resurrection men, the disgust clear in his face. After an extended breath, he said, "Still, she's an acceptable specimen from the neck down, wouldn't you say, Clementine?"

A woman in long cloak and nightcap stepped into the combined glow of candle and lamp. Clementine, Vine's assistant, moved almost silently across the room to peruse the corpse. She was as intimidating as Hawke remembered, stockily built for a woman, her face flat, nose squashed by some half-forgotten violence, beady eyes black and shining like those of a crow. She pursed her lips, assessing the condition. "She'll do."

Vine nodded curtly, pulling a leather pouch from the pocket of the apron he perpetually seemed to wear. "You'll take five for her."

It was not a question, but Blackbird shook his head all the same. He rounded his big shoulders, gathering himself to his full height. "We'll take eight."

"The product is damaged," Vine protested, pushing his spectacles further up the bridge of his nose.

"It is eight guineas for a large and five for a small." Blackbird nodded at the pale body. "This is a large."

"Six, then," Vine countered, "as a favour to Mister Szekely."

"Make it seven," said Blackbird, "and I won't tell Mister Szekely you tried to swindle him." He winked, the scar at the corner of his eye pulling taut so that his cheek puckered as though tugged on the end of a string. "As a favour to you."

Vine's expression tightened, but he said, "Two more guineas, Clementine, if you please."

Clementine left the table and swept from the room. She returned in a matter of seconds, bearing two more coins that she handed to her master. Vine dropped them into the purse with a grudging sigh, and tossed the full pouch to Blackbird.

"Now, gentlemen," Vine said, the noun uttered with an unconcealed sneer, "I bid you a good night, what's left of it." He looked at Blackbird. "Tell Mister Szekely that I shall see him this evening for King Lear at the Theatre Royal. The entr'acte to the fifth act will be performed by Monsieur Blanc's ensemble. A rare treat indeed."

Blackbird's expression signified that he gave not a fig for their high-minded entertainments, but nodded all the same, indicating with a perfunctory wave that the gang should take their leave.

A self-satisfied smile emerged upon Vine's face. "Not that you would appreciate such a thing."

Blackbird coughed up a lump of phlegm, spitting it onto the tiled floor before the anatomist. "Fuck off, Doctor," he said simply. "Think I'd want to watch a clown prance about to music? Tis the dogs for us."

Goaty's mangled mouth drew back in what might have been a grin. "And an ape."

"An ape?" Vine said, nonplussed.

"They're to bait an ape," Gilroy elaborated, Goaty's excitement reflected in his own voice. "A big thing. Mean as hell. Bright red arse and huge fangs, so the rumour goes. Fights like the devil."

Theophilus Vine wrinkled his pointed nose in revulsion. "How far mankind has fallen, eh?" Behind the doctor, Clementine muttered an amen.

Blackbird laughed grimly. "So say those who will shortly pull out the guts of a recently deceased young woman." He looked to Hawke, who was perusing a row of hooks, from which various grim-looking implements dangled. "You coming to the pit?"

"Home for me, I think," Hawke said, and he meant it. Black Horse Yard had served its purpose. It was time to return to Buckbridge Street.

Blackbird twisted his mouth perfunctorily. "Suit yourself."

Θ

But before he could return to St Giles, and before the ape would be terrorised to death to slake the blood-lust of a baying mob, Hawke had business south of the river. To that end, a little prior to midday, he took a drop of laudanum, then a boat from Coleharbour Stairs.

The day was cold and crisp, the light feeble, the sky grey as a wolf pelt, but the brown waters of the Thames, though they roared and swirled, were no match for the gruff boatman's expertise during a crossing that was as swift and uneventful as he could have hoped. He alighted at Horseshoe Alley, tossing the boatman a coin as he made his way up steps eroded by the feet of centuries. As he climbed, he checked the long blade, concealed beneath his greatcoat, gleaning confidence from the hard handle pressed at his waist. Bankside was no Seven Dials, especially during daylight, but that did not mean it was devoid of danger. The Surrey side of the great river often struck Hawke as something of a melting pot. A place to which communities from all parts of an ever-shrinking globe tended to gravitate, for work or trade, refuge or plain criminality. Folk came to London for the north bank, of course. For those streets that promised cobbles of gold. But

Southwark was where so often they ended up, that part of the city that was both within and without the metropolis, extending its tentacles ever southward, new homes and new industry filling the open spaces where once open fields had stretched. Hawke found Southwark exciting. A forward-looking community, seeing hope in the opening of each new brewhouse or factory, yet never managing to still the beat of its dark heart. It was not the lawless place of old, for the days of liberties that were outside the city's boundaries and beyond the reach of its elders were long gone, but the dubious entertainments on offer, the rows of gin palaces, the taverns, gaming dens and the countless brothels, each bearing testament to the south bank's earliest incarnation, continued to thrive unabated.

Hawke walked along Bankside, keeping the pungent river on his right, the square tower of St Saviour's piercing the hoary sky at his back. Down on the thin strip of cloying shoreline, a tribe of mudlarks waded through the filth, skinny legs black to the groin as they sought treasures in defiance of the cold. On his left loomed rows of buildings of various ages and styles, of homes, shops, mansions, churches and taverns, high and low, straight and leaning, fresh and decayed. The area had the feel of an architectural patchwork, straddling the ages, something that its counterpart to the north lacked after the scourge of the Great Fire. Already Hawke could see movement in the windows of the three and four storey tenements, shutters being thrust back to reveal the painted faces of prostitutes who duly began to call and whistle. Despite himself, he glanced up, catching the eye of one woman in particular, who beckoned him with a blown kiss and coquettish wink. He might have taken up the invitation, but time was of the essence, and he pressed on, her shrieked abuse ringing in his ears.

The roads hereabouts were busy with traffic. Sturdy dray carts in the main, transporting barrels of goods between Southwark and the moored barges that would take them eastwards, through the treacherous water that creamed at London Bridge's arches, and out to the docks. Many vehicles were branded with the same emblem, and, when one came close enough to make out, Hawke saw that it was a picture of an anchor. Corissa had told him to pass the Anchor

Brewery, the largest in the world, on his way to the Red Petal, so he watched one such cart thunder by, sweeping left and down a road barely wide enough to accommodate it. At the end of that thoroughfare, the cart drew to a halt before the ornate ironwork of a pair of huge gates, incongruous in the otherwise drab surroundings. The gates were marked with the same anchor symbol, and Hawke knew that he was heading in the right direction.

All the same, he resolved to stay close to the river to keep his bearings. After thirty more yards he encountered a blind woman, wrapped tight in a threadbare cloak, perched on a stool before an iron-bound rundlet from which she was selling curds and whey. A gaggle of black-faced chimney sweeps surrounded her, slurping the stuff from shallow wooden bowls, putting Hawke in mind of ravens at a discarded hunk of bread. The scene piqued his own sense of hunger, and he stopped, purchased a bowl-full for fortitude, and asked the boys the way to the bawdy house. Sure enough, the lads pointed the way, and he thanked them with a few pennies. Invigorated by the curds and whey, he quickened his step, striding into the busy jets of vapour that poured from his nostrils. He passed three drinking dens in succession, a net-maker's workshop and a sailcloth merchant, before crossing the yawning frontage of a vast warehouse, where a team of burly men with sleeves rolled to elbows lugged heavy-looking sacks from the back of a wagon. As Hawke drew nearer, the rich aroma of tea, coffee and cocoa supplanted the stink of the river, and he breathed deep, imagining the exotic climes of China, India, Ceylon and South America from whence this precious cargo had come. The leaves and beans would be graded in the warehouse, he supposed. Weighed and blended, roasted or ground, and then distributed to the corners of the Empire, returning as gold coins to fill a fat merchant's coffers. The distaste at the thought must have registered on Hawke's face, for he realised the warehousemen were sharing some jest as they watched him walk by, and he cast his eyes downward, eager to avoid confrontation.

He reached the Red Petal a few minutes later, which, like so many similar establishments, was a tall, jettied affair overlooking the Thames, with pale faces at windows open to the elements. A relief in the shape of a rose, its peeling paint faded to light pink, had been carved onto the lintel above a gloomy porch. Hawke approached, to be met by two thick-set fellows carrying cudgels, who emerged from the shadows above the single step.

"I would speak with the procurer, Mistress Yvette," Hawke said, taking a rearward pace to put daylight between himself and the weaponry. From further off came the clanging din of the foundry Corissa had mentioned, its metallic song underlying all else.

The heavies were tall and short, respectively, though both seemed like giants to Hawke with the extra foot of height afforded by the step. The bigger one, muscular arms rippling beneath a close-fitting white shirt, had a dark beard, severely canted nose and long, black hair that cascaded from beneath a battered tricorne hat. His bareheaded compatriot was as bald as an egg, almost as wide as the doorway, and wore a permanently sardonic grin, given by thick scarring at the corners of his mouth. It was he who spoke. "Would you, now?" His rasping voice, low and menacing, carried the hint of a

Cumbrian upbringing. He scratched a bestubbled cheek. "And who might you be, cully?"

Hawke said, still thinking of the foundry, "Smith."

The bald man chuckled. "'Course it is." His pebble eyes roved over Hawke. "Money first. To come up, you must cough up."

"I am not looking for girls," Hawke said.

"Boys, then?" the bald fellow replied, the scars upturning as he smirked. "We've plenty o' those too, if you can afford them. And we've a dwarf wench, if that pleases." His tongue protruded through chapped lips like a fat slug. "Great dexterity, I promise you."

Hawke shook his head. "The procurer. The *bawd*, gentlemen, if you please. I would speak with..." A malodorous wave washed over him before he could complete the sentence, and he covered his face with the crook of an arm. It was acidic in nature, eye-watering, and he gagged involuntarily as the men guarding the door broke into mocking laughter.

A woman's Irish brogue brought him back. "There is a vinegar manufactory some distance yonder."

Hawke chided himself for the reaction and straightened, removing his hat and swallowing down the bile that singed his throat. “Vinegar?”

The woman, exceptionally tall and clothed in garish yellow and pea green, had emerged from beyond the men with cudgels. They moved apart with obvious deference. She came to the edge of the step and nodded. “When the breeze takes it towards us, the stench can be quite something.” She was perhaps in her forties, with fair hair sprouting from the confines of a wide-brimmed bonnet. Her eyes were blue and bright, and Hawke thought she might once have been markedly attractive, had not the ravages of syphilis caused her skin to decay and her nose begin to cave. To conceal the damage, she fluttered a fan before her face, the flower motifs only adding to her gaudy appearance.

Hawke met her keen gaze, noting how she scrutinised him in the manner of one permanently anticipating danger. “You are Madam Yvette?” She gave the slightest nod and he went on, “I would enquire of your guards.”

"Enquire?" she said, an exotic bird perched betwixt two oxen.

"Do you have Frenchmen in your employ?"

The blue eyes narrowed above the fan's edge. "Is that a crime? The war is over. Peace reigns, praise the Lord."

"No crime," Hawke said. "I was told you had former French soldiers keeping the place safe."

She lowered the fan a touch, her expression visibly tightening. "Told by?" She edged off the step and out beyond the cover of the porch, glancing up and down the road. "Who sent you, Mister Smith?"

It would have been easy to invoke the name of Colan Szekely, for mention of their mutual employer would surely allay her fears, but the story of his unusual visit would eventually find its way back to the Hungarian's ears, and what then? Hawke said, "I work for Boris Milne, butcher up at Smithfield. His daughter was recently murdered, and he has engaged me to investigate."

Madam Yvette eyed him dubiously, raising the fan again. "And what qualifies you for this task?"

"I have experience in matters similar."

Amusement danced over her creased brow. "You are experienced in murder, Mister Smith?"

"In the detection of miscreants." Hawke glanced at the baleful guards. "I merely wish to speak with any Frenchmen in your employ. I accuse them of nothing. I seek no trouble."

"You speak French?" she asked.

"I wager they have English, or their usefulness hereabouts would be sore limited."

Madam Yvette gave a short bark of laughter. "Their usefulness extends only to their skill in throwing undesirables onto the street."

"And how do they decide who is to be desired and undesired?"

"The decision is mine," Madam Yvette said, the delicate flutter of her fan jarringly at odds with the steel in her tone.

Further along the street, a meeting of three men erupted into a spontaneous brawl. They collapsed together into the mud, scrabbling for eyes and throats, and groping for blades or firearms. Madam Yvette, alive to potential disruption to her business, made a clicking sound with her tongue and the guards pushed open the Red Petal's doors. She indicated that Hawke should follow. He stepped up and into the porch.

Inside the building, the light was warm and soft, and it took several moments for his eyes to become accustomed. He was pleased to smell the heady funk of perfumery and tobacco smoke in place of pungent vinegar.

“Fetch Paul,” Madam Yvette instructed the tall doorman with the beard and long hair. He took himself off along a dim passageway, while she fixed Hawke with an iron stare. “I’ll brook no discord in my establishment. I’ve a business to run, sir, and trouble affects profits.”

“I will give you no trouble if your men give me candour,” Hawke replied, calmly enough, though he was acutely aware of how close the bald, stocky man had come.

Madam Yvette made a sucking sound with her teeth, then abruptly nodded. “Top rooms. Do not worry. They are unlikely to be occupied until dusk.” She tilted her head to the side, watching Hawke. “Unless you’d like...?”

“No, thank you,” Hawke said. “I must not tarry.”

Madam Yvette told him to follow, and she led the way up a winding flight of stairs. Over her shoulder, she said quietly, "I've a mind to help you, Mister Smith, for I lost my own wee girl, many moons ago."

"Lost?" said Hawke, tiring by only the fifth or sixth step. How he hated stairs.

"Murdered," she said, without breaking stride, "like your butcher's daughter. Raped and throttled by her schoolmaster, would you believe?"

Hawke muttered a stunned oath. "I am sorry."

"It is done," Madam Yvette said flatly. "I could not help her. But perhaps I might help you."

They reached the first floor, where some of the rooms were already in use, despite the early hour, for shrieks, groans and good-natured laughter carried through the closed doors. Yvette took them up another staircase, which opened onto a narrow landing and three more doors. It was silent up here apart from their footsteps. One door creaked loudly as she pushed it open, and Hawke followed her inside.

Their muscle-bound escort did not accompany them, waiting instead in the corridor like a grim sentinel.

Hawke looked around. The chamber was barely furnished, save a low truckle bed occupying one corner. A single bay window projected from the room, glazed with diamond-shaped panels, through which beams of watery light came to cut the gloomy interior down the middle. He walked to it across chattering and uneven boards, propping a knee on the low sill to peer down at the Thames. At the water's edge, a pair of boatmen had moored their vessels side by side. They were dabbing at the dark surface between them, an oar each, and Hawke saw that they were working together to corral a package that spun and bobbed, buffeted by the unseen current. It was small and pale, a bundle of rags, and, though Hawke was too far away to make out any great detail, he recognised the shape well enough. "Is that a child?"

"Was once," Madam Yvette said, joining him at the smudged panes. She shrugged. "Stillborn. Newborn, mayhap. Unwanted, that's the thing. Plenty wash up along this stretch." She fluttered the delicate fan below her eye-line. "Not as if they've travelled far."

"From the..?"

"Whores?" she cut in with a note of confrontation. "Aye. Most." Then she gave a rueful laugh. "But a good few from betwixt wealthy thighs, too. They all look alike when they're floating 'pon Mammy Thames."

Footsteps outside. Murmured voices. They looked to the doorway to see the tall, hirsute guard returning from his errand, announcing himself with a cursory knock before entering. The man at his side, limping severely, was new to Hawke, and he presumed this must be Paul, a wiry fellow with brown hair, rotten teeth and boils blighting cheeks and chin.

Madam Yvette said, "Paul Garis and Serle Lamere. Good men, both." She shot the taller of the pair a sidewards glance. "They keep us safe."

So the bearded man from the porch, Lamere, had been French after all. Hawke nodded to each in turn. "Speak English?"

Lamere's expression did not change, but Garis gave a non-committal jerk of his narrow shoulders. "Little."

You know enough, Hawke thought. He eyed them both warily, for these were precisely the kind of men he was looking for. Could one of them be Betsy's killer? Or both? He held their twin gazes, trying in vain to distill thought from stance and expression, but both were implacable. "Why London?" he said after a half-dozen tense breaths, suddenly wondering if allowing himself to be cornered like this had been entirely advisable.

"On ships first," Paul Garis said, picking at an oozing boil that was erupting from amongst a patch of wispy hair below his bottom lip. "We came together, Serle and I. Unloading cargo at the wharves. But," he hesitated, looking a little embarrassed, "this work easier."

"This work?" Hawke said. "You mean brothels?"

Garis nodded. "And pay better. I have a wife now. English. London is my home."

Hawke looked at each man in turn. "Did you ever serve, during the war?"

"*Oui*," Garis said, evidently answering for Lamere as well as himself.

"Where?"

The Frenchman frowned. "Who would wish to know this?"

"Me," Hawke said bluntly, irritated by the sudden clamming up. He supposed the question might be a little unexpected, but it hardly posed any hostile intent.

After a moment's hesitation, Garis said, "Portugal and Spain." He glanced up at Lamere's bearded face. "Us both."

"Regiment?"

"Fifty-fourth."

"Can you prove this?"

Garis grunted. "Not something I flaunt in England, *Monsieur*. I would hardly wear my old uniform on the Strand."

Perhaps you wear it only to commit murder, Hawke mused, though he kept his own council.

The Frenchman went on, "I am abused by our customers every time I open my mouth, as it is." He grimaced. "Spat upon. Cursed to hell."

“Did the Fifty-Fourth serve in Italy?” Hawke asked, trying a different tack.

Garis said that it had not. “Serle and I were wounded at Vittoria.” He patted his upper left thigh, which presumably explained the limp. “Discharged then. The regiment went on to fight the Prussians and Austrians.” The hint of a shudder. “Then Waterloo. Without we two amongst its ranks, to our shame.”

Hawke dipped his head, deflated, for it seemed he had strolled up a dead-end. “Thank you for your time, *Monsieur* Garis. *Monsieur* Lamere.” He looked beyond them to Madam Yvette. “I apologise for the inconvenience. May I attend the necessaries before I take my leave?”

Yvette pointed out into the landing. “There is a piss-pot in the next room. Feel free, Mister Smith, so long as your aim is true. I’ve no wish to be mopping the floor before our first clients arrive.”

Θ

Hawke pissed as the footsteps of the others faded down the staircase. The room was narrow and rectangular with a single tiny window, in truth little more than a cupboard, but this was a house arranged for profit, and Madam Yvette had somehow managed to squeeze a small mattress on the floor beside the chamber pot. His mind turned as he relieved himself, wondering at the veracity of Garis' claims. The man seemed genuine, his answers offered quickly and without marked consideration, though the question around their military past had evidently rankled. Then again, if they were lying then he had little way to prove it. In all, he had discovered nothing of use, and he wondered what exactly he would tell Ruthven. Moreover, today was Tuesday. Tomorrow would be the first day of the Ember Week. The realisation chilled him to the marrow.

He cracked his spine, tucked in his shirt and fastened his breeches, leaning over the acrid-smelling pot to peer out of the window. Below, in a nameless alley, a three-legged dog was attempting to copulate with a piglet, which squealed and ran, dragging the mangy mongrel in its wake. Hawke snorted with laughter.

The first he knew of the cudgel was when it appeared beneath his chin, tickling the skin, its leather surface smooth and cold. He froze.

"What do you want with us?" a voice said close to his ear. The English was competent but heavily accented.

Hawke did not need to see who had spoken. "Serle Lamere, I presume?"

Lamere's bulky frame moved into view, his dark hair and beard like a lengthening shadow at the edge of Hawke's vision. He did not retract the cudgel. "Who sent you?"

"Boris Milne, as I told the bawd."

Lamere leaned in, his fetid breath as foul as the stink of urine. "Liar. I'll shatter your skull like an egg."

"Let me die with dignity then," Hawke said, fumbling frantically at his crotch. Part of him wanted to laugh at the absurdity of it all. He had survived so much, only to be bludgeoned to death while astride a privy.

To his surprise, Lamere seemed to consent, hesitating as he waited for his victim to button up. Except that Hawke had already made good on that account. When he ducked and spun, he brought the knife up from his waistband and slashed viciously at the Frenchman's forearm. Lamere reeled back, hissing a curse in his native tongue as blood blossomed like rose petals through his shirt sleeve. He tripped on the mattress, collapsing backwards onto it as the cudgel splashed in the slop bucket, his tricorne tumbling across the floor. Hawke kicked him in the face and advanced, taking a fistful of the felled man's collar and holding the blade beneath his chin.

"Mutilate a child, would you?" he hissed, aware that they had already made more commotion than was sensible. Now was therefore the time to play his hand.

"*Pourquoi*?" Lamere, suspended in Hawke's grip against the wall, grunted through hands latticed across a buffeted nose.

Hawke knelt on the mattress, leaning in, panting with the exertion. "*Benandanti*, fennel, sorghum." He shook the Frenchman hard. "Witchcraft!"

"*Merde*!" The fingers, blood leaching between them, slid away. "You are crazed." There was genuine bafflement in his expression, mixed with the shock of having been bested by so slight a figure. "Who are you?"

Hawke glanced at the open doorway, relieved to see that no one had come to investigate. He said, "Why attack me?" Another rough shake. "Talk, damn you!"

"Leave us alone, you dog," Lamere opined, his tone one of desperation. For all his relative size, he seemed utterly cowed. He stared up through an oily curtain of hair, eyes pleading. Bloody rivulets traced a path from both nostrils to gather on the bristles of his upper lip. "That is all we want."

"We?" Hawke echoed, finding it strange that Garis, likely formidable in his own right, would let Lamere fight for him. Then the image of Madam Yvette ghosted across his mind's eye. The way she had looked at Lamere. "You and the bawd," he murmured as the answer dawned. He sat back a little, though he made sure the blade did not flinch. “Speak plain, if you please, or there’ll be more blood in that bucket than piss.”

“You are not *Gendarmerie*?”

Hawke frowned. “Do I sound like a frog?”

“That does not matter,” Lamere said in a constricted voice, his lips a tight line so that his chin would not make contact with the blade. He blew away a bead of blood that tumbled across his lips. “They have agents everywhere.” Evidently he saw no guile in the Englishman’s face, for, after a long sigh, he simply said, “I ran.”

Hawke remembered the man’s wound. “From the army?” His answer was emblazoned upon Lamere’s pleading eyes. “You’re a deserter.”

Lamere made to nod, but thought better of it as the steel nicked him. “*Oui*. I took you for one of their hounds sent to hunt me down.”

“But Bonaparte’s armies have dissolved.”

Lamere’s head quivered in a suppressed shake of the head. “They give allegiance now to the restored monarchy. The old regiments persist. Old deserters are pursued with vigour. I feared you were here to take me away from her."

"Yvette. She's your woman?"

"*Oui.*"

Hawke took away the knife and released Lamere from his grip. "What I said was the truth." He stood up. "I hunt a child-murderer, not a deserter."

Lamere's face sagged as the tension drained. "You will not betray me?"

If only you knew how similar we are, Hawke thought, but he simply shook his head.

"I came," Lamere explained, straightening out his twisted collar, "as Paul told you, 'pon a ship. He had been discharged, wounded, while I had deserted my post. We decided to stay in London. It is a good city in which to hide." He clambered slowly to his feet, gingerly probing the wound at his forearm with reddened fingertips. "Worked as wharfmen on the Legal Quays, but my friend's injury was too bad. He needed softer employment."

"So he came to Southwark. Why did you follow?"

"The stevedores do not like we French. Common *crapauds*, they call us. They say we steal their jobs." He gave a wry little chuckle. "And their women."

Hawke understood. "You found the south bank more appealing."

"Bankside is a honey pot," Lamere replied. "It attracts every creature, for one reason or another. There are rich here and poor. French, Spanish, Bavarian. Orientals, Musselmen and Africans. Here we are accepted." He bent to fetch up his hat. When he placed it upon his head, he said, "And now Paul and I, we each of us is settled. He has his family."

"And you Madam Yvette."

"*Oui*."

Hawke kept hold of his blade, just in case, and glanced at the big man's slashed forearm. "I would apologise for that, but you'd have dashed out my brains given half the chance."

"For Yvette," Lamere agreed, "I would murder." He shrugged. "That does not make me a killer of children."

"No, it does not," Hawke said. As he spoke, an image of keen eyes above a fan's edge came to him. He said, "She is Irish."

"What of it?" Lamere said, nonplussed. "It is a big city of many different nations."

"Would she have England ousted from her homeland?"

Lamere gave a deep laugh as though amused by Hawke's stupidity. "She is a good Papist."

"Does she wear the harp?"

"Wear?" Lamere repeated, bemused by the question.

"The Celtic harp that is the symbol of her country," Hawke said, scrutinising the Frenchman's expression for a flicker of guile. "Might she display its image as a point of pride? Upon a piece of jewelry, perhaps?"

For answer, Lamere looked utterly baffled. Then his mouth pressed firm in sudden disgust. "You work for the government, yes?

Some kind of spy? She is no revolutionary, you English bastard. We want only to be left in peace."

Hawke stared hard at the brothel guard, but read nothing more than loathing in the man's bearded face. He stepped back, checking again the landing that led to his escape. It was empty, and he knew he should be relieved, but he felt a profound sense of deflation all the same. For a moment, when the cudgel had slid beneath his chin, he had found the murderer of Betsy Milne. At least that was what, in that split second, he had believed. He rubbed his face with a hand, suddenly tired. As he did so, he was struck. Not by a weapon, but by a thought. He looked up. "You said common *crapauds*."

"Toads."

"I meant the word common," said Hawke. "Are not all Frenchmen treated ill, a symptom of our recent conflict?"

"Gentlemen, *monsieur*, are welcomed with open arms," said Lamere, "if they bring sophistication to London society. Actors, architects, opera singers." He spat contemptuously, the spittle stained puce as it spattered the floor. “Not the kind of men who marched beneath the Emperor’s golden eagles, I promise you that.”

Θ

“Three days.” George Ruthven, Principal Patrol Officer for Bow Street Magistrate’s Court, dragged the tipstaff slowly along the iron bars. The prisoner seemed to bristle inside the stone alcove, ears pricking at the din, yellow eyes ablaze. “That is how long I have waited on you.”

Joshua Hawke, taking a cautious step back from the bars, offered a meek nod. “I am sorry, sir.”

“Dusk, Saturday, was the agreed time,” Ruthven went on, his staff’s slow toll like the ringing of a death knell. “The safe house on Red Lion Square was the agreed location.”

“I had nothing to tell, Mister Ruthven,” Hawke said. “Nothing to report.”

Ruthven propped the tipstaff under his arm, the vestige of his final jarring chime echoing off the surrounding stonework, before fading away, replaced by the faint caw of ravens and a perpetual low growl. “Then you attend the appointment, and you inform me of that fact.” He turned away from his contrite subordinate and stared into the cage. “Else I worry, Mister Hawke, d’you see? My mind goes a-wandering.”

The lion pounced. It had retreated to the rear of the alcove that had been sunk into the foot of the soaring battlements, haunches pressed up against the smooth stone, for all the world a cowed, pathetic creature. But it was waiting for its moment, and it sprung with such explosiveness, covering one end of its cell to the other in a single bound, straw and dust and dung clouding in its wake, that Hawke found himself recoiling in terror, stumbling haphazardly out onto a walkway of stone flags, there to sprawl amongst the sprouting weeds.

From the tower behind him, up high in the windows, came the laughter of guards. Ruthven laughed too. It was loud, raucous even, but as cold as the clanging of the tipstaff. He had not flinched when the enraged beast had pounced, and cared nothing still, though the lion, albeit a mangy and balding example of its species, snarled and clawed and battered at the rusty iron stanchions. With a sneer, he blew it a kiss, before looking down at Hawke. "When my mind wanders, I begin to sniff betrayal in the air."

"There is no betrayal," Hawke protested, hauling himself to his feet as the other animals in the row joined in a cacophony, agitated by the sudden violence. Three more lions were in the next alcove, and they circled it at a loping run, snapping madly at one another, while, further along, a massive tiger stalked in a blur of orange and black, pacing the same few yards over and over in mindless repetition.

"I presume, then," Ruthven suggested, "that you now feel able to make your report, or you would not have taken it upon yourself to interrupt my afternoon constitutional."

"I apologise for the nature of my visit," Hawke lied. When he had remembered Ruthven's weekly walk around the perimeter of the Tower, he had been thoroughly cheered by the knowledge that the intrusion would be unwelcome, and had duly taken a carriage to this south-easterly corner of the city's ancient Roman walls.

"Visit?" Ruthven echoed incredulously. "It is a god-damned liberty, Hawke, you impudent little bastard."

“Time, Mister Ruthven, sir. We fast run out of time.” He dipped his head in contrition. “It seemed most expedient.”

Ruthven sighed, glancing up and behind at the grey fastness within which they were hemmed. “Be quick with you.”

Hawke peered at the walls too. The Lion Tower on one flank and the castle’s outermost gate on the other, like cliffs of dressed masonry, thick and crenellated. The Tower of London was the symbol of supreme authority, a place that set him ill at ease, but, at least, it was an unlikely choice for the city’s miscreants to loiter, and therefore granted both himself and Ruthven a degree of anonymity. Here they were simply two more sightseers, come to marvel at the forbidding structures and the exotic beasts.

The menagerie itself no longer garnered the repute it had once enjoyed. No longer did gargantuan bears of pristine white chase fish in the Thames, or Elephants roam the outer ward, or apes swing and chatter in the Lion Tower’s upper chambers. Left to moulder, the majority of animals neglected and half-crazed, it could exhibit but a fraction of what once had been a celebrated collection. But a steady stream of onlookers filed past all the same, chattering with nervous excitement as they caught sight of the man-eating beasts in their prisons of stone and iron. The big lawman joined them, determined to continue his regular stroll, and Hawke jogged the first few steps to catch up. The lions flinched at his movement, the tiger did not break from its doleful circuits, and the paying public ignored him entirely. At Ruthven's right shoulder, he said, "I have made contact with folk who might possess knowledge of the kind of crime that we are dealing with. It smacks of pagan ritual, the like of which have not been seen for centuries."

"Wizards and warlocks?" Ruthven answered scathingly. "Superstition. I told you as much when first we discussed the Milne girl. But you think there is something in it?"

"Or it is one would pay homage to that kind of life, aye."

They passed a cage holding a vast cat with a glistening coat that was black as coal. It was licking the end of its huge tail, the thickness of a man's arm, with a long, pink tongue. Ruthven watched it with interest as he spoke. "Devil worshippers?"

Hawke made to reply, but they come upon a knot of six or seven women who had paused to stare at another cat, this time one with large black spots upon a coat of pale yellow. He held his peace until they had rounded the group. "The use of fennel and sorghum. We may look to Italy for its origin."

"Not Orientals then. Perhaps we'll forget Limehouse and look at Clerkenwell." Ruthven clicked his tongue. "Lot of Italians in Clerkenwell. I'll have the boys round a few up. Make an example or two."

Hawke digested the implication with building concern. It was precisely what Marco Totti had warned him would happen. "But the tosher-man, Varney Tapp...".

"Discovered with the body of Betsy Milne?"

"He was found to be clutching a brass button." That made Ruthven halt. It made him frown, too, so Hawke forged on before the officer could tie together the strands in his mind. "The button came from a French coat. Not the kind of thing a self-respecting Englishman or Italian would don on London's streets."

“They make fine coats in France,” Ruthven replied. “Besides, a warm coat is a warm coat. When you’re cold, dignity holds little import.” The self-satisfied smile crept up his broad face. “Something I’d expect you to appreciate.”

Hawke did not take the bait, his irritation counterbalanced by Ruthven’s failure to press him on the button’s provenance. “French regimental greatcoat. Infantry. So soon after the war, it is not the kind of thing a man openly wears if he values his limbs. All the same, one cannot deny that it may prove a straightening of our thread.”

Ruthven considered the summation for a moment, then nodded. “Either we assume it is nothing, a red herring, and we are left with the whole city to suspect...”

“Or we follow the path that takes us to French emigres who once served in Napoleon’s legions. Moreover, a man who may have taken part in the invasion of Russia.” He saw Ruthven’s puzzlement, and added, “The button comes from the 17th Regiment of the Line, a unit that was part of *La Grande Armée.*” There was more, of course. A connection to Ireland. But to reveal that Tapp had spoken to Milky

Mayhew before he died, contradicting the latter's original deposition, would risk exposing Mayhew to the full force of a vengeful Bow Street.

"A French veteran with an interest in Italian witchcraft," Ruthven was saying.

"Or an Italian witch who enlisted with the French legions."

"Or a madman with a penchant for military clothing, or simply a hotchpotch of coincidence." Ruthven breathed deeply as he digested the routes that might be taken, then strode on. "I will have the Patrol look into it."

"I have myself posed questions," Hawke said, out of breath and struggling to keep up.

"And?"

"There might be hundreds of Frenchmen at the Port. In the warehouses and wharves."

"Even so, Bow Street shall put out its feelers, as it were." Ruthven shot the sliver of a glance over his shoulder. "Good work, Mister Hawke. Good work indeed. Admirable, even."

"One question set me to thinking," Hawke went on, finding the notion of Ruthven's praise to be more stomach-churning than his scorn. "Perhaps it is not *that* kind of veteran we seek. There are gentlemen in the city too."

"Bonaparte's officers," Ruthven replied as they approached a pair of Yeoman Warders standing sentinel at a carved arch, resplendent in black and red cloaks, fearsome halberds in hand, "are not likely to be swanning about Mayfair in a plodder's greatcoat."

"Unless it is artifice," Hawke said. He lifted his topper to the guards, who ignored him. "A disguise."

"Strange disguise." Ruthven slowed, touching the rim of his own hat with the gleaming top of his tipstaff. The Warders stood deferentially aside.

"Precisely my thinking," Hawke went on, having offered sour stares to the sentries that were not so much as acknowledged, let alone returned. "Thus, I find myself considering another group. Not officers during the war, but not the kind to shoulder a musket or dig a latrine."

They were out of the walkway now, coming up to the final gate that would lead them onto Tower Hill. Ruthven spoke to more guards, who waved them through, then addressed Hawke. “Go on.”

“What about an actor or dancer?” Hawke suggested, reflecting upon the rancorous words of Serle Lamere, whose time in London had been blighted by prejudice, and whose bitterness was only intensified by the knowledge that those Frenchmen bringing with them a certain sense of refinement were afforded both welcome and advancement. “Or a regimental cook, employed now by a high class club out at St James.”

Ruthven grunted scornfully. “You’d have me deploy officers to Boodle’s or Brooks’s? Batter down the doors and arrest the staff?”

Hawke shook his head, not so naive as to think Bow Street would dare bring scandal to the thresholds of those venerated bastions of the political class. “But handled with a certain finesse, they strike me as worthy lines upon which to enquire.”

"Lines you are no longer free to cross," Ruthven jibed. All the same, the point had sunk in, for he added. "Very well. It is something to be considered."

Hawke licked lips that were suddenly dry. "To continue my work, I will require more funds."

Ruthven eyed him coolly. "Your work is concluded for now, says I. Besides, I advanced you plenty. If you chose to invest it in drink and opium, that is your own business. Back to the rookery with you, Mister Hawke. If you need money, rob some more graves. But keep your eyes peeled for a certain butcher, eh?"

"I told you, it was not Boris Milne who killed our men."

"Then?"

"I have a theory pertaining to the matter."

The corner of Ruthven's wide mouth lifted sardonically. "Oh? Indulge me, do."

"Goodbye, Mister Ruthven," Hawke said, bowing, and left.

Θ

The dramatic curvature of the crossing sweeper's spine was embossed upon the dirty fabric of his long coat. He loped awkwardly into the road as soon as a coin was forthcoming, tipping up his cap with the butt-end of his broom to reveal an African's dark face, creased deeply by the years and the work. He bent to the task, clearing a half-dozen steaming mounds of horse dung with an efficiency belying his crooked frame. The waiting gentleman, resplendent in burgundy tailcoat and ostentatiously tall hat, stepped smartly out once the road had been swept to his liking, adjusting a neckcloth of pristine white with one hand as he clacked a cane on the cobbles with the other.

"Took me an age to get here," Corissa Lott said, crossing the freshly spruced road behind the man who had paid. That man, oblivious to her presence, hooked a sharp right when he reached the far side, and quickly vanished, leaving her at the crossroads of Fore Street and Coleman Street with her companion, a slim fellow of average height and gaunt aspect, with brown, kindly eyes, thick brows and a closely shaven scalp beneath a topper that had seen better days. She gazed at streets teeming with traffic. "What's he about?"

“This is where he said,” Joshua Hawke answered. “You’ll recall he was to visit a cripple at the workhouse, then meet us directly.” He looked up and down the street. To his right, at the far end of the road, the steeple of St Giles Cripplegate dominated the scene, while a couple of hundred paces to his left, the empty shell of Bethlem Royal Hospital loomed above the patchy remains of the original London Wall. *Bedlam* was empty now, for its inmates had long since been moved to a new incarnation of the infamous asylum down at St George’s Fields in Southwark, but still those high, tiny windows, blocked by thick bars, seemed to leer at the road below with a sinister malice that made Hawke shudder. He quickly looked back at Corissa. “Besides, here is as good a place as any. Away from prying eyes.”

Corissa, well-wrapped in bonnet, gloves and pelisse, studied the traffic that swept before them in a ceaseless current of man, horse and vehicle. “More eyes here than you could count in a bloody lifetime.”

Hawke smiled. “Too many to notice us.” Seeing she was about to complain again, he went on, “We agreed to meet at four o’clock, and it is not quite the hour.”

“I hope we are not wasting our time,” she muttered.

“As do I,” Hawke agreed. “Either way, it provides opportunity to give the sewer murders some consideration.” He did not confide in her that, technically speaking, he did not need to consider anything about those heinous crimes. He was off the case, not that he had ever been on it in any official capacity. But now Ruthven had verbally cut him loose, he could creep back into the dark recesses of the rookery and never give Betsy Milne or Varney Tapp a second thought. Except that he had once been a thief-taker. Had once learnt his trade from that wily and irascible strongman, Joseph Nadin, and those instincts, so painstakingly acquired and honed, did not simply fail a man, regardless of how much he might blunt them with gin and shame.

Corissa’s eyes fixed on a point to the west. “There.”

Hawke followed her look, concerned that, despite the obscure choice of location, she had spied a face from the criminal world. He scanned the people at each shop front, perusing clothing, spices, wallflowers and lace, before his eyes came to rest, with abundant relief, upon a couple, approaching at a decorous pace, arm in arm. The gentleman, tall and bearded, seemed to stride in an ungainly manner, hobbling under his own weight. He flourished a wave with an arm that appeared to be double its normal length. "Before they arrive," Hawke said to Corissa. "Something Goaty mentioned."

She frowned. "Goaty?"

"He said you did not trust me. That I am not normal." Hawke could see consternation turn to anger on her features, but he ploughed on. "That kind of talk gets a man killed, Corissa, as well you know."

"I did doubt you," Corissa said. "Your loyalty. Your background."

The frank honesty disarmed Hawke, and for a second he just gaped. "But..."

"But that was before we spoke," she cut in, sparing him the garbled response. "That night at High Holborn. And I was right, wasn't I?" She jabbed his ribs with a finger. "You did have secrets. But I've kept them hid, as I said I would."

Hawke studied her face for treachery, but there was no guile in the brown eyes. He let his gaze sweep over her raven-black hair and bronze skin, feeling the pang of desire that was so strong and so dangerous, and in that moment, on the corner of this bustling road, Joshua Hawke felt a great urge to take her in his arms. He wanted, too, to confess all. To unload his other, deeper secrets. For the burden to be shared. He felt his face grow hot with embarrassment, and said instead, "Do you attend the play this evening?"

She frowned. "Shakespeare? Aye, of course, with Colan."

"At the Theatre Royal, I understand," he said stiffly, unable to stifle his jealousy. "Very nice."

"What's it to you?"

"There they are!" Ansell Brommett exclaimed beside his wife, Kitty. The pair, untangling their elbows, were wreathed in their own pipe smoke and both beamed. "Our unlikely comrades in arms!" To emphasise the appreciation of his own wit, the apothecary held up the limb that had looked so bizarre from a distance. In his hand he held another arm, human to every last detail, except that it was apparently hewn from wood. "Didn't fit the patient, damn it all. Muddled my measurements again." He shook his head in frustration. "Still, the poor fellow was not too distraught." He winked. "Armless enough." He received a thump in the side from his wife, at which he laughed, propping the prosthesis on his shoulder like the Yeomen Warders and their halberds, and indicating the large wicker basket, covered with a cloth, that swung in Kitty's hand. "A modest repast for us all to share. Mrs Brommett's idea. I hope you do not mind."

Kitty, snug against the cold in a long coat and shawl, let go of his hand and took the small clay pipe from between her teeth. "Of course they don't mind, Ansell, you daft brush."

Corissa turned away from Hawke and gave a little curtsy in acknowledgement. "And what a generous thought it is too."

"I like this girl!" Kitty declared. She winked at Hawke. "Keep a tight hold, Mister Hawke!"

Heat returned immediately to Hawke's cheeks, but his blushes were saved by Brommett, who sucked hard on his own pipe, exhaled a great, fragrant gust, and commanded them to follow him south, down Coleman Street. They went willingly, for it seemed churlish to dampen Brommett's forthright and jovial mood, and soon they were swinging east, into the confined passage of Great Bell Alley, the corner of which was taken up by a large grocer's shop, its creaking sign boasting of every essential a person could wish for. Hawke saw bundles of firewood and bottles of paraffin in the windows. There were barrels of tea, flour and sugar, all waiting to be portioned and wrapped for the discerning Londoner, and a multitude of smaller items crammed onto dark-painted shelves. Beyond the grocery were houses on both sides, big and small, new and old. The pale roundness of naked buttocks emerged from an upper window some yards ahead, and, as the owner of the arse yelled a warning, they skirted quickly into the street to avoid the inevitable fall of feaces. Upon clearing the offending house, Hawke realised that they were nearing the end of the row, and the vista opened into a wide space of well-kept lawns and fastidiously manicured greenery.

Ansell Brommett used his artificial arm to point the way. “Drapers Gardens. The perfect spot!”

Hawke followed contentedly enough, though he felt utterly incongruous as part of this group. Two women, strikingly different but attractive and vital in their own ways, and Brommett, who, despite his partial lameness, was straight-backed, well-dressed and confident. Hawke’s thin frame and rough clothing made him the poor relation, and he wondered if passers by would take him for some kind of sharper, inveigling himself amongst the gentle folk in order to lighten their pockets, or worse. Behind him, Corissa was complementing Kitty on her straw hat, which was tied at her chin with green ribbon. Kitty declared, “What say you, lass? A Brommett in a bonnet!”

Corissa’s laugh was polite but genuine, its usual edge blunted. A sound that he had never before heard leave her mouth. It was like dawn birdsong. He did not catch her reply, but it clearly amused Kitty, and the exchange made him smile.

The final units in the row were shops. One was a tailor of high quality, to judge by the garments on display, while the other was a music shop, selling all manner of instruments, as well as a prodigious selection of printed music, the latter propped on various kinds of stand, from plain square-shaped structures to highly stylised, ostentatious pieces that looked more like the wood carvings of Grinling Gibbons than functional paper holders. Hawke stared at them, and at the gleaming brass, the ornate flutes, and the beautifully crafted string instruments. They were gorgeous things, and he imagined they must, in the right hands, make music to lift the soul. And yet something therein gave him disquiet. Something jarred, but he could not think what.

The shops left in their wake, they entered the gardens and reached a pair of empty benches positioned at the fringe of a gravel path that surrounded a circular pond, at the centre of which stood an ornamental cherub, wings spread, spitting a jet of water skyward. Brommett sat down, laying the false arm on the stones so that he might plunder the picnic basket. Beckoning his wife to sit at his side, he crammed a hunk of cheese into his mouth, saying to Hawke, "On the matter of the deaths of your," he hesitated, "associates, I have considered many possibilities. First, a poniard."

"Too wide," Kitty said.

Brommett nodded. "And the blades are typically triangular or square. Your wounds appeared circular?"

"So far as I could tell," Hawke replied.

"Saddlers and cobblers," Brommett suggested, "both make use of large needles to punch stitching through leather."

"But those kinds of implements," Hawke said, "cannot explain the strange markings upon the skin." He scratched his armpit as an unseen creature scurried therein. "I had considered an awl or some kind of rivet."

"But?" Brommett prompted.

"But my thoughts have since wandered down a different path."

"Then let us eat in amity while we ruminate," Brommett said, patting his stomach. "Sit, Mister Hawke, and lead us down this mysterious path."

"First," Hawke answered as he perched awkwardly on the next bench, "might we consider the matter of Betsy Milne?" He could feel the eyes of passers-by on him, scrutinising his appearance, fearing his intentions. He forced himself to ignore them. "I met with Ruthven."

Brommett's brow lifted. "And?"

Hawke took off his hat, tapping the rim against his thigh to beat away the dust. "I explained the French army button. Suggested leads that they may follow. They'll find nothing." He shifted his rump so that Corissa could sit down. She was close, her thigh scraping his, and he could smell the hint of lavender. It was a moment to savour. A fragment of time that would soon pass, fading into memory, but Hawke would cherish it. He had not felt this alive for years. Not since before that fateful Manchester day. "The search remains too broad."

Brommett scratched his beard. "And all the while the clock ticks." He delved in the basket again, earning a slapped hand for his trouble. "Tomorrow is Wednesday, the first ember day of Advent."

"He does not need reminding, Ansell," Kitty admonished, still attempting to defend the victuals from her husband's marauding fingers. In the end she moved the entire basket, ignoring Brommett's faux fury, and began to distribute small buns and brightly polished apples.

Hawke bit into one of the buns. It had a deliciously sweet glaze, though it hurt his decayed molar. "No matter." He replaced the hat, acutely aware that a pate of stubble was not a common style in Drapers Gardens. "It is true that the killer may strike at any time, and I have failed."

"The Runners have failed," Corissa corrected him. "This was not your business, Joshua. Not your fight."

And yet, he thought, it has become my business. Was it Ruthven's disinterest that had done it? His concern for a scapegoat rather than justice? Was it Marco Totti's pleading eyes, so full of fear? Or the raging desperation of Boris Milne, revenge the only matter on his mind? Perhaps it was all of those things. A potent concoction, made all the more intoxicating by Hawke's own past. By the screamed entreaties of innocents, cowering before a sword held high, poised for the final stroke. In the end, he said simply, "I have made it my fight."

“Here,” Brommett interjected, tossing a miniature meat pie to each of them. “Now, what do we have?”

“Next to nothing,” Hawke said gloomily. “Betsy Milne is killed, but snatches at the fiend’s coat in the throes of her death, seizing a button.”

Brommett nodded. “The tosher-man...”

“Varney Tapp,” Kitty prompted.

“Varney Tapp,” Brommett nodded, “finds this button with her body but is killed, either by her murderer, or in an unrelated attack.”

Kitty went on, “The button finds its way to Milky Mayhew.”

“And Mayhew,” Hawke said, “gives it to me.” He held his peace as an elegant couple, arm in arm, strolled past, steps crunching rhythmically on the tiny pebbles. They paid the unlikely foursome no heed, regarding instead an advertisement that had been fastened to some railings near the pond. He waited until they had moved on. “Mayhew adds that Tapp’s killer wore a brooch in the shape of an Irish harp.”

"But you cannot narrow your search with the Irish connection," Brommett suggested. "There must be tens of thousands of Irish in London."

Kitty gave a bleak chuckle. "They do not call St Giles the Holy Land for nothing."

"So I must bend my thought to the smaller groups," Hawke said. "French and Italian. How can it be further refined?" He looked at the sky for inspiration, finding none in its grey fastness, and at the naked trees and the cherub's rushing fountain. Then he stared at the advertisement, squinting to read the block type, and realised that it announced an evening of blood sport. Three vicious badgers and a man-eating ape would be pitted against the dogs. It was the event his fellow resurrectionists were due to attend.

"If our prey is a native of Northern Italy," Brommett's voice scythed across Hawke's thoughts, "then it is more difficult. Stories of the *Benandanti* cult may have been passed down. An oral tradition."

"But," Kitty added brightly, perhaps a response to Hawke's glum countenance, "if our evil-doer is French, we may seek a literate person."

"Scholarly, even," her husband agreed.

Hawke looked from one to the other. "How so?"

"If it is a French soldier," Brommett replied, "they have taken the time to learn of the *Benandanti*. Of the rituals associated with the cult."

"That would fit," Hawke said, his voice low and slow as he mulled the possibility.

"Fit?" Corissa echoed.

"I have been considering the connection to Napoleon's army," Hawke explained, "given the coat button. It seems unlikely that a common infantryman would wear his old coat in this city. Not without first replacing the military buttons. And an officer would not own such a coat. Which leaves who? The non-commissioned officers, the surgeons, the cooks. All valued members of English society now.

Mixing with the kind of folk who would not take a second glance at a man's buttons to determine his worth."

Kitty nodded enthusiastically. "And all learned, literate types."

"A useful seam to mine," Brommett said thoughtfully. "We must identify men of that ilk."

"It is not the locating that will prove difficult," Hawke said, "for I have already asked much the same of Ruthven. The task is in gaining access to them."

"Will not Mister Ruthven attend to that issue also?" Kitty Brommett asked.

"Perhaps," Hawke said. "At least he claims he will. But he is just as likely to send a mob into Clerkenwell to purge it of Italians, then claim justice is served."

"That would be simpler," Brommett agreed bleakly. He stooped to collect the prosthesis, then used it to tap Hawke's topper. "Then we must double our efforts. And do enlighten us as to your notion regarding these strange wounds that have us so vexed." He twisted to kiss his wife on the cheek. “But only on full stomachs, my love! Come come, do not be shy with the pie!”

Kitty punched him, he yowled and Corissa guffawed. Hawke, silently, thought of the music shop at the end of Great Bell Alley.

CHAPTER EIGHT

WEDNESDAY

Hawke returned to his tiny lodgings after the impromptu meal at Drapers Gardens. It was the first time he had set foot in the decrepit tenement for several days, and it felt strange being back in the mouldering attic that was his home. A feeling made more profound by the room's newfound spaciousness, Lucas's mattress and personal effects having been sold or incinerated. At the end of it all, Hawke thought, they were all mere vassals, possessing nothing that was not, ultimately, Szekely's to dispose of at a whim. Only an expansive black circle was left of his friend. A tide mark of blood that tainted the uneven floorboards.

Hawke took a pipe during the evening, lying on his bed and staring at the smoke that roiled about the decaying and stained ceiling beams, trying in vain to unravel the tangled strands of Betsy Milne's bizarre death. Then he had slept away the first part of the night, dreaming fitfully of massed crowds, painted banners and slashing sabres. He had woken with a throbbing skull, a beating drum that kept time with his heartbeat. Hardly a surprise, he supposed, given his rare abstention from laudanum. Gin alone, he had promised himself, and then only enough to steady his nerve and his hand. He felt sick, but at least he could see and think with some measure of clarity.

Now it was the first few minutes of a new day. One of the final three Ember Days of the year. He lit a pair of candles and went to piss in a steaming metal pail in the corner of the room, then padded across to the single little window that looked down onto Buckbridge Street and the rest of the rookery, wondering if, at this moment, an innocent child was being hunted through the streets. Maybe the pursuit was already over, the fennel and sorghum meticulously prepared, each stalk laid out for the wrapping. He breathed deep, warding off the gut-knotting sense of failure. His breath clouded the glass and he wiped it with a sleeve, revealing the silhouettes of chimney pots and spires, gilt-edged by moonlight. Revealing, too, the movement of figures down on the street. He leaned into the glass, squinting to improve the detail. That familiar shiver again, creeping down his neck.

A knock at the door. Hawke turned, boards creaking under his bare heels. He glanced at his hat, coat and boots, piled together at the foot of the bed, but decided breeches and shirt would suffice. Would bring a note of authenticity.

He leaned into the door, pressing his cheek up against a slat so splintered that it offered a range of viable spy-holes.

On the far side, a woman's voice said, "My apologies for the hour."

"Miss Clementine?" Hawke answered. Her tall, stocky frame might have belonged to a man in the anonymity of the dark passage, but he recognised her wide face with its flattened nose, lit as it was in the watery light from a window somewhere along the landing. He stepped back and slid free the bolt.

"The same." Clementine glanced furtively over both shoulders as she stepped into the room. She carried a basket, much akin to the one from which Kitty Brommett had produced so many delicacies the day before. She wore layers against the cold; woollen gloves, and a heavy, hooded travel cloak over her dress. Her bonnet sat at a slight angle so that a patch of silver-flecked brown curls sprouted at one side of her head. "I bring a message from Doctor Vine."

Hawke watched her as she walked further. "For me?"

Clementine reached the middle of the chamber before turning back to regard him, those little black eyes glinting in the candlelight. "For your employer," she corrected herself. "Only, Mister Szekely's lodgings are not known to us."

"But mine are?"

"Aye." Her broad face and broken nose took on something of a gargoyle's glower in the shifting shadows. "You might recall that you informed Doctor Vine some weeks ago."

"No, Miss Clementine," Hawke said, turning to close the door, "I do not."

"It is of a most urgent nature," she blustered irritably, moving to the side so that her back was flush against a mildewed wall. She set down the basket. "I apologise for the disturbance at such an hour, but I will be only moments." She touched fingers to her lips. "Gracious, sir, but my haste gives me a terrible thirst. Might I trouble you for something to drink?"

Hawke offered an embarrassed smile, indicating a small table near his bed, upon which a glass bottle stood, three-quarters full. "I have gin, madam, and nothing more."

"Then gin will suffice, with thanks."

Hawke crossed the room. Clementine, as anticipated, followed. He could sense her working around to the rear. Instead of grasping the bottle, he grasped his knife. When he twisted on his heels she was right behind him, looming over him, a matter of a yard away, having covered the open space with shocking speed. Clementine's club-like fist was aloft, poised beside her right ear, and in it, like a flash of quicksilver in the tremulous flame-glow, he saw the slender blade. It was long and sharp, like a huge needle. Hawke wrenched himself violently away, performing a ragged pirouette, driving his left forearm up to block her strike and slashing at Clementine with the blade as he went. There was no aim in it, only wildness borne out of desperation, but he felt his knife jolt against something rigid, then snag and grind - clothing, flesh, bone? - and he was on the floor, tumbling, scrabbling for purchase, scrambling to his feet, and thanking God for the resolve to stay free of opium's warm embrace. Just for tonight.

When he set himself, gasping for breath like a drowning man, he could feel moisture just above his left wrist and knew, though the moment's panic suppressed any pain, that the great needle had pierced his flesh. But he did not care, not yet, for it was enough that he was alive. Clementine was bleeding too, the upper side of her left hand gaping red as if a huge ruby had been attached to her glove. It was no more fatal a wound than the one she had inflicted upon Hawke, but it aggrieved her all the same, for her lips were paired back in a rictus grin of anguish as she cradled the injured flesh. Still, he noticed, she clutched the long needle, still she would be able to wield it, and in that moment she seemed to register him beyond her own pain, and her face tightened into a stony mask. She let the damaged hand dangle at her side and raised the weapon anew. Hawke followed suit, bending his knees, licking dry lips, and trying desperately to anticipate her next move. They circled one another, like the giant cats he had seen at the Tower Menagerie. There were drops of blood on the floor, glimmering burgundy patches in the candlelight, macabre chain-links connecting attacker and victim.

Clementine was bigger than Hawke. Probably stronger too. She eyed him with bellicose intensity, panting audibly, then shrank into herself, coiling, ready to pounce. Hawke gritted his teeth, braced for whatever might come. It was with disbelief, then, that he saw her reel back, skittering away from him to dive for the edge of the room. For a heartbeat he was frozen by sheer surprise, but then he saw that she was making for the basket she had carefully positioned beside the wall, and he knew instantly what it contained. He gave chase, but she turned before he could close with her, snarling, black eyes reflecting the candle flames like red-hot coals, and the slender blade had vanished from her grip, replaced by a heavy cleaver, the kind used in the butchery trade, its edge gleaming silver, bragging of a whetstone's recent caress. Hawke saw Butcher Milne in his mind's eye, the threats he had made at *The Bell* in Smithfield, and he saw Lucas and Harlowe too. Saw their yawning wounds. Knew that such a fate would be his own.

Clementine growled, a low, visceral sound, and took a step towards him.

It was then that Blackbird said, "Stay there, bitch, or I'll blow your fucking brains out."

Clementine froze on the spot.

She did not want to. She wanted to leap like an enraged lion and chop Hawke to slivers. The conflict was etched in every taut line of her face. But Blackbird, huge and grim-faced, had swaggered through the doorway like an avenging angel, and she was not mad enough to do anything but his bidding.

Blackbird brandished a blunderbuss, fully cocked. It was short and stout, with a flared brass muzzle that would ensure a wide spread of shot. Not a weapon of precision, but in the hands of an expert, in the confines of this little chamber, its carnage would be unspeakable. And so, staring dumbly into the flintlock's gaping maw, Clementine lifted her hands.

Hawke felt his legs start to tremble, relief as potent as fear had been. "Christ's blood, Blackbird, but you took your time."

Blackbird snorted. "Bested by a woman."

"I was not bested," Hawke began, but his protest was cut short by the appearance of another, far more diminutive, form that stepped out from behind the dark-skinned resurrectionist.

"So this is our persecutor?" Corissa Lott said, regarding Clementine with curiosity. She seemed incongruous in this grim place of spattered blood and buckled walls, so resplendent was she in a long-sleeved evening gown of white gauze, satin roses sown onto one shoulder and its corresponding hip. She wore pink shoes, to match the roses, and fine white gloves, and in her hand she held a silk reticule. The little tasselled bag, embroidered at its edges with a floral design that was shot through with silver thread, seemed utterly unsuitable for the item she took from it. Pulling free the pistol that she had once rammed in Hawke's own face, she cocked it and brought it level with Clementine's heaving chest.

Blackbird made a sucking sound with his teeth. "You were in the right of it, *Solly-yom*. My compliments. I shall inform Szekely." He looked at Clementine. "You follow him here?"

"She followed Lucas," Hawke said. "The night he died."

"I followed him," Clementine said with admirable calm, "then I killed him."

"Why?" Corissa asked.

"She is a Giltspur," Hawke answered for their captive. "The gang are behind this."

"The Giltspurs," Blackbird's gravel-hewn voice echoed. "I knew it. I blasted knew it."

Clementine twitched her right hand so that the cleaver, shimmering orange in the dim light, drew a luminous line in Blackbird's direction. "The nigger possesses more wit than the rest of you combined."

“The Giltspur Boys ordered our deaths,” Hawke went on, “but Clementine wields the knife.” He turned to her, meeting her brazen gaze. “Or should I say the surgical probe?”

“Surgical what?” Blackbird grunted sceptically as he fished in a pocket for a quid of tobacco which he stuffed into the corner of his mouth.

“Probe,” Hawke replied. He wiped the knife on his thigh and sheathed it, inspecting the damage to his wrist. Just like the wounds inflicted upon Lucas and Harlowe, it was impossible to gauge the full depth of the puncture, but, when he squeezed the edges, the hole welled with bloody beads that plummeted to speck his bare toes. “The kind of tool used in dissection.” He scanned the floor, eyes quickly settling on the weapon, and he stooped to collect it. “The kind plunged once, twice into the living flesh of Lucas and Harlowe.” He stared at the object, holding it up to the nearest candle. It was red and slick with his blood. Its etched markings, carved by an undeniable expert into the wooden handle, were smeared crimson, but legible enough, proving what he already knew. Because he had known Clementine would come, had guessed it. Yet the speed and ferocity of her attack had still managed to catch him ill-prepared. The probe had come so close, so perilously close, to his neck, as it had done Harlowe before him, and Lucas, in this very room, that he could barely bring himself to look away. "The Giltspur Boys wanted us all dead, but wanted to avoid an all-out war with Szekely."

"So they sent a woman," Corissa continued, "known to each of us. Not a friend, but not a threat by any stretch."

"And they put the rumour about that Butcher Milne is killing resurrectionists in revenge for his daughter's death, but I've seen Milne with my own eyes. He makes threats, but he has done nothing. It is grief that talks through him."

Blackbird screwed up his pulpy face in confusion. "But our lads were killed with a butcher's hatchet." He jerked the blunderbuss at the weapon in Clementine's raised hand. "Like that."

"Not so," Hawke said. "Look closer." Now that he could see the weapon without the blur and whirl of mortal danger, the jagged teeth became clear. He waited for Blackbird and Corissa to notice the serrations, then added, "It is a bone saw."

"From the anatomy theatre again," Corissa said. "Harlowe's wounds were too ragged to have been inflicted by a smooth edge. That's what you told me."

Hawke inverted the probe so that its handle was enveloped within his palm, the slender shaft nestling flush against the inside length of his forearm, utterly concealed. "She inveigles herself into the room, then works her way round the back of her mark with the probe." He flicked up his hand, recreating the downward stabbing motion with which she had tried to impale him. "Stabs the neck, thus. The victim is incapacitated. With the task made simpler," his eyes slid towards the basket, "takes the larger blade, concealed therein, and finishes the matter."

Blackbird moved closer to the basket, crouching to inspect it, though the blunderbuss remained steadily trained on Clementine. "Cunning bitch," he said, almost whispering. He looked up, and for the first time Hawke saw genuine horror ghost over the man's hitherto implacable features. "Chops them up with the bone saw when they can't fight back. Jesus wept."

Hawke nodded. "And makes it look as though an angry, grief-stricken butcher has taken leave of his senses and made merry with his cleaver."

"How did you know?" Blackbird asked.

"Someone told me recently that it was wise to do away with those privy to one's dirtiest secrets." It had been Ruthven. Puffed up and proud on that misty morning outside Newgate, with not a moment's consideration to the hunt for a killer of criminals. But it was his words that inadvertently lit a fuse within Hawke's mind, even if that had not been his intent. So Hawke had considered Goaty as a possible suspect, fearing personal enmity had tipped into direct action. A ruse, perhaps, in order to frame him and eradicate a rival. But even Goaty's usual hostility had been muted after Harlowe's death, concern for his own welfare apparently genuine. It set Hawke's suspicions to the others. To Gilroy Penley and Blackbird, and even Corissa. But each and every one of them would not have dared challenge Colan

Szekely for supremacy. Which left Szekely himself. Was the softly-spoken Hungarian callous enough to wipe out his own gang in order to further some hidden agenda? Absolutely, Hawke had decided. But there seemed no obvious reason to do so, and a stranger method of dispatching said gang he could not fathom.

"It made me think of Theophilus Vine," Hawke continued, deciding it best not to dwell on the alternatives while those candidates were in the room. "Perhaps he no longer wished to treat with resurrectionists. Wanted all trace of us gone."

Blackbird made a scornful grunt. "Vine's school cannot exist without fresh corpses."

"Indeed," Hawke said, "and if he rid himself of our group, then another would have to be engaged." He shifted his gaze to the tall, bleeding woman who returned his stare belligerently. "Then I saw Clementine. Two days ago, at Covent Garden. Playing lookout for a party of rough looking men, one of whom I recalled from the night at Hockley-in-the-Hole." He glanced at Corissa. "Wounded in the neck."

"The Giltspur Boys we fought," she said, the trauma of recollection quietening her voice.

"The man you stabbed did not die after all," said Hawke. He turned to the huge West Indian. "Another man had a hook for a hand."

"Ran into him at the graveyard that night, didn't we?" Blackbird confirmed Hawke's recollection. He whistled softly, absently fingering the trigger of his blunderbuss. "Shit on a stick."

Something else had struck Hawke too. After his dalliance with the pot-girl at the *Swan and Cygnet*, she had mentioned her fear of being poked and prodded by doctors. It had brought him back to Vine's anatomy theatre, and the wondrous array of slim, wickedly sharp tools at the doctor's disposal. All of them freely available for Clementine to borrow as she saw fit. And all of them made bespoke for Vine, at doubtless a pretty price. Each piece bore the initials 'TV' marked deep into every handle. A simple but elegant zig-zagging pattern carved into every hilt, at the base of the blade's shaft. The same pattern that had been stamped upon the flesh of Clementine's victims as she had stabbed with all her might, effectively tattooing them with her master's mark.

Hawke had run the idea past Ansell and Kitty Brommett, Corissa too, whilst soaking up the serenity of Drapers Gardens, and they, in turn, had responded with such affirmation that it had served to solidify the theory. By then, of course, he had already alerted Blackbird, having whispered the outline of his suspicion to the gang leader after lifting the body of the farrier's wife. That was why Blackbird had declared his attendance at the baiting, and why Hawke had overtly stated that he would be at home. They needed Clementine to hear. Needed her to know that he would be alone, probably in an opium stupor, while his only allies were at some back-alley dog-pit, inebriated and useless.

"Seamus O'Neill, the lad Colan killed," Corissa said to Clementine. "Who was he to you?"

"My cousin," Clementine answered, and for the first time a tremor crossed her features.

Corissa swallowed falteringly, an unpleasant realisation evidently dawning. “You anatomised him.”

Clementine’s face seemed to crumble, the stoic façade melting away, and she half collapsed, bracing hands upon her knees for support. “A good boy. Deserved neither his fate, nor,” the words were stunted, interspersed with sobs, “what came after.”

Corissa looked at Hawke, her face morphing from rigid determination to revulsion, and even the beginnings of compassion.

And that was when Clementine went for the door.

Blackbird had inadvertently provided a clear escape route by moving to the basket, and Clementine, launching from her crouch like an over-sized frog, made a darting run that was impressive for one of her size. But Corissa’s pistol was up like lightning, the octagonal muzzle hovering steadily a yard from the would-be assassin’s flattened nose. Even so, Hawke thought the bigger woman would duck her head and charge like a stampeding bull, but she pulled up at the last moment with a snarl of frustration, eyeing the gun barrel with seething malevolence.

"Drop it," Corissa commanded, meaning the bone saw. Clementine did as she was told, the weapon clattering loudly on the wooden floor. Corissa carefully shuffled round to block the path to the door, keeping her pistol arm out, straight and unflinching. When she was satisfied, she said, "The Giltspurs will be coming for us."

"They're doing that already," Blackbird growled.

"Openly, then," Corissa said. "They'll know Colan killed Seamus, and it will be war."

Clementine grinned nastily as she wiped away the last vestiges of tears. "Oh, they know." The black eyes glided sideways to regard Hawke. "Covent Garden? That's what we're looking for. Why we were there. Your people." Her voice was slow as she relished every word. "Dead men walking, all of you."

"What now?" Hawke asked Blackbird. He had predicted their quarry would turn out to be Clementine, had meticulously set the trap, but he had given no thought to the aftermath. Clementine visibly bristled, setting her jaw and squaring her shoulders in expectation of summary violence.

“Let Szekely decide,” Blackbird replied after a moment’s consideration. “He’ll want words with Doc Vine, I shouldn’t wonder. How that big wench managed to sneak out with his probes and saws.”

“I doubt it will ruin their dealings,” Corissa said bitterly. “Only tonight they talked business throughout King Lear.”

Hawke looked at her afresh, as if the abrasive pang of jealousy he now felt had scoured clean his eyes. For the first time he properly noticed the gown she wore, and saw that tresses of her raven-black hair had been curled by an expert hand, framing the face, the rest tied back in a severe chignon to expose her slender neck. She was dressed for high society. For Colan Szekely. “And do not forget Monsieur Blanc’s ensemble,” he muttered.

“Fat chance, the haughty bastard,” Corissa scoffed, apparently missing the sourness in his tone. “Every musician clothed more colourfully than a peacock. More gold brocade than down at Horse Guards. More plumage on show than instruments.” She chuckled, shaking her head at the memory of the concert. “Ribbons on their wrists and brooches on their chests.”

Hawke gaped at her. He felt as though he had been struck by lightning. “Brooches?”

Clementine dropped to the floor. She sprawled on the boards, and for a heartbeat Hawke thought she must be suffering a seizure of some kind. But then she was at Corissa’s ankle, wrenching out and up, and Corissa toppled backwards with a shriek, pink shoes skittering away, white satin petticoat flashing bright. The pistol fired, missing the tie beam and punching through the roof, a flurry of plaster and wood splinters fluttering down like snow. Then the larger of the women was up, and she had retrieved the bone saw, its serrations bright, and she scrambled onto Corissa Lott, slithering over her, mauling her in an effort to bring down the brutish weapon.

Corissa bucked and writhed, lashed up with her feet, her cries muffled beneath the weight of her assailant. Her arms were outstretched, clasping and clawing, desperately scaffolding Clementine’s good hand to prevent the blow. Clementine roared furiously as she tried to bring the saw to bear. She dragged up her injured hand. The motion pulled apart the wound so that blood welled and spilt over them both, smearing Corissa's cheeks as she attempted to gouge her enemy's eyes.

Hawke, mind reeling, and stunned by the sudden ferocity of the attack, had dithered, but he realised that he still clutched the probe. He bounded forwards, raising the skinny implement with its vicious point, ready to plunge it deep between Clementine's shoulders. In his peripheral vision he glimpsed Blackbird, nonchalantly raising the blunderbuss.

The world exploded.

There was no warmth to the blast, just a gust of pressure, of force, as if a gale had swept through the rookery, and Hawke was tumbling away, snatched up and tossed about like a dry leaf. He was vaguely aware of the hardness of the floorboards under his back. The high beams spun above him, wreathed in fingers of white smoke. Voices, male and female, melded into each other.

Pain. Searing, white-hot pain. He tried to remember where he had stashed the laudanum. Then all was quiet.

CHAPTER NINE

FRIDAY

Hawke woke with a start. The world swam.

He peeled his tongue off the roof of a mouth that felt like parchment, and lay flat and still as he tried to deduce where he was and how exactly he had arrived. His left side, from lowest rib to pelvis, throbbed beneath fresh sheets, reminding him of Clementine's attack, the fight that followed and the shot that had ended it. The images swooped and twisted in his head like a murmuration of starlings. Taking form then melting away, real but ephemeral. He stared at the ceiling, blinking clear the heavy dregs of sleep, and knew instantly that he was not at home on Buckbridge Street. No rotten, worm-eaten beams here, but broad panels, unblemished by time or treatment, and painted a mellow orange.

Two windows, shutters thrown back, allowed light into the room. They also carried the taste of tobacco on the breeze, and the hammering, shouts, clangs and whistles of construction work. With a surprising amount of effort, he managed to turn his head towards them, seeing a sky of milky grey that could have been dawn or dusk, though the din of the builders suggested the former. He rolled his head again - gingerly, so as to discourage the perpetual spinning sensation - and inspected the room. It was a bedchamber, sparsely but tastefully furnished, with a plain rug on the floor, two chairs beside his mattress, and a desk on one side of the room. On the other was a substantial chest, nestled against the wall beneath a portrait of the old king. On the wall opposite Hawke there was a chimney piece carved of dark wood, suspended above which was a large mirror that made the room seem as though it went on forever. The hearth beneath had been recently stoked, flames dancing as if to celebrate Hawke's wakefulness.

With no hope of identifying his surroundings, Hawke drew a fortifying breath and set himself the task of discovering his wounds. He moved in increments, retreating and sallying by turns, inching off the bed with preemptive oaths and winces, beginning with his arms and letting his head and shoulders follow. The pain was all in his left side, quite low, but too ambiguous to pinpoint, so he gritted his teeth, panting fast, and propped up onto his elbows to leverage his upper body, a little at a time, until he had lifted his whole torso. The covers slid down and bunched at his waist to reveal a naked but undamaged chest. He steadied himself against a wave of nausea, praying it had come as a result of sitting upright, and was not a sign of genuine sickness. The pain had refined into a white-hot stabbing sensation. Hawke swallowed back a groundswell of bile. He felt peculiar, quite apart from his own body, as though he looked down upon himself, and a great urge to collapse and shut his eyes assailed him.

He cursed himself for a contemptible coward and dragged back the sheets, raking his eyes down the length of his body. There were bandages, stained a rusty colour on the left flank, enveloping his midriff and extending down, over the angular sharpness of his pelvis, to finish around his buttocks. He put a hand to the stain, snaking his fingers gently over the surface of the dressing, and was reprimanded by a hot flare of pain so searing that it stopped his head spinning in that moment, dragging his mind free of the groggy miasma. He hissed through his teeth, imagining steam billowing up from the wound like that which had flurried from the water drums at Babcock and Bull, the smithy on Fleet Street. But that seemed like weeks ago. Perhaps, he thought, it was. Cold dread rose through his body as he thought of Corissa. Was she hurt? Dead? Had Clementine escaped, somehow protected by his own stupidity? And what of the Ember Week? Had it come and gone? Were more children lying in other sewers, wrapped in vines and mutilated beyond recognition? And all the while, Hawke had slept, uncaring and impotent.

The worry and the guilt, churning together like the ingredients of a most potent tincture, caused a knot to form in his guts. He swung a leg over the side of the bed. It hurt, but it was bearable, and he let the other one follow. He cringed as he pushed up, a low growl escaping unbidden from his chest as his side burned like hellfire. Mercifully, his back cracked without persuasion.

And then he was walking. Slowly, falteringly, but the steps came, for he would permit no refusal. He reached the window and looked out. It could have been any street in London. Taverns, homes and shops. The building opposite was high and leaning, caged from foundation to roof in scaffolding. Nearby, a team of workmen dug the ground, leaving the roadway half blocked by a huge pile of spoil, over which urchins picked in their search for plunder.

"He stirs," the man said. "Holy Mother be praised."

Hawke cricked his neck, so rapidly did he twist to see Colan Szekely, who had somehow reached the chair at his bedside unnoticed. The man was truly a wraith, he thought with a new pang of sickness. "Mister Szekely, sir, I..."

"Hush, my dear *Sólyom*," Szekely said, smooth as a snake. He was clothed all in black, but had removed his hat and gloves. His chalk-white hands and skull seemed positively ethereal in the dimness of the room. The thin facial scar looked like a thread of silver tugging between eyelid and mouth. His lips, by contrast, were a purple slash as they widened into a smile above a plate of boiled potatoes and greens that he held beneath his nose to sniff. "Conserve your strength." He offered Hawke the food, along with a little fork. "You have suffered much."

Hawke sidled back to the bed and took the plate, resting it on his lap. He was ravenous, but Szekely's sudden presence made him too anxious to eat. "I was shot."

Out on the street, a man broke into slurred song, the verse bawdy and out of tune. Szekely seemed not to notice. "By Blackbird, of all people." He half-smiled. "His aim was ever dubious."

"He was aiming at Clem-"

"I am aware of all that transpired. Indeed, he confessed to nearly offing my beloved, which would have been a singular tragedy."

Hawke relived the moment Blackbird had fired. Or, rather, he remembered the noise. Ear-splitting, teeth-aching, heart-stopping. The flash had blinded him and he could still smell a trace of smoke. The blunderbuss could be a true fiend in a confined space. What differentiated it from a musket was the distinctly flared muzzle, a feature designed to enable rapid reloading while on the move; on horseback or atop a coach. It was what made it the weapon of choice for postal coachmen in their perpetual battle with highwaymen and footpads. But what it also provided was an increase in the spread of shot. The tiny lead balls, packed tightly like fish-eggs in the barrel, would fan outwards when the trigger was pulled, rendering them next to worthless at long range, but shockingly effective when the target was close. They could take a door off its hinges, a head off its shoulders.

He felt himself flush as the memory crystallised. "Miss Lott?"

"Is well, all told," Szekely said. "She has nursed you attentively."

"Clementine?"

"Not quite as fortunate." Szekely leaned back and adjusted the silken scarf about his neck. "Took the brunt of the shot, despite your valiant efforts to shield her."

"I assure you, Mister Szekely, I..." Hawke stammered, desperate to head off any hint of collusion with the murderess.

Szekely dabbed his lips with a slender, lily-white finger. "Hush hush hush. A jest and nothing more." He tutted softly. "Sweet Clementine. Clementine O'Neill, to give her her proper name. The wee bullets made the devil of a mess of her. Looked like a shark took a nibble, truth be told. She is very much dead, dear *Sólyom*." He spread his pale palms in a gesture of resignation. "But we are now at war. Her blood will not be the last drop to taint the Thames."

Hawke peered around the room again. "Where am I, sir?"

"Arundel Street. Little drinking ken called *The Lion*. You know it?"

"Aye."

"It is my good fortune to own the place."

"How did I come to be here?"

"Blackbird brought you, bless his heart. Over his shoulder like sack of turnips." The corners of Szekely's baby-blue eyes crinkled. "Made for a pleasant change, I shouldn't wonder, carrying a live body for once." He leaned in a little, as if conspiring with Hawke. "If I didn't know him better, I'd say he felt a touch guilty for blasting you almost to oblivion. Now hush, I tell you. Recover yourself. There are graves to be emptied. Profits to be made." He stood abruptly, retrieving gloves and hat. All that black against his porcelain skin made him look like a magpie. He glanced at the doorway, making a soft clicking sound with his tongue, as if to hail someone. “I simply wished to assess your progress, and I am heartened by what I see.” He bowed low. “There will be a reward, dear *Sólyom*. Rooting out Clementine and her foul scheme was a grand service to render. It shall not be forgotten. Now, business requires me elsewhere.”

Szekely vanished as rapidly as he had arrived, leaving Hawke to stare dumbly at the empty doorway. Outside, a workman dropped a shovel or hammer, the heavy tool clattering all the way down the scaffolding. Hawke almost jumped out of his skin. The residual anxiety of a meeting with the Irish-Hungarian would linger cruelly. This time, at least, it was mingled with a profound sense of relief. Clementine was dead; Szekely was, for now, satisfied.

Corissa Lott entered the room. The warm cinnamon tone of her skin contrasted so starkly with Szekely’s that Hawke took an involuntary intake of breath. He was immediately embarrassed, acutely self-aware, and yet entirely unable to tear his gaze from her. She crossed the room like moving sunlight, a gentle waft of lavender accompanying her as she took a seat.

As mesmerised as he was, Hawke caught the glimpse of a grimace as it inhabited her features. “You’re hurt.”

She had been holding a scroll of some kind, which she dropped so that she could touch a hand to her shoulder. “A piece of shot clipped me. Still in there.” She smiled wanly. “A souvenir.”

“God damn it all, Corissa, I am sorry. I...”

She stayed him with a scornful snort. “Sorry? That bastard would have killed me in a heartbeat if it meant killing Clementine too.”

“Szekely would-”

“Colan Szekely would discipline Blackbird for the inconvenience. Dock him a week’s wages if he felt particularly put out. Oh, do not be so naive, Joshua,” she added peevishly. “It is very well to have a woman on his arm. A half-caste to-boot. Adds a little mystery to his persona. But he would find a replacement in an hour or two.” Her almond eyes narrowed with amusement, skewering him. “Of course, you have impressed him in this business. A possible leader of men, and a clever one too. Which makes you a rival to Mister Blackbird. Better grow some eyes in the back of your skull."

"Christ," Hawke sighed, rubbing a hand over new stubble. "Does it never end?"

"You know better than that."

Hawke acknowledged the fact with a rueful grunt. The world of the St Giles body-snatchers might not be the one he would choose, were he given his time again, but it was the one in which he now lived, and violence, vengeance and death were as elemental as the air he breathed. The reality made him think upon those who had not asked to be embroiled in Szekely's web. "Does he know of the help I have received?"

She shook her head. "He cares only that the immediate threat has gone. Your apothecary and his good wife are safe in anonymity."

"Good." Hawke looked down at his bandages, the top part of which was still on show above the sheet. "I believe I have you to thank for this."

She frowned. "You did not see Goaty in here, hour upon hour, cleaning your wounds and changing the dressing."

He laughed. It hurt. "Thank you, Corissa."

"You saved my life," she said. "Took the shot that was meant for me."

"I did not know he was going to bloody shoot."

She gasped. "Chivalry is truly dead." To his surprise, she leaned in, placing her hand on his leg. "It may have been an accident, Joshua, but it happened all the same." Then she got up, moved in, kissed his forehead.

Hawke was dumbfounded and terrified all at once. He searched the door for Szekely but saw no-one. "How long have I been here?" he blurted eventually, obfuscating to give a chance for the heat to leave his cheeks.

She had taken her seat once more. "Two days."

"The Ember Week..."

"Has begun."

"And?"

Corissa bent to reach a hand to the floor, bringing up what he had first thought was a scroll. It turned out to be a rolled newspaper. She unfurled it and handed it over. “Trouble.”

The Morning Post was cock-a-hoop with rabble-rousing relish as it described the descent of a dozen of Bow Street’s finest upon the Italian neighbourhood in Clerkenwell. Hawke read quickly, scanning the black lines of text for salient information, all the while feeling his heart sink into his stomach. “A mob followed them in?”

“Aye,” Corissa replied. “A whole crowd by torchlight. Ransacked a few homes, dragged out a few men of the right age. Butcher Milne was there too, so Colan tells me. One or two Italians got a hiding for good measure, but lucky none were strung up there and then.”

“The right age for what?”

“Murder.”

Pressure grew behind his ribs, making his breaths shallow. “There’s been another?”

She shook her head. “The magistrates got nervous. Folk are demanding answers. Justice. And the papers whipped them up so as riots looked likely.”

So Ruthven made good on his threat, Hawke thought. Better to sacrifice one community than risk seeing the whole city burn. He swore softly. “They are scapegoats.”

“Aye, that may be, but you said yourself that these strange vines, this witchery, is an Italian vice. Might the Runners not stumble upon the true murderer in spite of it all?”

“They might,” Hawke conceded bleakly. In his head he ran through what he knew. A child grotesquely murdered. Pagan practises harking back to Medieval Italy. A French military button. An Irish harp. There was much here, and yet there was nothing. And now it no longer mattered, because George Ruthven had decided to close the case and take the plaudits. Hawke had been dismissed, and a perpetrator had been decided upon, regardless of guilt or innocence.

Exhausted and frustrated in equal measure, Hawke flung the Morning Post petulantly away. It flapped in the air, turning inside out, then skidded on the smooth floorboards, finishing in a crumpled pile like the carcass of a shot pheasant. Two pages of advertisements found themselves at the outermost. Hawke stared at the bolder examples. A product guaranteeing the simplest and most complete shoe blacking available, a cordial for women that promised the dissolution of crow's feet in ten regular doses, the announcement of a much-vaunted prize-fight between an English champion and his American counterpart.

A theatre production on Drury Lane. Shakespeare's King Lear.

Hawke's eyes latched onto the notice as if grappling hooks had been flung from between the bold type. Corissa was saying something, but she might as well have shouted from the scaffolding across the road. He only saw the newspaper. Only heard his own voice. After a short while, she touched his shoulder, shaking him gently.

Hawke looked round. "I need to go to the Theatre Royal."

Θ

Between Corissa and the hackney driver they managed to manhandle Hawke into the otherwise empty vehicle, the coach listing slightly as he clambered awkwardly aboard. Corissa joined him on the bench, snapping orders through the window before swiping shut the leather drapes. In Hawke's desperation he had professed utter disinterest in whether they were spotted leaving *The Lion* by one of Szekely's people, but that did not mean she would entertain complete carelessness.

They thundered north on Arundel Street, a portentous wind, foul and biting, rushing up from the Thames at their backs. Hawke grunted and winced as they juddered over cobbles, swerved pedestrians and picked a haphazard route between rival hackneys, brightly coloured coaches and lumbering ox-carts. He cursed the streets and cursed his wounds, breaking out in a sweat that was cooled by the rushing air to make him shiver uncontrollably. But it was worth the discomfort, he told himself. Speed was all.

They turned west onto The Strand and were immediately snarled in a sluggish current of traffic as the road rounded St Clement Danes, the church named for its early Norse parishioners, now a grand edifice, towering over the community with its steeple and domes.

Hawke banged the roof with his fist, bellowing for the driver to force a way through, but he knew it was futile. He would have leapt out and run for it had he been physically able, but it hurt badly enough just to walk, and he quickly abandoned the notion.

"Shall I?" Corissa asked, reaching for the door, evidently reading the conflict on his face.

"No," Hawke replied. "Too dangerous."

She sat back with a sour look. "Better explain, then, Joshua."

"The murderer of Betsy Milne."

Her jaw slackened. "Is at the theatre?"

"I realised that night, when Clementine attacked me. You said something. The musicians playing the entr'acte. You likened them to peacocks."

Corissa's brow furrowed as she searched her memory. "Monsieur Blanc's ensemble?"

"They wore brooches, you said."

"And ribbons," she nodded, "feathers, lace."

“*Brooches*, Corissa,” Hawke said, hissing as one of the hackney’s wheels bounced over a pot-hole. “The killer wore a brooch.”

“In the shape of a harp,” she answered dismissively. “No harpists in the ensemble, Joshua. And none as would don a brooch of that kind, lest they be accused of being an Irish traitor.”

And that was the crux of it, Hawke had come to understand. He leaned closer to her, their knees touching as he clung to the edge of the bench. “It wasn’t a harp, the tosher-man saw.” He was almost whispering in his earnestness. “It resembled one, but he was mistaken. What design were Blanc’s brooches?”

She bit her lower lip hard enough for the plump flesh to blanch. “I do not recall.”

“My money is on a stand.”

“Stand?”

“To hold the sheets of music. When we were in Drapers Gardens with the Brommetts, we walked past a music shop, do you recall?”

Her nose wrinkled. “Vaguely.”

“Something rankled when I looked into the shop window. Something in the back of my mind. I couldn’t place it.” He paused, grimacing, as the hackney swung a violent right into Catherine Street. They immediately ground to a halt. He leaned out of the window to see that they were behind a pair of young lads, both barefoot and toting sticks, driving a flock of lily-white geese up the middle of the road. Back inside, he said, “But the other night, just before Clementine lunged for you, it all made sense. Through all this,” he flapped a hand at his damaged midriff, though it was concealed now by his shabby clothes, “the thought escaped me, but seeing the advertisement for King Lear, in the Morning Post, it hit me like a punch in the face. The shop at Drapers Gardens had a music stand in the window, Corissa. It was shaped like a lyre.”

“I know the kind,” she said dubiously.

“And what does a lyre-style music stand resemble?”

Her wide, brown eyes did not waver from his, though their pupils seemed to dilate and contract as the notion settled. "A harp," she murmured.

"Don't you see? It isn't an Irish connection we seek, but a musical one."

"And Blanc's ensemble are French to a man," Corissa said. She put a hand to her mouth as though she had witnessed something terrible, mulling the theory while the geese outside honked and squawked to the bellows of the two boys. The hand went down suddenly, gripping Hawke's knee. "Wait. French musicians are hardly rare."

"But we know some play the Theatre Royal this very day," Hawke countered, determined she would not water down his conviction while he was resolute enough to overcome the pain. "And we know these don brooches, possibly ones shaped like harps. So let us begin here."

The geese turned noisily into an adjacent alley, and the way was clear. As the hackney coach accelerated, Catherine Street became

Brydges Street, and almost immediately the large, rectangular structure of the theatre rose out from amongst the other rooftops and chimneys.

"I will go in," Hawke said. "Bow Street is a stone's throw from here. Will you take a message to Ruthven?"

For a moment it looked as though Corissa might demur, such was her antipathy towards the Runners, but she could hardly escape the entreaty in his face. She nodded, adding, "If you tell me what Peterloo means to you."

Hawke was about to pull back the curtain to check on their progress, but he found that he could do nothing more than grip the leather, letting his weight hang from it as he digested her statement. He tried to look at her, but his eyes would not leave the coach floor. He opened his mouth. No words would come.

"You have been delirious these last two days," she said, taking the initiative while he worked his jaw dumbly. "Thrashing and sweating and sobbing like a baby. All the time returning to one word.

Peterloo. Peterloo." The name was like a lightning bolt striking his skull, making him flinch and cower. "Peterloo."

"Did we not all hear about it?" he managed to answer. He could sense the lack of authenticity in his own words. "All read of it in the newspapers?"

"But we do not all dream of it," she said coldly, cutting him off. "Do not take me for a fool, Joshua. We have come this far, you and I."

He dragged his gaze up to meet hers. "What do you know of that day?"

"A great throng, broken apart most heinously by soldiers in their cups."

The final words were vicious and bitter, but Hawke knew she had him cornered. He could no longer hide. "Cavalry," he corrected her. "The Manchester and Salford Yeomanry broke the crowd, ably supported by the 15th Hussars. There were foot soldiers too, in reserve." He laughed, grimly and without a trace of mirth. "And artillery. Artillery! All to quell a peaceful protest." In an instant he was no longer in London, but St Peter's Square, Manchester. He could hear the crowd's chants, smell horseflesh and sweat, feel his own fear. "Near a score killed. Women and children too. Cut to pieces by sabres, trampled by hooves. More than seven hundred grievous hurt." He knew moisture was beginning to prick his eyes, but he could do nothing to stop it. "All they wanted was freedom from poverty."

Corissa looked at him pityingly. Her hand was still on his knee. "You were there, weren't you?"

"To my shame."

"Shame?" she echoed in disbelief. "Surely there can be nothing more honourable than defiance in the face of the law, when that law oppresses the people. I know folk died, but folk die all the time. Think of our own rookery. It stinks of death. But you..." she cast her gaze away, searching for the right superlatives, "you faced down the bastards' swords. The blood shed that day meant something."

The hackney came to a halt, the driver calling their destination down to them. Through a gap in the curtain, Hawke could see that they were outside the fresh new Doric portico that welcomed theatregoers at the Brydges Street entrance. Immediately beside the coach were a pair of huge doors, studded with rivets the size of fists, beneath arches filled with stained glass as elaborate as to be found in any high church chancel or nave. He realised in that moment that he could step out of the vehicle right now. Could evade further questioning. Could let her believe what she chose to believe.

And yet. “I saw that terrible day, Corissa,” he heard himself say. The deed was done. No turning back. “Saw it from the saddle.”

“From...” she began, hesitating as the truth dawned. She simply stared, dumbfounded. Emotion rippled across her face. For a moment she looked as though she might vomit, then it seemed likely she would strike him, then only horror, only revulsion showed where once empathy - admiration, even - had been.

Hawke wanted to take her by the shoulders and make her see what he had seen. He wanted to tell her of the crowd. What a host it had been. Tens of thousands, gathered with one mind and voice. He wanted to describe the music that accompanied them that day, joyful and uplifting. The flags that fluttered across St Peter’s Square, their colours and slogans proclaiming liberty for all. Such a thing he had never beheld. Never even imagined. Then Henry Hunt, that famed orator for whom they had all come, stepped onto the stage, bowing briefly as he took off his white hat and addressed the people with booming voice.

Hawke did not take Corissa by the shoulders. He slumped back, staring again at the floor. "I was there as a member of the Yeomanry, under command of Joseph Nadin, my employer. I was one of his thief-takers by day." He swallowed, the motion thick and cloying. "Someone, an officer, snapped. Panicked. The fateful order was given."

And that was about the size of it. Hawke remembered how the horsemen surged forth, aiming to apprehend Hunt, but it was a fool's errand. Perhaps the officers had expected the mass of bodies to part like the Red Sea before Moses, but none moved. They could not move, such was the density of the crowd, and then the cavalry were upon them, sabres drawn, and madness took hold. He tried to meet Corissa's gaze, but she turned away. He opened his mouth, but the words were stillborn on his tongue. How could he possibly describe the horror of defenceless heads shielded from slashing swords by bare arms? How could he make her understand just how much blood flowed onto St Peter's Square, making the ground slick and treacherous? How could he begin to describe the screams?

Hawke had screamed too. At first to cow the people in the hope that they would move, but his screams had turned to pleas, hoarse and desperate, as the first limbs had been cleaved open. He had wheeled his mount about, blocking the blades of his comrades with that of his own, spitting forlorn orders for the men to relent. To withdraw. To see sense. But they were full of rage, the Yeomanry and Hussars. Many were full of ale too. In that, at least, Corissa had been right. And all of them were assailed by fear at such a vast gathering. In the whites of the peoples' eyes they saw not terror, but insurrection. Revolution.

Could he tell Corissa how the whole thing lasted just a few minutes, and that all that was left was a field of caps and hats, bonnets, ragged flags, bits of dresses and coats, bloody shawls and lost shoes? The hustings stood there empty, banners slashed, bearing silent witness to the carnage. And the bodies, of course. Crushed, mangled, mutilated. Many moaning as they bled. Young ones calling for mothers. Women wailing for their children. Men searching for wives amongst the dead and dying.

He wanted to say all that and so much more. That Joseph Nadin, hearing of his actions, had stripped him of his rank and threatened him with imprisonment or worse. That he had lost everything at Peterloo, and that he had vowed never to pass a day sober again, so overwhelmed by shame was he.

He had forgotten the Theatre Royal. Forgotten the musicians of Monsieur Blanc's ensemble. "I will never forgive myself."

Corissa pushed open the coach door. "Don't tell me. You were only following orders." She stepped out onto the street. Looking back at him, her face a mask of disdain, she said, "The boots. You told me you were a deserter."

"I am," Hawke said meekly. "From the Yeomanry. Corissa, I..."

"I'll go to Bow Street and fetch your man," she snapped, leaving him to gape at the open door.

Θ

"My men have searched the premises thoroughly, as you requested, though it vexed me to do so," Principal Patrol Officer George Ruthven said to Hawke after conferring with a skinny subordinate who looked barely out of his teens. Hawke had waited outside the theatre, under the grand columns of the portico, for the sneering porters had not granted him entry until the large, red-cheeked man in blue coat and yellow waistcoat had stalked imperiously down from Bow Street. On seeing Ruthven, and the tipstaff he twirled expertly in one meaty paw, they had immediately exchanged arrogance for mewling deference, and allowed Hawke, Ruthven and three other Runners inside. Now, though, standing in the Theatre Royal's spacious, and ostentatious, entrance hall, Ruthven glowered at Hawke with a look of pure thunder on his broad face. "The musicians have gone. Am I permitted to return to my real work, or is there a troop of unruly fairies you'd like me to hunt down?"

Hawke ignored both the jibe and the junior Runner's half-suppressed snigger. "Gone?" He stared past them, beyond the second and third officers who loitered by cold gas lamps and ornamental palm trees, and through the big doors that opened onto the playhouse itself. The interior was sumptuously decorated in gold, green and crimson. He could glimpse a portion of the wide stage, flanked by the galleries and private boxes. He imagined the place filling with society's cream. All there to unwittingly bask in the musical skill of a secret child-killer. "King Lear is scheduled for tonight."

"The players continue," Ruthven responded, irritation turning his voice to a growl. "The musicians do not. Monsieur Blanc has taken his parcel of minstrels to the coast, so they tell me. Portsmouth and a ship bound for the grandest stages the north has to offer." He adjusted his black cravat, shouldered the tipstaff, and looked past Hawke to the exit. "Our business is concluded, sirrah."

"Will you not pursue them?" spluttered Hawke, aghast.

Ruthven rounded on him. “Pursue? This coat buttons over a great many other duties, Mister Hawke. None of which constitute trekking across country on a wild goose chase.”

“Sir, this is no wild goose chase.” Hawke started forwards, wanting to grasp the lawman by his lapels, but tremors of pain stirred in his hip and side. “It is...”

The tipstaff’s gleaming top, like the heavy head of a medieval mace, jabbed hard into Hawke’s sternum. “Your mulatto punk gave me chapter and verse, and, I confess, I was intrigued enough for a stroll of a few hundred yards. But now that I see you. Now that I speak to the proprietors of this venerable establishment, and consider what you are actually attempting to suggest.” He shook his head, clearly rueful that he had indulged such a flight of fancy. “It is a figment of your opium-addled imagination.” His voice grew louder by the word. “Brooches and witchcraft and French soldiers? The matter has been dealt with by my officers. This,” he waved the staff at the hall’s high, ornate ceiling, “this foolery, is a waste of my time. The people are content that justice has been done, and you, sirrah, might be best served by a stay in Bedlam."

"Justice?" Hawke repeated in astonishment. "You knock down a few doors in Clerkenwell and drag out any Italian man you find?"

Ruthven's eyes darkened. His red face turned a deeper hue, contrasting starkly with his sandy hair. "Careful there." The tipstaff returned to Hawke's chest. "It's been a while since this thing cracked a skull, but it is not beneath me."

Hawke tensed, acutely aware that Ruthven was as capable of swift violence as he was immune from its consequences. Yet he had come this far. To retreat now would be to abandon all hope of snaring the real killer. "It is the Ember Week," he said imploringly. "The time when the murderer may strike. Please, I beg of you, listen to me, Mister Ruthven."

"He will not strike," Ruthven retorted angrily, "because he *cannot* strike. He is in jail. We have a score of Italians under lock and key, and the murderer of Betsy Milne will be rooted out from among their number."

"Let me follow Blanc's group, Mister Ruthven," Hawke persevered. "Do not spare your officers; send me. I'll go to Portsmouth willingly."

Ruthven laughed. It was a grating, mirthless, mocking sound. "And who will fund this expedition? You? Colan Szekely, perhaps? Will you not be busy pillaging the caskets of decent Londoners?" He pulled back his shoulders, drawing himself up to his full, imposing height. "Fly away, Hawke," he commanded imperiously. "I will send word if and when your dubious services become required. Should you drink yourself into an early grave beforehand, be cheered that you have value to someone." He winked. "The anatomy schools will pay handsomely for a corpse with a shrivelled liver to inspect."

"Sir!" a shrill, breathless cry came from the entranceway, interrupting them both. "Mister Ruthven, sir!"

Hawke and Ruthven parted, turning to regard the big doors, through which a grubby-cheeked boy with an elfin face and moth-eaten clothes scampered, the porters snapping like bulldogs at his heels. Ruthven ordered the men to relent, then addressed the boy. "What is it?"

"Cor'ner's asked you to attend him, forthwith, Mister Ruthven."

"Oh?"

The boy shifted uneasily from one flap-soled shoe to the other, grime-caked toes on display like so many new potatoes. "There's been another one."

Time seemed to stand still for Joshua Hawke. His stomach convulsed as his heart palpitated wildly. The skin at his neck fluttered as though a hundred butterflies simultaneously alighted from the nape, and the pain in his side vanished. He wanted to quiz the messenger, to confirm that he had been right all along, and yet that confirmation was what he feared most. In the end, he said nothing, because Ruthven cleared his gravelly throat.

"Another one?"

The boy nodded. "By Temple Church, sir. A lad, younger than me." A look of raw fear caused his gaunt features to quiver. "Tied up with plants, sir."

George Ruthven nodded once, dismissed the messenger with a brusque wave, and looked down at Hawke. "Are you fit to travel?"

"Aye, sir."

"Then it is settled. You'll accompany my men to Portsmouth and apprehend this fiend." George Ruthven set his jaw. "Do not return until this dog has been brought to heel."

Hawke wanted to slap Ruthven. To tell him to shove his command where the sun did not shine. To crow that he, Hawke, had been right when the hero of Cato Street had blundered blindly from one false accusation to the next. But he could do none of that. Because the murderer of Betsy Milne, of Varney Tapp, and of this latest poor wretch was still at large. In the end, he simply nodded. "I'll run the bastard to ground, Mister Ruthven. You have my word."

Huge thanks to all who put up with me while I produced this book.

You know who you are.

Thanks in advance to you kind folk who've given Corpse Thief a run.

I really hope it was a decent read.

Look out for **Part Two**!

A bit about the 'real' history used as the backdrop for Corpse Thief...

Body Snatchers

Hawke is a resurrectionist. Also known as a body snatcher, grave robber or sack-'em-up man. As morbid an occupation as it may seem, it was a real and thriving (illegal) business by the early 19th Century, and a terrible fear for the loved ones of the recently deceased.

Before the Anatomy Act of 1832, the only legal supply of corpses for anatomical purposes in the UK were those condemned to death and dissection by the courts. This was all well and good during the previous century's era of the *Bloody Code*, when hundreds were executed for relatively trivial crimes, but by the time of Joshua Hawke's arrival in London, the numbers had diminished sharply, which meant that there were nowhere near enough corpses to meet the demand from medical schools and private anatomical schools.

With this clear shortfall in supply, the criminal fraternity quickly arrived upon the (very lucrative) solution. Not least because cemeteries were often overcrowded, meaning fresh graves were shallow and easily accessible. Moreover, interfering with a grave was not, at this time, regarded as a felony. The corresponding punishments were well worth the risk.

Peterloo

The Peterloo Massacre took place at St Peter's Field, Manchester, in the summer of 1819.

As mentioned in the book, the end of the Napoleonic Wars had seen Britain struggle with chronic unemployment and periods of famine. By 1819, the economy was in such a mess that people were beginning to look to more radical politics for a change in their fortunes. One of the groups that responded most vigorously to this desire for parliamentary reform was the Manchester Patriotic Union, who organised a demonstration to be addressed by the well-known radical orator, Henry Hunt. Thus, on 16th August, a huge crowd - somewhere between sixty and eighty thousand - gathered to demand (amongst others things) the reform of parliamentary representation.

Shortly after the meeting began, local authorities summoned the Manchester and Salford Yeomanry to arrest Hunt and several of the rally's key figures. As Hawke tells Corissa, things went badly wrong, and the Yeomanry charged the crowd, arresting Hunt, but injuring a woman and killing a child in the process. With chaos ensuing, the 15th Hussars were sent to disperse the multitude. They also went in at the charge, killing 15people and injuring hundreds more.

The massacre was dubbed 'Peterloo' by the horrified press, in an ironic comparison to the Battle of Waterloo. Eyewitnesses did, however, report seeing one cavalryman turn against the tide, trying in vain to stop the carnage. That man was never identified.

Joshua Hawke will return...

27189237R00262

Printed in Great Britain
by Amazon